Maxwell's Return

Maxwell's Return

M J Trow

Text copyright © 2014 M J Trow

All Rights Reserved

ISBN-13: 978-1-909869-91-2

This edition first published in 2014 by:

Thistle Publishing
36 Great Smith Street
London
SW1P 3BU

Chapter One

The silence was almost deafening before the black car with heavily tinted windows purred up to the kerb. The driver jumped out and opened first a rear door and then the boot. He emptied the contents and dumped them unceremoniously on the grass, still damp from the rain of earlier in the night which was waiting for the summer sun before it could evaporate. The passengers, rudely awakened by the discreet and padded slam of the boot lid, tumbled out from the luxurious back seats and were still blinking on the path as the car sped away. One of them looked around, puzzled, feeling that something was missing but before he could put his loss into words, the car, having turned to go back to the town and then on into the countryside beyond, pulled in again and the rear door opened, silently, eerily, all by itself. The man looked in, then reached in, grasped something left on the back seat and pulled it out, depositing it with a grunt at his feet. The car pulled away again and soon it was just an array of brake lights and indicators at the top of the slight rise.

The houses all looked down with blank eyes at the little group huddled together on the path and they looked back, with eyes scarcely less blank. The woman hitched her child up higher on one shoulder and balanced his weight with her bag over the other. The man picked up their bags and the forgotten luggage from the car, which was now beginning to growl. The low, threatening noise began to rise in volume and voles and shrews for streets around raised questing whiskers to the sky. Memories are short in the world of vermin, but even these twenty generations on, they knew their enemy and the message flew by means of snickers and squeaks beyond human hearing, by messages embedded in the constant dribble of urine, spread through wainscoting and undergrowth.

'Metternich's back! Run! Hide!'

And they all knew they couldn't do both.

Chapter Two

Jacquie Carpenter-Maxwell was still sleeping the sleep of the seriously jet-lagged with Nolan tucked snuggly into the curve of her body when her husband slipped out of the room. Still in his pyjamas, Maxwell crept up the stairs to the attic room, where his Light Brigade had been waiting for almost a year for his return, the half-finished Troop Sergeant Major John Linkon lying on his back beside his harness-less horse under a cloth, waiting for the last licks of paint that would make him almost live again. Maxwell picked up Lord Cardigan, sitting Ronald as patiently as ever. He had been finished now for years and he turned him to the window, checking for dust. There was none. Hector Gold, his other half of the exchange which had kept him away from Leighford, from Columbine and from his 54mm Brigade, had kept them pristine. He looked across the diorama and then gave them a second look. All was not quite as he had left it. Right at the very edge of the valley, almost off the table but in the direction of the Sapouné Heights, had his attic been big enough, was a new figure, standing, horseless, gazing at the men. Maxwell walked round to where the little man stood and crouched down to look him in the eye. He wasn't a soldier, he was a civilian, a battle-walker, a travelling gentleman, a *schlachtenbummler* as the Germans have it and he was the very image of Hector Gold, down to his blond hair and, to Maxwell's delight, a cheeky wink. Extending a careful finger, he patted the little man on the head. All the way across the Atlantic, he had worried about what he would find when he reached his house, his school, his own historians, his Sixth Form. His stomach had knotted from time to time and he had found it hard to concentrate on *Monsters' University*, although Nolan had insisted that he would be asking questions later. But now he knew that he had left everything in the right hands. He winked back at Hector Gold, TG *par excellence* and went downstairs to put on the kettle and restart his normal life.

Hector had even filled the fridge, although it did have a slightly transatlantic flavour, with a preponderance of maple syrup and some rather brightly coloured juice. But no doubt Nolan would greet them all with whoops of delight. A hot coffee steaming in his hand, he wandered into the sitting room and pulled back the curtains. They had gone straight to bed the night before, having let Metternich out to renew old acquaintance with small and vulnerable creatures of the night and to rout the army of interlopers who would doubtless have invaded his territory during his absence. The room was still dark. He had no idea what time it was, but the light in the attic had seemed to him to suggest around about seven – he had lost the knack, temporarily, of telling the time from the sky. In Los Angeles, the time was night or smog – it was hard to be more accurate.

He walked around the back of the sofa and set his coffee down on the table, then threw himself back into the embrace of his favourite chair. He closed his eyes and leaned back with a sigh as the cushions moulded themselves to his contours as though he had never been away. Then, he opened his eyes and looked ahead with a smile still lingering on his lips.

Then he screamed. He would say later that it was more of a manly shout, but it was definitely a scream, as everyone in the house at the time would attest. He screamed because stretched out on the sofa, her head pillowed on a cushion, was an old lady, hair tidily held in a net, a small bubble of saliva growing and diminishing at the corner of her mouth with every breath. He had hardly time to register that fact before she was screaming too. Struggling upright, she clutched the blanket she was sleeping under up to her chin and stared with wild eyes about her.

'Mrs Troubridge!' Maxwell felt his heart lurch back into a more normal rhythm. 'What …?' He almost used the cliché he avoided on pain of death, then couldn't help himself after all. 'What are you doing here?'

'Careful, Max,' said a voice to his left. 'She'll have to kill you now.' Jacquie stood there, in rumpled pyjamas, the pillow still printed on one cheek and her hair on end. 'Mrs Troubridge. Have you been there all night? We had no idea.' She turned to her husband. 'Max. A cup of tea for Mrs Troubridge.' Maxwell's heart descended from his mouth. Never mind all night; he was afraid she'd been there all year.

The old lady still sat there wide-eyed and clutching her blanket, despite the fact that she was fully clothed beneath it. 'Jacquie,' she said, focussing her eyes one by one. 'I was expecting you last night, dear. I thought it would be nice to be here to welcome you, to let you know everything was all right while you were away, but I …' she looked down at the drool marks on the cushion and hurriedly turned it over, '… I must have dropped off for a minute.'

'We got in last night, but there was a mix-up with the taxi from the airport. We had a chauffeur-driven car in the end, because it was the taxi-firm's fault, but it took a while to arrange. As it was, the driver nearly drove off with Metternich.'

Mrs Troubridge's face clouded over. She and Metternich had a history which had not always been a happy one and she had half-hoped that the animal might have been in quarantine for at least a while; or, better still, gone feral in the Rockies. She had enjoyed her time with no vole-innards on her doormat. 'Nolan is well,' she stated. Her boy – now him she *had* missed.

'Nolan is blooming,' Jacquie said. 'He sounds a bit … American at times, Mrs Troubridge. But that will wear off soon enough, I expect.'

'By the end of the week, or he's off to the orphanage.' Maxwell gave a coffee to his wife and a tea to Mrs Troubridge, made in a pot, with the requisite number of spoonsful of loose tea. Jetlag was no excuse for making a bad cup of tea and he knew Mrs Troubridge would take no prisoners. There were after all, standards.

'Max has been fighting a rather rearguard action,' Jacquie told her neighbour. 'It started with a Cookie Box but he soon knew that wouldn't work.'

'A cookie box?' Mrs Troubridge was confused. She knew Mr Maxwell was a little unusual, but surely he wouldn't refuse his child food.

'It worked like a swearbox,' the instigator of the system explained. 'Every time Nole used an American word where an English one would do perfectly well, he had to put ten cents in the Cookie Box. It came out of his pocket money, but within a week he already owed us for the next two months, so we stopped doing it.'

'And anyway,' Jacquie took up the tale, 'he had to mix with all the other children, so it wasn't fair on him. And now he's back, Mrs Whatmough will soon knock him back into shape. He sounds quite cute, as a matter of fact.'

As if on cue, a wail came down the stairs. 'Mom! I mean, Mummy!'

'Ah, the voice of the turtle is heard in the land,' Maxwell said. 'Ladies, after you …'

But Mrs Troubridge, showing a rare and remarkable turn of speed, was already through the door and heading for the stairs.

That morning went by in a haze of phone calls and emails. Jacquie still had three weeks left before she had to report for duty at the Nick, but Henry Hall had left a message on the answerphone nonetheless. It didn't actually spell out that the DCI would like to see her sooner; the catalogue of illness and disaster that had apparently befallen every third person in or out of uniform was only so that she knew how everyone was, of course. She wasn't to worry about a thing – she must enjoy her next three weeks; oh yes, please don't even think of coming in to work. She rang back and left a message on *his* answerphone, promising to drop by on Monday. The emails were largely from the people they had just left, hoping they had got home okay, not to be strangers; many people found they had business trips coming up. Was Leighford near London at all? It's a village somewhere, isn't it? They would love to drop by. Jacquie sighed as she thought of the hotel she seemed to be opening, but with only a few exceptions, everyone would be welcome. There were even some emails from the teachers at the school Maxwell had honoured with his presence. They all began in the same way; - 'Hi Jacquie, can you let Max know I've been in touch ...' His technophobia had survived its sojourn Stateside and was still alive and well. As he kept telling them, 'If it was good enough for Edison . . .' She wouldn't be the one to blow his cover, and so she replied in the third person, as though by dictation.

Maxwell was downstairs in the kitchen, starting on the washing. He was not New in the sense of Man but he knew his limitations and sticking on a load of washing was a simple way of doing his bit. Nolan had been clamped to the ironing-board bosom of Mrs Troubridge since, and partly during, breakfast, but he had now disappeared with the loyal Plocker, with whom he had had a regular Skype call every Sunday while they had been away. Plocker had not asked for a present, nor expected one; getting Nolan back had been enough for him. Nevertheless, the bag of variously highly coloured American sweets had been gratefully received and Maxwell sent a silent apology to Mrs Plocker, who would have to deal with two little boys high on sugar and e-numbers for the rest of the day and halfway through the night.

As he sorted the loads into coloureds and whites, he let his mind wander and soon his living phantasm was strolling down the familiar corridors, peering round doors, checking that all was well with his world. Judging by the house, which was actually rather cleaner than when the Maxwell family had left it, Hector did not like chaos in any part of his life, so he had no fears for the welfare of his historians. His Sixth Form he knew would have flourished in the maternal care of Helen Maitland, the bulwark the kids called The Fridge. Leighford High was like a living thing, though, and if one part was not functioning, then there was a chance that the whole thing might crash and burn. He had heard of the depredations of Mr Gove, but didn't worry overmuch about that – he had seen things come, he had seen things go; O levels, CSE, GCSE, A2, AS, CPVE, CFEE, the Baccalaureate; when it was all said and done, an exam was an exam and an able student an able student. No, what he worried about was what Legs Diamond might have got away with while he had no one to curb his excesses with a mixture of contempt and mulish refusal to comply. There would be Elf and Safety notices everywhere; decaffeinated coffee in every machine; an iPad in every sweaty fist, textspeak the norm in every essay. Wikipedia quotes would have taken over. He felt a cold sweat run down his spine and he straightened up from his laundry pile. Shoving the whites into the drum, with the obligatory red sock for good measure, he added the gel, twirled some dials and pressed the button. Then he hot-footed it to the sitting room and snatched up the phone, punching in numbers he hadn't used for many months but yet came back to him without a second thought.

'Hello?'

'Hello. Helen, Max here.'

'Max!' He could hear the grin on her face. 'I didn't think you were back just yet.'

'Back in body, dear heart. My head is still on a pillow somewhere in Los Angeles. We'll get back together soon, I hope.'

'How are Jacquie and Nolan?'

'I gather that small boys don't do jet lag. He is off with his mate on a sleepover. Jacquie is catching up on emails, calls, you know how it is. How are you?'

'We're fine and before you ask me, so is the Sixth Form. We only had one pregnancy … oh, I think you knew about that before you went …'

'Tamzin?'

'No, in that case, two pregnancies, I suppose I should say. The results look as if they will be up this year – talking of which, Paul and Hector got on like houses on fire and the historians are all doing well. It was like having you around, but less trouble.' Her chuckle warmed his ear. 'You have missed some great weather – apparently we are in for an Indian summer, so you won't feel it too badly.'

'Feel it?'

'The cold.'

'My dear woman, I have never been so cold in my life as I have been for the past seven months. Air conditioning has kept us in Arctic temperatures. It was like the Donner party all over again. I'd eaten Nole's leg before I realised what was happening. The only time the *real* temperature kicks in in California is during the quick dash to the car and from the car at school or at the shops.'

'The Mall.'

'Wash your mouth out, Mrs Maitland. I have managed to retrain half of one of America's largest cities to use correct vocabulary – I don't want to have to start again with you. I did inform them that the only Mall in the world was the Pall variety that leads directly to the Palace.'

'The staff at Leighford are all expecting you to come back with an American accent. I should qualify that,' she said hurriedly, as his indrawn breath threatened retribution. 'The younger staff. Hector has been telling them how his colleagues have been training you in the finer points of Yank Speak. The rest of us know that you will have been training them on how to Talk Proper.'

'You betchya,' Maxwell drawled, much after Cletus Spuckler from *The Simpsons*.

Helen laughed. 'I hope you did that deliberately, Max,' she said. 'I have fifty pee riding on you.'

'Fifty pee!' he said, horrified. 'Fifty pee! Surely you have more confidence in me than that? Oh ye of little faith.'

'They capped the bet,' she said. 'As always, you have kept everyone guessing! But you rang me for a reason, I would imagine. You must have lots to do.'

'Most of the luggage isn't here yet. We sent it on by carrier; I'm not quite sure how we managed to leave with a suitcase each and now need DHL to get us back, but apparently there was a lot of stuff we couldn't leave behind. Nolan's scooter, for example.'

'He's that age, Max. He'll be cycling around behind you soon, you just wait.'

'So, to answer your question, there isn't a lot to do. We managed to dislodge Mrs Troubridge eventually. Hector seems to have actually trained Mrs B to clean, so the place is like a new pin.'

'Hector has been doing his own cleaning, I understand,' Helen said.

'Mrs B ...'

'Mrs B is in what you would doubtless call rude health,' Helen reassured him. 'She didn't hold with cleaning for foreigners, especially them Yanks wot got her auntie into trouble in the War and then left her holding the baby. Them Yanks don't care, apparently. No woman's safe with them, even when they look like they couldn't knock the skin of a rice pudding, like that Mr Gold. Her family wouldn't have her in the house along of him. It wasn't right.' Helen Maitland couldn't do an impeccable Mrs B like Maxwell could, but it was near enough, although the spectacle did make him feel slightly nauseous.

'I suppose Hector was a little short-sighted,' he mused.

'Yes,' Helen agreed, 'but not stone-blind. In fact, he was happy to fend for himself. I understand it was how he managed at home anyway.'

Maxwell had met his wife – he could believe that.

'He was sorry to have to go back. We were wondering . . .'

'Yes?'

'Well . . . it wasn't anything you did, was it? That the school wouldn't spring for another year?'

'No.' Maxwell was outraged. He had dragged that school kicking and screaming back years. 'No, it was all to do with funding. They were cutting staff and I didn't think it was fair that Hector's post should be judged by me. And of course, with the divorce going through . . .'

'He seemed very pleased with that.'

'Rightly so, I should think. No, it was time we got back. Jacquie was having a good time, a few lectures, working with the DA; all good for the CV but not what she's used to. We're not sorry to be back.'

'So … I suppose you're after the goss.'

'If you have the time.'

'Not for all of it,' she said. 'But I suppose you've heard the main points, anyway.'

'Not really. You know me and emails. Paul and Hector just got on with it and obviously you had no problems, so I haven't really been in touch with anyone.'

'Well, Legs hasn't done anything too heinous, you might be glad to hear. Charlotte …'

'Who?'

'Thingee Two,' Helen Maitland translated. 'Afternoon Thingee. You know, the one with blonde hair.'

'Of course,' Maxwell said, clicking his fingers. 'Pregnant?'

'Naturally. She was an accident waiting to happen.'

'Andrew Baines, PE.'

'Good Lord, Max!' She was astounded. 'How on earth did you know that? I've only just found out.'

'Ah ha,' Maxwell tapped the side of his nose, despite the fact that there was no one to see, 'We have our ways. Body language, heart, body language. I won't embarrass you by mentioning the thinness of track suit bottoms – let my nuance be enough.'

'I'll know where to look, next time,' she muttered. 'Where was I?'

'Lascivious PE teachers.'

'Hmm. Let me think. You saw the thing about Bernard Ryan in the paper, I expect?'

Maxwell blinked. 'What thing?'

'You missed it? I thought Sylv was sending you the *Leighford Advertiser* out.'

'She did, but for some reason, our neighbour took rather a shine to it, so it often disappeared from the letterbox.'

'Oh, well, if you missed it … it's a bit complicated, Max. It will take longer than a phone call to fill you in. Look, why don't …?'

A shrill peal rang through the house. 'There's someone at the door, Helen,' Maxwell said. 'I'll get that and give you a call later. Bernard *Ryan*, you say?'

'I do,' she said. 'Answer the door, Max, and I'll wait to hear from you. I'll see if I can find some backnumbers so that I can get everything in the right order.'

The bell shrilled again, accompanied by Jacquie's call, asking him to answer it. 'Must go,' he said, putting the phone down. Trust him to have used the only non-cordless in the place. Then he made for the stairs, muttering 'Bernard *Ryan?*' to himself, trying to make it sound like sense.

Maxwell reached the bottom of the stairs just as the bell pealed for the fourth time. He threw open the door to remonstrate with whatever lowlife was outside but instead of a neighbourhood urchin, his doorstep was decorated with Sylvia Matthews and two bulging Asda bags. They stood there for a moment, grinning at each other before Maxwell dived forward and grabbed the shopping, which he dumped in the hall before grabbing Sylvia in a hug which was once all she longed for. He planted a kiss on each cheek and pulled her inside.

'Where's Guy?' he asked, sticking his head out and looking ostentatiously left and right.

'In Brighton,' she said. 'He has a new job, Head of Department, no less, and he has gone in to suss out his office. Bless him, he's taken in a little bit of carpet for under his desk. He's learned a lot from you, over the years.'

Maxwell's square of carpet was famous throughout Leighford High School. School hierarchy dictated that only the most upper of the upper echelons had carpet in their office, so Maxwell had provided his own. It was a physical symbol of the Revolt of the Middle Managers. Along with a kettle that boiled in less than thirty minutes and a tin to keep the biscuits dry. Of such things are legends made.

'Well, it's lovely to see you,' Maxwell said. And it was; they didn't make school nurses like Sylvia Matthews any more. He ushered her up the stairs. 'I'll leave the bags down here, shall I?'

'No, no,' she said, turning. 'It's stuff for you. I know Hector was going to fill the fridge but he is so …'

'... American,' Maxwell completed her thought. 'Yes, he is a tad, oops, a little. However, Nolan was delighted to find a fridge full of Gatorade and a cupboard full of Oreos and granola but personally if I never drink another crocodile pee I shall be a happy man.'

'Crocodile pee?'

'I always assumed that that was the main ingredient in Gatorade, but I may be wrong.' He peered into the bag and saw with delight rashers of unsmoked bacon, thick cut and gave her another hug. Home at last. 'I must take issue with you, though, Sylv,' he said. 'Why didn't you let me know about Bernard?'

'I did. I sent you the *Advertiser*. It knows more or less what I know.'

'We didn't get that issue. The chap next door took rather a shine to the rag and pinched it half the time.'

'Strange neighbours you must have had. I wonder what he liked about it?'

'I think he thought it was deeply satirical. Remember our favourite headline?'

'*Spaniel Uninjured*,' they chorused.

'So, you missed the story,' she said.

'Yes. Fill me in.'

'I don't know all the ins and outs,' she said, 'but it all started back in June, or at least that's when we heard of it. I understand that the actual beginning of it all was before that.'

'Tell me as if you were writing it down,' Maxwell advised, pointing at a chair for her to sit on. 'Begin at the beginning and go on till you come to the end: then stop, as the King of Hearts would say.'

'All right, then. I'll do my best. Hindsight is a wonderful thing.'

'Twenty twenty,' Maxwell agreed and settled back, looking expectant.

Sylvia looked at him. 'Do you know anything about this, Max?' she asked.

'No,' he said, frowning. 'Why?'

'Because this isn't some juicy goss about him running away with one of the dinner ladies or similar. It's serious.'

The Head of Sixth Form sat up straighter and looked her in the eye. 'Go on,' he said. 'I really am listening.'

'Well,' she began, 'it turned out that Bernard had been doing some home tutoring. Not for the money, one would assume, on his salary, but for the satisfaction, company, whatever it might be. He didn't advertise, just took on kids whose parents knew him or friends of theirs knew him – word of mouth, you know, the usual thing.'

'He lives alone, doesn't he?' Maxwell checked.

'Yes. I think in the early days he used to have a lodger, a flatmate, call it what you will. But since he became first deputy, he hasn't needed the money and I think like most of us he didn't really like virtual strangers in the house.'

'No girlfriend?'

'Again, possibly at one time, but not at the moment. Where was I?'

'Bernard tutoring.'

'Right. Yes. So, he did a bit of tutoring and he was coming up to the exams so he wasn't doing so much. One evening, or so the story goes, he was getting ready to go out when one of his tutees – is that a word?'

'Possibly,' Maxwell said, doubtfully.

'One of the kids he tutored came round in a state. She was crying, a bit hysterical, in fact, and begged him to let her stay. He was doubtful but he has been a teacher now for …'

'Allegedly,' Maxwell put in.

'Indeed, but even he knows the score re kids and homes, I should hope. Anyway, he was doubtful, but he mopped her up and heard her out. Apparently, some family member, he wasn't sure who, was … well, behaving inappropriately towards her. This person had always been touchy feely, but had recently upped the game.'

'Nasty,' Maxwell agreed. 'One of ours?'

'No. She went to St Olave's, along the coast.'

'That's a boarding school, surely?'

'Well, yes,' she agreed. 'But they do have about 20 percent day girls. She was one of those. So, as you know, Bernard has nothing to do with pastoral, especially the girls, so he was at somewhat of a loss. She was adamant that she didn't want the police involved, in fact she said if he called the police, she would deny it and accuse him if any medical examination should show that she had had sex.'

Maxwell looked serious. 'Don't tell me he called the police and she … how old is she, by the way?'

'She was fourteen.'

'Was?'

'I'm jumping ahead in my story. He calmed her down and said she could stay the night as long as she told her parents where she was. She wouldn't do that, but she did agree that she would let them know she was safe, but not tell them where. He settled for that, because he could see that otherwise she would just run and he preferred that she was somewhere safe, not wandering the streets.'

'How do you know so much?'

'Again, Max, story, in order, telling of.'

'Sorry.'

'He had to go out, a long-standing arrangement, or so it seems, that he couldn't break. When he got back, in the wee small hours, she was gone.'

'Note?'

'Nothing. He assumed she had gone home, had second thoughts, whatever happens in the heads of fourteen year old girls. He had worried that … well, perhaps she had designs on him. You know what they can be like.'

'Bernard?' Maxwell's eyebrow disappeared under his hair.

'You don't use the same eyes as a teenager, Max. Bernard is not unattractive in a … well, he is attractive to some, I'm sure.' She raised her hands and let them fall. 'I've lost my thread again.'

'She had gone.'

'Yes. Right. The next morning, he came to see me about it. To ask me what he should do. I advised that he should ring the parents, find out if she was all right, and do it now. He rang from my office.'

'And?'

'And Henry Hall answered the phone. The girl, whose name was Josie Blakemore, by the way, had been found dead on the beach that morning, by the rather clichéd man walking his dog. Bernard tried to bluff it out, but of course, DCI Hall couldn't help but wonder why he was ringing and so it all came out. At least, I assume it did, because I haven't seen Bernard since the police came to pick him up from school.'

'My God!' Maxwell was aghast. It all sounded like an episode of *Law & Order*. 'Is he in custody?'

'No. They questioned him under caution, or so I understand. But they couldn't arrest him; there was no forensic evidence to connect him with the murder, although of course his DNA was on her clothes and hers was at his house. He's on gardening leave until … well, I don't know for how long. I can hardly think that they seriously suspect him, but it was a rather strange story that he had to tell …'

And a voice from behind her added, 'And worse than that, he has no alibi.'

Chapter Three

High tide on the beach at Willow Bay lapped the roots of the trees which the previous winter's storms had brought tumbling down the cliffs to make a giant's log-pile on the sand. Too new to be driftwood, too sodden to be firewood, the branches and roots tangled together just a little more with each incoming wave and made a Gordian knot of huge proportions. Sometimes completely submerged, at Spring tides and in storm conditions, the trunks had not become home to the usual beach-dwelling creatures such as rats and foxes, searching for new habitats as houses took over their normal ones. But something was moving in there, swaying in the water as it ebbed and flowed. It looked at first sight like an exotic flower, an orchid perhaps, as it waved, languid and pale, among the roots. It seemed to be beckoning, then dismissing the crabs that scuttled along the roots and burrowed under the trunks driven deep into the sand by the trees' fall from the sunshine on the cliff above. One crab, braver perhaps than the rest, approached the white thing and, scenting food, began to carefully pick delicate morsels from it, feeding itself with deft movements of its claws. If no one found it soon, the hand, then the arm, then the whole body of the dead girl would be bone.

'No alibi?' Maxwell asked, raising an eyebrow. He turned to Sylvia. 'Didn't you say he went out on a long-standing appointment?'

'Yes,' Sylvia said. 'But that's only what he told me, what I've heard since.' She looked across at Jacquie who had thrown herself down in the chair opposite. 'You look fresh as a daisy,' she said. 'No jetlag?'

'Yes,' Jacquie smiled. 'But I am trying very hard to rise above. How are you Sylv? Thanks for all the little reminders of home while we were away. Did Max tell you how much our neighbour loved the *Leighford Advertiser*?'

'There certainly is no accounting for taste,' the school nurse laughed.

'He must have taken the one about Bernard. I can't believe it went into detail, even so. Even the *Advertiser* has some scruples, surely.'

'Not so much scruples as absolutely rubbish reporting,' Sylvia said. 'You may have missed it in any case, because they called him Ronald Ryan, but they did say he was a Deputy at Leighford High and so I'm sure, like everyone else, you would have put two and two together. They didn't say it was in connection with the murder, either. Just said he had been suspended pending investigations into something that they were not allowed to report in detail.'

'And since that could only be fingers in the till or fingers in the knickers,' Maxwell continued, with an apologetic shrug at his two favourite women, 'everyone made their own decisions as to what it might be.'

'Well, it was a little worse than that,' Sylvia said. 'They put it on the same page as the body being found and said that a forty one year old man was helping police with their enquiries. They said she had been to visit her Business Studies tutor before she disappeared. Then in Bernard's piece, they said he was a forty one year old Business Studies teacher and the damage was done.'

Maxwell looked steadily at his wife. 'And, dear heart, if I may say so, you seem to have a few extra details yourself. I thought you weren't going back to work for another three weeks.'

She met his gaze. This may be a case of who blinked first. 'I'm glad Sylv's here,' she said, 'because she can be my witness when I say that I am not going to tell you anything about this case and I don't want you involved. Right, Sylv?'

Sylvia Matthews nodded but knew she wouldn't be called upon to ever stand up in even an unofficial Maxwell family court to swear to it. Max would get involved, of course. Jacquie would end up telling him everything and it might even end up that Bernard Ryan would yet be all right. Sylvia Matthews liked most people, but she didn't like the deputy head who was often unfair and vengeful. There was no such thing in his book as water under the bridge and he could hold a grudge for England. But even so, she had seen the look on his face when the police came for him and her maternal instinct had made her want to run to him and hold him close. The little boy he once had been – that even he had once been – looked out from behind his geeky glasses and she could have cried for him. In fact, later, at home and safely in Guy's arms, she had. But to Jacquie, she just said, 'Right.'

'Does this have anything at all to do with the three week thing?' Maxwell asked mildly.

'Not precisely, no,' Jacquie said, shifting a little in her chair. Sylvia sighed. The DI had blinked first and the rest, very appropriately, would be history.

'So you've spoken to Henry, then?'

'You've spoken to Helen. Sylvia,' Jacquie made a dramatic gesture with her arm and nearly knocked his mug out of his hand, 'is actually here.'

'So, what did Henry have to say?'

'He's well.'

'And?'

'And the family, of course.'

'And?'

'And ... well, he did mention that there are a lot of people off sick – summer colds, apparently – and ...'

'So you will be going in on ...?' Maxwell waited politely, his blandest expression firmly pinned on his face.

Jacquie took a deep swig of coffee, muttering something into her mug.

'Hmm?' Maxwell leaned forward. 'I didn't quite catch that. Sounded like "Chocolate, elephant, pencil" if I may quote Jeremy Hardy at this juncture.'

Jacquie cleared her throat and straightened her back. 'Monday,' she enunciated. 'I said I might pop in.'

'Monday!' Maxwell said. 'Jacquie I really thought we had agreed …'

'I don't need a holiday,' she said. 'The exchange was a holiday, to all intents and purposes. I learned a lot, of course I did, but they wrapped me in cotton wool.' She turned to Sylvia to explain. 'I couldn't carry a weapon, or, as you still call them over here, a gun, so there were limited options for what I could do. I worked mainly with the special unit assigned to the DA's office, so we were mainly interviewing. Very different from our methods here.'

'And sadly, very unlike any *Law & Order* episode I have ever seen,' Maxwell cut in. 'They do use those things for smashing down doors, though. I would love to have one of those.'

'Perhaps for Christmas,' Jacquie said, patting his knee.

Sylvia looked perplexed. 'Why would you want one?' she asked.

'Why would you *not?*' Maxwell asked, making vague swinging motions in the air.

'He's a funny age,' Jacquie said. 'As it was, I had to stop him talking to my temporary colleagues about the – and I quote – "balls up" they made over the Bobby Kennedy shooting.'

'When was that again?' Sylvia asked.

'Before your time,' Maxwell assured her.

'So, as I was saying,' Jacquie brought them back to the here and now, 'I don't need a holiday, I haven't been working hard at all. And Henry is pretty desperate, with staff on maternity leave, off with bugs, stress, you name it. So,' and she raised a pre-emptive finger at Maxwell before he could speak, 'I am going back on Monday, ad hoc hours, no night calls and the leave will re-accrue. So that's it. No arguing.'

'I know better than to even try,' Maxwell said. 'I'm surprised you made it Monday. I was expecting you to go back this afternoon.'

'Don't be silly. It's Saturday.'

'And what does that have to do with the price of fish? However, this does rather open the door for me going in to get the results.'

'Had you planned not to?' she said, archly.

Sylvia watched the match with a wry smile. 'I think that makes it deuce,' she said. 'Do you need any help with Nole?'

'Results day might be a help,' Maxwell said, 'but aren't you normally there to wipe noses?'

'Noses, tears, the whole lot, yes,' she said. 'We'll talk – I think Guy will be free, or perhaps Mrs Troubridge – how is she, by the way? I kept meaning to look in, but Hector seemed to be on it.'

'She's blooming. A little disappointed to see the Count back, I fear, but of course over the moon to get the Boy back. She was asleep in here this morning; I nearly had a heart attack.'

'I forgot to ask about Metternich – how did he get on in LA?'

'Racoons were a challenge at first, but he soon got the hang of them. Skunks, he came to an arrangement with. I'm not sure whether there are still mountain lions around, but if so, there are probably fewer now. He had a whale of a time. Has an American accent, of course, but we're hoping it will pass.'

Sylvia looked confused. 'Are we still talking about Metternich? Or has Nolan got an American accent.'

'Of course,' Maxwell looked quizzical. 'They both have.'

Jacquie began to relax. The conversation had taken a rather more domestic turn and Bernard Ryan's lack of alibi, which she should never have allowed to slip out anyway, seemed to have been forgotten.

'Have you got loads of pictures?' Sylvia asked.

'I'm making an online album,' Jacquie said. 'We managed to get out and about quite a bit.'

'So, what's this about Bernard having no alibi, then?' Maxwell asked, with his sunniest smile.

Later that evening, with Nolan away on a sleepover and Metternich sprawled over all three cushions of the sofa, his front legs stretched over his head and his back legs turned to the side in a Yoga position of his own devising, Maxwell returned to the question he had been dropping into the conversation all afternoon and through a takeaway dinner. Jacquie turned to face him, chin cupped in her hand, elbow resting on the arm of the chair. Her hair was a cloud of chestnut and the low light from the table lamp on the table between them made her eyes glow. She looked across at Maxwell, one of the two loves of her life – Metternich stirred in his sleep and half opened a steely eye – make that three loves of her life and she knew that she would give in soon. But the rules of the game stated quite clearly in para 4 subsection iiia that there had to be at least one more attempt. Her months with the LA DA (inevitably christened by Maxwell La-di-da) had not been wasted. She could now slow any investigation for weeks, by invoking laws and precedents without number; and that was before she reached for her motion to suppress. She blinked slowly twice and spoke.

'I'm sorry,' she drawled, just a hint of California in her voice. 'What was that?'

He narrowed his eyes at her and she was yet again reminded of his similarity to Metternich. 'I said, so Bernard Ryan has no alibi, then?'

'Does he not?' She feigned innocence. 'I did not know that!'

'Jacquie!' he shouted, making Metternich jump in his sleep. 'Sorry, Count,' he said, 'but really. A man has to jump through hoops here just to get some basic information. You said that he had no alibi. I said ...'

She flapped a hand at him and fell back against the cushions of her chair. 'Yes, yes, all right. I give in. Bernard Ryan has no alibi.' She picked up a magazine from her lap and started to read, skimming the pages with unseeing eyes until she heard him take in another breath, prior to asking again. With a smile, she turned back to him. 'I don't see why you shouldn't know. It's not as if he is really a suspect. If Diamond has any sense, he will have him reinstated by the time term starts.'

'But . . . he told Sylvia he was out on a long-standing arrangement or some such thing. That's an alibi, isn't it?'

'It's an excuse,' she corrected him. 'A ruse. A story. A reason. Any number of things. But unless we can get corroborating evidence from anyone who saw him at this so-called long standing arrangement, there is one thing it isn't.' She watched him, waiting for a response. 'What isn't it?' she prompted.

'An alibi.' He was frowning. 'But . . .'

'No buts. He hasn't got an alibi. I haven't seen the case notes, but I imagine that he probably just wanted to get away from a potentially dodgy situation with a fourteen year old girl. The worst he is is a heartless bastard, but surely you knew that already.'

Maxwell took a deep breath and then let it out again without speaking. Then he tried again. 'He is a heartless bastard, yes, of course he is,' he agreed. 'But only with staff. He would sell us all down the river without a moment's thought. He lives by rule books and lists and government guidelines. He has never met a health and safety initiative he doesn't like. I would imagine that he sleeps with Mr Gove's latest edict under his pillow every night. But . . . but . . .'

'But?'

'But this was a child. She needed him and he went out and left her. That doesn't sound like the Bernard Ryan I know. He should have called someone, social services, God forbid or at least Legs. He knew he had done wrong, or why would he have gone to Sylv the next morning? I just don't think he would have abandoned a child. That's all.'

Jacquie gave him a long, hard look. She had lived with this man for years now and loved him for longer than that. She knew that he would never leave a child in distress alone and she knew that most people wouldn't. There were teachers who were in it for the money, but heaven knew why; there were surely easier ways of earning a crust. There were teachers who didn't have the brains God gave sheep when it came to doing the right thing. Maxwell's heart was on his sleeve and she loved him for it. Bernard Ryan's heart was made of stone, but his head was not and so she reluctantly had to agree with her husband. If Bernard Ryan couldn't come up with an alibi, there was something wrong somewhere. She raised an eyebrow at him and reached for the phone. After a moment's pause, he nodded and she dialled.

After only one or two rings, Henry Hall was on the line.

'Jacquie. You really don't need to come in until Monday, you know,' he said, raising a finger at the sergeant hovering in the doorway.

He listened in his usual silent way, absorbing every word, not interrupting with even a grunt.

'Well, Maxwell should know, I agree, but . . .'

The phone muttered in his ear.

'But doesn't this make it worse for Ryan? If he is behaving out of character?'

The sergeant shuffled his feet and Hall raised a finger again.

'I do see what you mean. I think. But he isn't really a suspect, Jacquie. I can see that a concrete alibi might make it easier for him to get back to work, but as far as we are concerned, it makes no difference. I'll make a note, though.' He coughed discreetly. 'And . . . we will be seeing you, Monday?'

The phone muttered again.

'Good. We've just had someone call in – a body on the beach. Nothing much, I don't think. They're not even sure it's a body. It will turn out to be a tangle of clothes or something, caught up in that landslip at Willow Bay.'

This time the phone asked a question.

'I think you were away. There was a storm and some trees came down the cliff. No one hurt but there was a bit of a kerfuffle for a while. You know what it's like. Missing people, are they buried under the rubble? The usual.'

He glanced up as a civilian receptionist appeared in his doorway and spoke in a low voice to the sergeant, whose head came up in surprise. He gestured to Hall, who spoke rather more urgently.

'It looks like something has come up, Jacquie,' he said. 'I'll see you on Monday. 'Bye,' and he rang off, keeping the phone in his hand, as if at the ready. He looked at the sergeant, who was looking portentous. 'What?'

'It's not just clothes, guv,' the man said. 'It's a body. It's another one.'

Maxwell raised an eyebrow at his wife. 'That sounded a little like the bum's rush,' he remarked, his voice as inflection-free as he could make it.

'No,' she said, putting the receiver down slowly. 'It . . . well, they seem to have found a body on the beach. No biggie.'

'No biggie?' Maxwell queried. 'I know we are by the sea here, heart, but even so, bodies on the beach . . . surely not an everyday occurrence. You're not in California now, you know.'

'There were less than three hundred homicides . . .' she caught the eyebrow again as it whizzed upwards, 'murders in LA last year, as a matter of fact,' she said. 'They have the lowest h-murder rate for a city of that size in the world.'

Maxwell didn't move. He merely sat looking the picture of rapt attention. Then he slumped. 'You didn't say it,' he whined.

'What?'

'So there.'

'So there, what?'

'No, I expected you to say "so there". They have the latest h-murder – I'm assuming that is just murder you mean there, rather than the much rarer h-murder,' and he ducked as the magazine whooshed past his head, 'murder rate for a city of that size in the world, *so there*! But you didn't.'

'Well, they have.'

'Dear heart, of course they have. And I bet when the figures come out for this year, the rate will have gone down further still. But if my own ridiculously full brain can come up with a figure, then I would reply that the whole of England and Wales had less than twice that. So, that's why I must repeat that a body on the beach is certainly not 'no biggie'.'

She shrugged a shoulder and reached for the magazine. It wasn't there, having slid harmlessly down behind Maxwell's chair when she flung it.

'So, would you like me to fish your magazine out, or would you like your jacket?'

She looked at him and then gave a sigh. 'Jacket,' she murmured, then reached up her arms to him. 'I do love you, Peter Maxwell.'

'And I love you, Detective Inspector Carpenter-Maxwell. Just as well, eh?' Planting a kiss on her nose, he went upstairs to fish her jacket out of the wardrobe. He knew she would never make it until Monday. But never mind; this would give him the moral high ground and would grease the wheels when it came to wheedling details out of her. Even after all this time, she still wasn't up to all his little games and long may that situation flourish. He wiped the smile off his face and went back down to where she stood in the lounge, already twirling the car keys.

'Don't wait up,' she said as she made for the stairs.

'I'm not even sure what the time is,' he said. 'I may go up and do some modelling. Or I might also suddenly fall over fast asleep. Expect me where you find me.' He blew a kiss and watched her safely down the stairs. There wasn't much he could do to keep her safe at work but he did what he could. The door slammed and he waited to hear the car engine start before going back into the sitting room. The phone was ringing.

'War Office.'

'And don't think that just fetching my jacket and letting me go in to work gives you the moral high ground,' his wife's voice sounded softly in his ear. 'I'm wise to your tricks, Peter Maxwell.'

'Ha. Ha.' He put the phone down and spoke to the room in general. 'And yet you still fall for them, dear heart,' he said. 'Luckily for me.' And he twirled on his toes and made for the attic and TSM Linkon.

DI Jacquie Carpenter-Maxwell let the car coast to a halt at the kerb where only twenty four hours before the hire-car had dropped them after their eleven hour journey. It seemed almost unbelievable that Los Angeles was only a few days ago; already, it felt like another life time. And here she was, back in harness and a dead girl on the beach. No, correction; *another* dead girl on the beach, albeit under different circumstances. The new sergeant, Jason Briggs, had been already suited and booted to go off and arrest Bernard Ryan but in the end he had been countermanded by Henry Hall. Hall didn't believe in coincidence, gut reactions, coppers' noses or anything else of that nature. Nor did he believe that Yakult was good for him, but he dutifully drank the horrible stuff every day, just to please his wife. So, had Briggs had any decent reason for pulling Ryan in, he would have let him do it, in that same spirit. But apart from the no smoke without fire reason – another aphorism for which Henry Hall had no time – Briggs had nothing, so Bernard Ryan could spend another night in blissful ignorance of the axe that was undoubtedly about to fall.

Jacquie suppressed a little smile as she eased the car door quietly to. It had been very gratifying, the genuinely happy faces she had met when she walked in to Leighford Nick. No one was happier than Henry Hall but she had to judge by the faint twitch at the corner of his mouth and the double flicker on the flat lenses of his glasses as he dipped his head before she knew just how much he had missed her. A lot.

'Jacquie,' he had said as he pulled out a chair. 'I'm not sure you know Jason.'

'Ermm, no.' She could have added, 'only by repute.' The emails from her colleagues had not painted a very attractive picture. Crawler. Brown-noser. Smartarse. But time would tell. 'Hello, Jason,' she said as he extended a hand.

'Ma'am.' He had touched her fingers briefly, but that was that. She couldn't blame him. He would have been filling her shoes while she was away and it was never easy to step back down again. And it still felt odd to be called 'Ma'am'.

'Thanks for coming in, Jacquie,' Hall had said, and clearly meant it. 'We're down to the wire as far as personnel go. So many out sick you would hardly credit. God knows what it'll be like when the flu season kicks in. Still, you're back now so let's get on.'

Jacquie knew that that would be the last she would ever hear about her absence. And now, here she was, creeping up her own stairs, checking instinctively for innards. Metternich had settled back into the routine of Columbine without a hitch. Presumably, cats didn't have any truck with jetlag. When you spend twenty out of every twenty four hours asleep and the other four disembowelling things, jetlag is for other people. The great beast met her at the top of the stairs with a querulous miaow.

'All right, all right,' she whispered. 'Did you have your sachet last night?'

The animal looked at her wistfully. It had been rumoured in their neighbourhood in LA that Antonio Banderas had been seen in the yard taking lessons in cute looks from Metternich. The miaow this time was just a mime, as he clearly had not the strength to make a noise.

Jacquie looked at him and pursed her lips then went into the kitchen. 'I think you're lying,' she whispered severely. 'How do I know? Because your tail flicked to the left and down – always a sign whatever they say on *Lie To Me*. But just this once you can have the benefit of the doubt.' She pulled out a sachet of his favourite food and emptied it into his bowl. He nudged her with his substantial backend and dived right in. She kicked off her shoes and trod softly on the bottom stair, listening, then remembered that Nole was at Plocker's for the night. She could just pick up the soft breathing of her husband from their bedroom, the soft breathing that other people might call snoring, but she was too well brought up. She undressed in Nolan's room and then slid open the door to her own bedroom and slipped in alongside Maxwell, who murmured in his sleep and budged over to give her more room.

'A'ri'?' he asked.

'Yes, fine,' she muttered, turning her back so he could fit around her like a spoon.

'Henry a'ri'?'

'Mm-hm.' She was dropping off already. Heaven knew what time it was, on this continent or any other. She waited for another few seconds for the other question, but it never came. She closed her eyes and offered up a silent prayer to the god of jetlag. She would at least be spared the third degree until the morning.

'So,' the curtains flew back with a rattle and DI Carpenter-Maxwell screwed up her eyes against the August sunshine. 'A body on the beach, eh? Have they arrested Bernard yet?' She looked up to see Maxwell looming over her with a tray and a smell of coffee and toast filled the room. She struggled upright.

'I thought we agreed . . .'

'Of course we did. But you know how it is,' he smiled at her and pushed a small errant lock of hair behind her ear. 'I can't help asking.' He paused and looked at her. Antonio Banderas had not been in the yard in vain. 'You can't help telling me what I need to know.' His Svengali impression was among the best in the world.

She took a slurp of coffee. 'Not much to tell,' she said. She looked at the tray. 'No strawberry jam?'

'Soz, heart,' Maxwell said. 'Just grape jelly. It will be a while before we completely exorcise the American within. There's peanut butter, look.'

'Okay.' Jacquie was famished, having missed many meals, she wasn't sure which ones.

'So, not much to tell,' he prompted.

'Not as yet. There was a body on the beach, caught up in the driftwood and whathaveyou at Willow Bay. There had been a significant cliff fall back in the spring but that was by the way. The body had been there around two or three weeks, the forensics guys thought. Hard to tell because the tide only reaches there when it is really high and they have got to work it out. There are no charts for that kind of situation.' She took a huge bite of toast, jelly and peanut butter and sighed. 'I do miss the food, you know, already.'

Maxwell smiled. Had their forebears fought the War of Independence in vain? 'The fridge is full of it, as are all the cupboards. Sylv's back bacon is fighting a rearguard action, I'm afraid.'

'We can cook fusion style,' Jacquie said.

'So, this body . . .'

'You're relentless, you know that?'

Maxwell decided to consider it a compliment.

'They have an ID already, because this girl had been posted as missing three weeks ago in Brighton. The time of death seems to fit with her having died straight away, but we'll have confirmation soon, I hope.'

Maxwell sat on the edge of the bed and gazed at her. 'Are you well?' he asked.

'Yes. Why do you ask?'

'Because I am not having to prise all of this out of you with hot pokers and other Torquemada-like devices.'

'Well, she probably won't be ours, will she?' Jacquie said, starting to butter her second slice of toast. 'She went into the water at the Brighton end and just washed up on Willow Bay beach. The murderer, if there is one, will live in Brighton, the crime will have been committed in Brighton. Henry will have a friendly meeting with the Brighton boys and da daaaaaaa – we hand her back.'

'If there is one?' Maxwell asked. 'Does it look accidental, then?'

'Well, she was dressed for a night on the town. She's not a working girl. In fact, girl is the word; she was just fourteen. But like all of them, she looked a lot more with all the slap on. She had a sparkly thing,' she sketched the shape of a boob tube with her half-eaten toast, 'and a skirt up to her tonsils. And a pair of fuck-me shoes, pardon my French. She could have just drunk too much and fallen in.'

Maxwell looked dubious. 'Fourteen, though,' he muttered.

'Surely, Max,' she said, leaning back, 'surely I don't have to tell you what these girls can be like?'

'No,' he said, shaking his head, 'you don't, unfortunately. I just can't see a fourteen year old going out on the piss on her own. And at that age, I would think that at least one of her mates would have coughed to her mum. Or on Facebook. Whichever is the sooner.'

'That might turn out to be the case,' Jacquie said, wiping her mouth and offering up the tray. 'Henry is getting the notes across today and by tomorrow, we'll have the autopsy . . .'

'PM.'

'Yes, PM, sorry . . . results through, hopefully, although it probably won't help us much. The alcohol levels for example will have degraded by now. Any DNA will be helpful, but that won't be ready for ages and of course we need to have a suspect before we can make a match.' She kicked Maxwell lightly to move him off the bed and he got up, holding the tray, still looking thoughtful. She stood up and reached over to give him a kiss. 'Let's forget about dead girls today, shall we, and get the photos sorted. I've promised them to Mum and Sandy and the girls.'

Maxwell turned and walked to the top of the stairs with the tray. Forget about a dead girl. How do you begin to do that?

Chapter Four

Jim Astley looked over his half-moon glasses at Donald and asked him the question his assistant knew he would ask. As he had left the house that morning, in answer to the call, he had told his temporarily significant other that he would say it, and now here he was, saying it. 'Why have we been called in on a Sunday for this, Donald? This girl has been dead for weeks.'

'I have no idea,' Donald said with a shrug that set his fat layers wobbling. 'I got the call. I came in. That's what we do, isn't it?'

'Well, yes, of course we do. But . . .' Astley looked down at the girl on his stainless steel table and shook his head. 'What is it they say? If you don't have the murderer within forty eight hours, you'll never have him? This girl has been dead for weeks.' He was beginning to sound like the stuck records of his own misspent youth.

'They're still working it out,' Donald said, looking down at his crib sheet, 'but they are estimating three weeks, just shy of, because of when she was reported missing.'

Astley looked over his glasses again. 'They've been looking for this girl? They need to look harder next time.'

'She went missing in Brighton,' Donald explained. 'She was on the database, but . . . well, I suppose the police have more things to do than look in piles of driftwood for missing persons from along the coast.' Donald had almost said 'better things' but he knew his Jim Astley and he knew what phrases set him off. That was one of them. Others included 'he only killed his wife' and 'he's had a good innings'.

'Hmm, Brighton. Will they be wanting her back?' Astley sounded hopeful. He hated bodies that had been in the water. He hated the adipocere, he hated the gooseskin, he hated in particular the nibbles that crabs took out of their fingers and ears. He looked closer at the face and could see no signs of long immersion at this stage, although there was definite nibbling.

Again, Donald looked at his sheet. 'It's a bit up in the air at the moment,' he said. 'She was a Brighton resident, lived with her . . . oh, that's unusual, with her sister, the one who called her in as missing, as far as I can see. Well, yes, she lived there, but they can't find her on any CCTV on the Night in Question and according to all of her friends, she wasn't out with them.'

'So she may have gone out for a night on the tiles here, instead. Tell me, Donald, you probably have more of a nightlife than I do, would anyone come to Leighford for fun if they could go to Brighton?'

Donald chose to ignore the 'probably'. *Everyone* had a better nightlife than Jim Astley, whose drunken wife kept him on tenterhooks every time they went anywhere. Since the debacle at the last Christmas party, they didn't go out much any more. And then, there had been that business at the Golf Club. So he answered the question in the spirit in which it had been posed. 'I would only come here rather than stay there, if you follow, if I didn't want to meet anyone I knew. This child lived with her sister, so sister might go out to clubs and they might bump into each other. Not so likely with a mum or dad. But a sister . . . that's different. I often bump into my sister, for example, my mum not so much. Mind you, she's dead, so . . .'

'Thank you, Donald. You said "child".'

'Fourteen.'

Astley lifted the sheet that covered the girl from neck to ankle and looked. He shook his head, sadly. 'I had no idea, Donald. This is just a little girl.'

'Yes,' Donald said. He and his boss shared little, but they still could share sadness for a young life wasted and lying cold on their slab. 'Her clothes are over there. She was dressed to party, I must say.'

Astley looked over his shoulder at the pathetically small bundles containing boob tube, tiny skirt, tinier panties. The shoes with almost unbelievable heels were perched on top, each one separately bagged. He gripped the side of his table and leaned forward, head hanging. 'I hate these, Donald. More and more each day, I hate them.'

The big man put out a tentative hand and rested it on his boss's shoulder. After a second or two, he gave him just one pat and then withdrew it. After another second, Astley blew out a breath and lifted his head again.

'Right, Donald,' he said. 'Let's do this thing.'

Not quite time to hang up the microscope yet.

'Jacquie?'

'Guv?'

'Have we got the PM report on Mollie Adamson yet?'

'It's come through as an email – you should have it somewhere.' She looked at Henry Hall, bland and imperturbable and wondered why she had ended up with two of the three men in her life hating emails.

'Can you give me the gist?'

'It was hard for them to be precise. She had eaten with her sister just before she went out and the stomach contents imply that she had died within about four hours of that meal. She didn't drown, they are sure of that, so she didn't fall in or get thrown in while she was alive. She didn't die exactly where she was found, but not far away – she had lain on her side for perhaps half an hour before being moved. There were signs of sexual activity but not rape – there was no bruising or other signs so we have to assume it was consensual. As far as could be told, she was sexually active and had been for some while . . .'

'She was fourteen, yes?'

Jacquie turned from the screen and looked at the man. Father of boys as he was, he still saw fourteen year old girls playing with Barbies, the triumph of hope over experience. 'Yes,' she said, shortly.

He sighed. 'But no cause of death?'

'They think manual strangulation. It's hard to tell for sure because there are no fingermarks. The hyoid is broken, that's about all they have to go on. They think the killer muffled his hand with a scarf or something.'

Hall slammed his hand on his desk. 'These television programmes, they go into all the details of how to escape detection. Soon there won't be a forensic test they can't avoid. The silent witnesses are getting more silent every day. DNA?'

'There was semen, but it is degraded and they doubt they'll be able to get much. Anyway . . .'

'. . . we need the killer first. I know. So,' he decided to try another avenue, 'does she have any links with Josie Blakemore? School? Friends?'

'Nothing yet. Brighton police are at the school as we speak.'

'How are we handling this? Is it theirs or ours?'

She gave a rueful smile. 'Ours, I guess. With a lot of help from them, hopefully. They will deal with the preliminary interviews, we'll deal with the forensics. It would be nice to think *su casa, mi casa* but there are, after all, still forty two separate police forces in this great country of ours. After that, who knows?'

Hall was mentally counting heads – now Jacquie was back he at least had someone he could lean on; he had missed her more than he had expected. He had had three long relationships with women in his life – with his mother, his wife and Jacquie. And sometimes he wondered which one he had spent most time with. 'Let's hope there isn't an after that,' he said, shuffling papers on his desk. 'Let's hope they call soon and say that someone has coughed.'

'Coughed? Have you been watching reruns of the *Sweeney* again?' she asked, smiling.

'Just to pick up some tips.' He didn't smile, but she knew he was smiling on the inside. Peter Maxwell would have launched into an entire dialogue between Carter and Regan.

'Well, let's hope, then,' she said. 'Apparently, the sister wants to identify the body. Jim Astley isn't happy – it's not pretty.'

'Surely, we've done fingerprints . . .' Hall's voice died away as he remembered there were no fingertips to speak of. 'DNA? Clothes?'

'She's adamant. She says the clothes aren't her sister's and it's all a horrible mistake.'

'Denial. I see. Well, make sure you take her, Jacquie. Jason isn't . . .'

'I know, guv. I know. I'm meeting her at the hospital in an hour.'

He looked down at the papers on his desk. 'Thank you, Jacquie,' he said, formally. The meeting was over. Then, as she was halfway through the door, 'I've missed you.'

She turned to look at him, but he was busy with papers. 'Right back atchya,' she whispered, then closed the door and was gone.

Nolan and his father were rebonding with Leighford. Nolan had had a whale of a time in Los Angeles and in the first three weeks had gone up two grades at school. Not so much due to his innate genius as to the fact that anyone who had been taught even for ten minutes by Mrs Whatmough and her staff had to be streets ahead of any Californian child. Or indeed, any child in the world. Mrs Whatmough took no prisoners so any four year old who couldn't recite the twelve times table backwards in his sleep was soon out on his ear. Nolan should have had seven bells knocked out of him in the school yard every day but he was not his father's child for nothing and he soon had all the eleven-year old girls in the palm of his hand and there is not a seven year old boy in the land stupid enough to take on a gaggle of girls, so he survived. He soon had an American accent, was a handy pitcher in Little League and considered no day had begun properly without blueberry pancakes and a pile of bacon a mile high. Maxwell was working to remove the accent, wouldn't know a baseball rule if it got up and bit him on the leg but was up there in the queue when the pancakes were being handed out, so it would all come right in the end. Meanwhile, they were enjoying the park, the sweetshop and the beach in more or less that order.

'Dads?'

'Nole?'

'Will we be going back to America?'

'I hope so, mate. We've got enough invitations to last us years.'

'What, to live?' Young though he was, Nolan Maxwell was good at keeping his voice level. His father sometimes thought that there was a residual DNA insert from Henry Hall in there somewhere – like people got to look like their pets.

'Would you like to go there to live?'

'Hmm, no, not really. Their sea isn't right. And it's a bit hot. I liked the food, though.'

'We can do the food, I suppose . . .'

'Plocker liked the American sweets.'

'Plocker likes all sweets. That's why he's always at the dentist.'

'And he is quite fat.'

'Pleasantly portly,' Maxwell said, smiling.

Nolan jumped by his side, chanting. 'Pleasantly Portly Plocker.'

'Don't tell him I said so,' Maxwell said, hurriedly.

'He's called Fatty at school.'

'Does Mrs Whatmough allow that?' Maxwell was surprised.

'No, not really. We have to whisper it.'

Maxwell forebore to tell his only child that Mrs Whatmough could hear a pin drop in another county; let him find that out for himself. Meanwhile, a dad and his boy could kick along the edge of the tide until they disappeared over the horizon.

Jacquie Carpenter-Maxwell loved her job but there were parts of it she hated and the task she now faced was one of them. Mollie Adamson's sister was already waiting for her when she got to Leighford General and she had to walk the length of the corridor towards her with a suitable expression locked onto her face. She held out her hand and introduced herself when she was within earshot and the woman stood and took a step towards her. Her hand was cool and dry and she gripped firmly.

'Caroline Morton,' she said. 'Mollie's sister.'

'Hello.' At this point in every cop show she'd watched in the States, someone would say 'We're sorry for your loss' with that impossibly flat delivery. Better to say nothing at all. Jacquie made a few mental notes. Married. That was a surprise. Somehow, she had expected the two sisters to be closer in age. She had imagined a rather Mills and Boon scenario of a recently dead mother, sister who had just left school giving up her future to care for her younger sibling. This didn't seem to be the case. This woman was in her late twenties at the youngest. She could be much more.

'Half sister, perhaps I should say,' Caroline Morton explained. 'We had the same father, different mothers.'

'I see,' Jacquie said. 'I didn't know . . .'

'I told Brighton police all this at the time,' the woman said, rather coldly.

'I do understand,' Jacquie said, feeling as if she was on her back foot. 'We are still synchronizing notes. Our main concern was to find out cause of death, that kind of thing. Time has already been lost and I'm sure you are aware . . .'

'That the first forty eight hours are vital, yes. That ship has sailed, though, hasn't it?'

Detective Inspector Jacquie Carpenter-Maxwell smiled tightly at the woman in front of her and refocused her expectations. This would not be a tear-filled experience, with a sobbing, sodden woman sipping machine-made tea in an anteroom. This was not what she was expecting at all and she silently beat herself over the head for not having read the file completely. Never assume, she told herself – she was definitely the ass here. 'We have made strides as far as forensics go,' she said tersely. 'Would you like to have a chat with me first or go and see your sister's body?'

'If it is my sister,' the woman riposted.

'You doubt it?'

'Well, they certainly weren't her clothes,' she said. 'I told the police, she had gone out in a sweatshirt and jeans, espadrilles. The clothes they showed me pictures of yesterday . . . well, Mollie didn't own any clothes like that.'

'Perhaps a friend . . .?'

'Nor her friends. Mollie wasn't that kind of girl.'

'So, you'd like to see . . . the girl . . . first?'

'Of course.' The woman looked down her nose at Jacquie. 'Because when it turns out not to be Mollie, you won't need to talk to me, will you?'

'Er . . . no. No, I won't. Would you just excuse me for a moment. I'll just go and alert the assistant to . . .'

'I rang ahead,' the woman said. 'They're ready for us.'

Jacquie looked askance at her. This woman couldn't be this cold, surely. What was her job, for God's sake? 'How did you get the number, may I ask?' she said.

'I see you are very unprepared, DI . . . it is DI, is it? . . . DI Carpenter-Maxwell. I am a solicitor. Partner in Morton and Morton in Brighton. Perhaps you've heard of us?'

'No.'

'We specialise in criminal cases. I'm surprised we have never crossed paths before. However, that is by the way. Shall we go and see this body?'

Jacquie fell into step alongside the woman and thought she had rarely wanted quite so much to poke someone in the eye. Caroline Morton was almost a head taller than Jacquie and could walk in killer heels faster than most women could manage in trainers, but Jacquie refused to scuttle along trying to keep up. So they arrived at the viewing window a few seconds apart. Jacquie rang the bell and Donald appeared like a genii from a bottle.

'DI Carpenter . . . Maxwell.' Donald still carried a torch for Jacquie and he found it hard to get his tongue around the dreaded name that told him she was out of his reach for ever. 'How are you? We've missed you.'

Before Jacquie could open her mouth, Caroline Morton cut in. 'If we could dispense with the pleasantries,' she said, 'I am here to make an identification. Or rather, probably not make an identification. If you could get on with it. I have appointments for later today.'

Donald bridled and went back through the door marked 'Staff only', slamming it to behind him. Then, a curtain was drawn back to reveal a shrouded figure on a trolley. Donald's disembodied voice came through a small speaker to one side. 'If you're ready?' he said. Usually, he would have asked the relative if they were sure, that this was not going to be pretty, that they could wait for DNA but this woman had really pissed him off so let her see what she would see. He waddled into view and pulled the sheet back to reveal what lay beneath. He hoped Jacquie was ready for it. He wouldn't upset her for the world.

Jacquie drew in a sharp breath. She had seen sights like this many time, but repetition never took the edge off it. The girl's face was almost unmarked, aside from the signs of decomposition. Crabs had eaten away the visible ear and had started work around the nostrils and lips but it was clear that if this girl was known to you, you couldn't help but recognise her. She had a simple gold hoop in one ear-lobe, hanging there by a thread of skin. Her pale hair was pulled back from her forehead and her eyes were closed, Jacquie suspected with packing behind the lids, to hide the fact that the sockets were now empty. She glanced to one side and saw the ivory profile of the solicitor beside her. Before she could speak, the woman nodded her head, just once and turned away.

Jacquie nodded to Donald, who replaced the sheet and pulled the curtain back across the window. 'Is that your half-sister, Mrs Morton?' she asked.

The woman took a deep breath through her nose and dipped her chin, clearing her throat. 'Yes,' she said, quietly. 'Yes, it is Mollie.' She turned to look at Jacquie and there were tears in her eyes but they didn't fall. 'Can we . . . can we go somewhere quiet? I think we need to talk.'

'Well?' Jim Astley looked up as Donald came into the room, slamming the door behind him. 'Did the police get the name right?'

'Yes.' Donald turned and busied himself in the corner, cleaning things already clean, stacking things already stacked. His back, so huge it blocked out the light, was eloquence itself.

'Problem?' Astley was eating a sandwich and had no mouth free for niceties.

Donald turned and struck a dramatic pose, hands behind him on the edge of his desk. 'That sister! What a piece of work. She was rude to me, she was rude to . . . Jacquie.' Donald always paused before he spoke the Detective Inspector's name. He was like a kid on his first crush. Astley wondered what his current significant other looked like. On past showing they had all had a touch of Jacquie Carpenter-Maxwell about them, but seen in a funny mirror. No one who *really* looked like her would live with Donald.

'Ah.' Astley waited but there was no more. 'But it is the right girl.'

'Yes,' the big man agreed. 'She did have the grace to go a bit white round the gills. But . . . well, solicitor, what you gonna do?'

'What indeed, Donald.' Astley returned to his sandwich. 'What indeed?'

Jacquie had taken Caroline Morton into the grubby little room at the foot of the stairs which was up for grabs whenever anyone wanted a quiet word. It had once been a lunch-room for the smokers and it still bore a faint whiff of tobacco even after all the years that had passed since the last puff had been puffed and the last dog-end had been ground underfoot. Jacquie wondered occasionally whether there was a smokers' room in a police museum somewhere, looking just as quaint as the photographs they used to take of dead peoples' eyes, looking for the reflections of murderers. It was only a matter of time. Caroline Morton looked around with a wrinkled nose before finally choosing the least vile chair.

'Would you like a coffee?' Jacquie asked. 'Tea?'

The woman shook her head, to the DI's relief.

'I'm sorry you had to see your sister . . .' Jacquie began but the solicitor raised a hand to stop her.

'I asked for it,' she said. 'I have no one to blame but myself. My husband did tell me not to come. He . . .' she lowered her head for a moment, 'he offered to come instead, but I stopped him. I was so sure it wasn't Mollie. So sure that it was . . . well,' she sniffed and looked at Jacquie with a rueful smile on her lips, 'someone else's kid. Some other poor soul who would get the knock on the door. Some might say it served me right. For thinking it couldn't happen to me.'

'I'm sure no one would say such a thing,' Jacquie said, automatically.

'You seem a nice woman,' the solicitor said, unexpectedly. 'Perhaps you wouldn't say it, but I would. I have. And I expect I will again. However,' and she sat up a little straighter and pulled her skirt down over her knees, 'we're not here to talk about me. You want to know a bit more about Mollie, I expect.'

'Please.' Jacquie wished she had a recorder here, or someone to take notes. But this woman was in the mood to talk now and who knew when she would feel like this again. She would have to trust to her memory.

'Mollie was my half-sister, my father's daughter by his other wife. That's what we always called her, my mother and I, his *other* wife, although in fact he was married to her for longer than he was to my mother. They were very young when they had me, in fact they got married because of me and it was not going to work from the start. I was only four when they separated, six when he married Mollie's mother. He was always good to me, though, and so was she. My mother remarried but she always bore a grudge. Anyway, I had left school when Mollie came along. My father and Mollie's mother tried for years, miscarriage after miscarriage, before they finally had Molly. So they were delighted, of course, and I was made her godmother at her christening, which was lovely of them.' She looked at Jacquie and dabbed at her eyes. 'Could I have some coffee, do you think? Black, one sugar.'

Jacquie was surprised. The ice-maiden seemed to be thawing. She got up and went in search of a machine that worked and when she came back, Caroline Morton was on the phone.

'Yes. Yes, thank you. That's kind. Please ring my secretary and she will reschedule. Mm hm. Yes. 'Bye.' She slid the phone into her bag. 'I don't feel like case conferences this afternoon, as it turns out,' she said, with a watery smile. She reached out and took the coffee, lifting the lid and peering in.

'It looks a bit murky,' Jacquie said, 'but it tastes all right.'

'Thank you. I was just checking by habit. My husband always seemed to have difficulty in believing I really take it black. Anyway,' with a skill born of long practice, she was straight back into the story, 'once I was at university, I didn't go home to my mother's house much. She was on *other* husband number three by this time and it was all a bit much. He was a piece of work and I haven't seen him since she died.'

Jacquie made a sympathetic face.

'Two years ago now. We hadn't really spoken in years, although to be fair she tried to keep in touch. I see more of my second stepfather than any other member of the family, as a matter of fact. Mike's a nice man, he . . . anyway, he's not really part of the story. I tended to go home to my father's house when I went home at all, so I saw quite a lot of Mollie as she grew up. She was a sweet little thing. Then, about two years ago . . . no, a bit less, because my mother had just died . . . Eileen, Mollie's mother, found a lump in her breast. She ignored it. It killed her. Just like that. About a year ago.'

Jacquie found she was almost holding her breath. This woman who looked so cool and sophisticated had a shell that she had had to grow to keep the world away, not through choice, but for self-preservation.

'My father couldn't cope. At the funeral, he was like a zombie. He asked me to look after Mollie for the night and went home and shot himself.' She bit her lips and then took a swig of scalding coffee. 'Just like that. At least he had the decency to make sure Mollie was with me and my husband. Mark. He's known Mollie since she was born, more or less. We have been together since university and . . . well, he's always known her. And she's been with me ever since. I went back to the house and brought all her things away. We sold it and the proceeds have been invested to give her an income . . .' She took another gulp and carried on. 'And to send her to school. She was going to start boarding at St Olave's in September.'

'St Olave's?' That rang a bell.

'Yes. She was in some little tin-pot private thing when she came to us and we left her there for a while, although it was quite a drive each day to get her there and back. But she needed some stability, you see. She was going to St Olave's one day a week last term, just to get used to it. We wouldn't have sent her there if she didn't like it.'

'And did she?'

'What?'

'Like it?'

'She had made a few friends, as far as you can in one day a week for seven or eight weeks. But she was looking forward to it, yes. She was a bit young for her age, we always thought. We thought that boarding would be good for her. Stand her on her own two feet.'

Jacquie thought back to the shoes, the boob tube and the micro-mini, all bagged up waiting for the eager attentions of Angus at the main lab and wondered where her sister had got that idea from.

'That's why . . . why we couldn't believe it was her. Not in those clothes. Do you think that the . . . murderer . . . dressed her like that? You hear such things. Hell,' she suddenly shouted, 'we've got *clients* who would do that.' She looked at Jacquie and smiled. 'I wish I still smoked,' she said with a hoarse laugh.

'We don't think she was dressed after death, no,' Jacquie said, carefully. 'When the lab really get to work, we will know more. But the weeks of immersion, if you don't mind my speaking frankly, have done us no favours. Much of what was there has now gone, in the sense of fingerprints, DNA, fibres, hairs. I don't have to tell you, I'm sure.'

'But was she dressed like that?' her sister said. 'They weren't her clothes.'

'Did she have pocket money?' Jacquie asked.

'Yes . . . well, not pocket money. An allowance.'

'Have you checked how much of it she was spending?'

'No. It was hers, to do with as she wanted.' Caroline Morton suddenly saw the point. 'Do you think she was buying clothes like that to go out with . . . men. Well, boys.'

Jacquie shrugged with a gentle smile. 'She was fourteen,' she said. 'She had lost both parents, she had moved house, she was moving school. I'm sure she loved you and your husband, but you must see that she had gone through a lot. Perhaps she just wanted some company where no one knew her history. Where people didn't try to be kind and thoughtful all the time. It is possible to love someone too much. To wrap them in too much cotton-wool.'

'The Brighton police didn't tell me much . . . I don't know how to ask . . .'

'She wasn't raped, no,' Jacquie said.

'But?' This woman was good.

'I really don't think I ought to tell you any more,' Jacquie said, edging forward in the chair, prior to getting up. 'If we need to speak to you . . .'

'Rubbish,' the woman said, crisply, suddenly all professional. 'You haven't asked me about when she went out that last night. About whether she went out a lot. Who with. All that kind of thing. I want to *tell* you.' She was almost shouting and Jacquie sat back down, resigned.

In a monotone, Caroline Morton told Jacquie everything about Mollie's last weeks. How she had been excited about changing schools. How they had gone out shopping for uniform, for new underwear, sports wear, shoes. Not for boob tubes and micro-minis. Not for fuck-me shoes. Just hockey sticks and big pants. Sometimes tears trickled down her cheeks. Sometimes she smiled or even laughed. But at no time in the story did she tell of Mollie having sex on the beach, of coming back with sand in her hair and a guilty look in her eye. The story was of a virginal little girl, who had one night got dolled up like a working girl and gone out and got herself killed.

Chapter Five

Maxwell teased the lock of chestnut hair away from his lip. He had already nearly choked to death on a mixture of Titian and Southern Comfort and he was anxious not to repeat the experience. His wife lay along the sofa, her head on his chest, the cat on hers. Neither of them would be going anywhere anytime soon if Metternich had his way. Nolan was in bed, bathed and cherubic, looking as though butter wouldn't melt in his mouth. The Maxwells should have both been on holiday, but that was not the Maxwell way. Duty was calling and they couldn't turn a deaf ear.

'Results tomorrow, then,' Jacquie said, easing Metternich so that his leg was not sticking into her rib. He rewarded her with a low growl.

'Helen says they should be good,' Maxwell said. 'Hector's a good teacher. His kids back home were very well taught.'

'That's good.' She sighed a small sigh and waited.

'I might see Bernard tomorrow,' he said, casually.

There it was. Finally, he had let fall the second shoe.

'I mean, he usually comes in for results. Unless he is still on gardening leave of course.'

She kept up her masterly inactivity. He reached round and put his cold glass on her forehead.

'Jacquie? Dearest? Do you hear me?'

'I can't look round, because of the cat.'

'I don't want to see you – oh, any more than usual, I mean, which is a lot, of course – I just want to hear you tell me that Bernard is now a free man.'

'In that case, I'm afraid you will just have to want, Max. I can't lie to you, he is still very much suspended. Legs rang Henry up today to ask what he should do for the new term.'

'But surely . . . he didn't have anything to do with this other girl, did he?'

'The other girl is still a bit of an enigma. She is much more complicated than we thought. Her sister knew nothing of what we have to call her secret life, although that sounds a bit True Movie for my liking. Henry is trying to get Brighton to take it back, but they rightly say that just because she set off from there doesn't mean she met her murderer there. In fact, her murderer is more likely to come from Leighford. Who else would know about that landslip in Willow Bay?'

'Where does Bernard fit in, though?'

'His lack of alibi is still there, like the elephant in the room.'

Pinned down as he was, Maxwell couldn't react to the pachyderm remark. Usually, he would fling cushions hither and yon, looking for the pesky creature and priming his invisible twelve-bore. He settled for flicking her on the top of her head.

'Ow. I know, no elephant. But you get the general drift. If what he told Sylv is true, why won't he tell us where he went? He just says it's private.'

'Well, sometimes it just *is*.'

'I agree,' she said. 'But when you are a suspect in a murder case, two murder cases, pretty much, you would think that he would tell us. It wouldn't go any further. It's not as if we would let the world know where he had gone.'

'He might worry you would tell me.'

'I wasn't here when he was pulled in. For all he knew, we wouldn't be back for months.'

'True.' Maxwell took another sip of his drink. 'I have known Bernard Ryan for more years than I care to remember, but in fact, you know, I don't know him at all. I don't even know where he lives.'

'Across the Dam.'

'Swish. Married?' He answered himself. 'No, I know that one. He's single.'

'Correct.'

'Parents? Siblings? Cat? Dog? Significant other? Nothing. He's just a pain in the arse who works at Leighford High School. That's it.'

'He teaches Business Studies.'

'Allegedly. I have never known a man more adept at avoiding actually having anything to do with kids.'

'And yet,' she pointed out, 'he did tutoring.'

'Yes,' he said, tapping his glass on his teeth. 'Why did he do that?'

Jacquie bridled and put her hand down to restrain the cat. 'Don't do that, Max. Metternich doesn't like the noise. And I don't like the claws.'

'Sorry, both. Did you check Bernard's bank records?'

'This is sounding very much like you finding things out that you shouldn't know,' she remarked smoothly.

'I could always ask Bernard,' he said.

'You don't even know where he lives,' she said.

'Thingie would tell me. Up at the school. *She* knows everything.' He sounded terribly like Violet Elizabeth Bott.

'Possibly. Yes, we did check his bank statements. He is very well off, thank you very much. Why aren't you a deputy head? I could become a lady of leisure.'

'I can see you doing that,' he laughed, pulling the errant lock of hair gently. 'So, he gets a big salary. That doesn't mean he is comfortably off.'

'It does, actually,' she said. 'He goes on holiday once a year, although to fairly fancy places. Usually at Christmas, somewhere hot. He has the occasional weekend away, again somewhere quite swish, but he can easily afford it. Plus the money he gets from tutoring. He puts it all in the bank, with a note to identify it. All above board.'

'On *Law and Order* they have credit card slips.'

'Come up to date, you old dinosaur,' she said, reaching down and patting his leg, the most she dared do with Metternich poised on her chest. 'It's all done with swiping and heaven knows what. And it does look as if Bernard uses cash quite a lot, for shopping and whathaveyou.'

'Something to hide!' Maxwell said, triumphantly.

'Prefers cash,' she returned. 'People still do. *You* for example.'

'Does he have an alibi for the second girl?'

'Who knows? We're not sure when it would need to be for. And anyway, Max, can you really see Bernard as a serial killer? As a predator of young girls?'

Maxwell pursed his lips and looked up at the ceiling, whistling silently. Bernard Ryan had been a thorn in his side for years, handing out risk assessments, creating paperwork and forms to be filled in in triplicate for the slightest reason. Legs Diamond he could work with; even Dierdre Lessing, God rest her evil soul, had had her good points, but Bernard Ryan was not a nice man. He always saw the worst in people and Maxwell was a great believer in the theory that people who only saw the bad only had bad within themselves. But, a serial killer and predator of young girls . . .?

'No. No, I can't.'

'Precisely. Neither can I. But he'll have to come up with an alibi for the first murder if he is ever to get back to school. Or wait until we find the real killer, of course, which could be never.' She lay there for another moment or two and then asked, 'Max? Can you do me a favour?'

'Anything, dear one. What can I do to help, oh fount of my being?'

'Can you move the cat? Quickly. I need to sneeze and he'll have the skin off my chest if I take him by surprise like that.'

Maxwell moved with stealth but precision and whipped the huge animal up in the air in the nick of time. Jacquie's sneeze could have woken the dead and Metternich reacted as she knew he must, but it was Maxwell's forearm that took the brunt. She was still applying tea tree ointment to the scratches when the phone rang.

Jacquie got there first. 'Hello? Oh, Jason. Hello.' She raised an eyebrow at Maxwell who swirled his drink and tried to look as if he wasn't there.

'You have? Do you need me? Thanks. I appreciate that. I'll see you tomorrow. 'Bye.'

She put the phone down and stood there, screwing the top on the tea tree ointment slowly.

'That was Jason.'

'The Argonaut?'

'No.'

'The new sergeant.'

'Yes. Well, not that new. New to me.'

'And?'

'They've not managed to isolate any DNA from the second girl yet, but they have a blood group. Apparently, our man was conveniently a secretor.'

'Now there's a phrase I haven't heard in quite a while,' Maxwell remarked.

'No. I would imagine Angus had to get his text books out for this one. They are still trying to use various methods to get a useable amount of material, but for now we just have a blood group. And as it is quite unusual, they are going to pick up a suspect now.'

Maxwell didn't ask, he told. 'Bernard Ryan.'

Jacquie nodded. 'Bernard Ryan. He'll be on his way back to the Nick by now.' She looked at him. 'I'm sorry, Max. This means no more cosy little chats about murder.'

'Darn. Whatever can we do instead?' He spoke lightly, but she could hear the tension in his voice. He was asking himself if he could possibly have been so wrong about the man. If someone he had seen for at the very least two hundred days of every year, for years and years . . . if that someone could really be a person who stalked little girls, groomed them, had sex with them and then threw their strangled bodies onto a beach? If he was so wrong about this man, what else was he wrong about?

'Max . . .'

'It's no good, Jacquie. I hate to say it, because the man *is* a shit, but he didn't do it.'

She didn't answer.

'He just didn't. That's it and all about it.'

Thursday, Thursday. Hate that day. Peter Maxwell had just come back from the land of Mama Cass and it was as though he had never been away. He had taken his trusty bicycle, the steed he called White Surrey, out of mothballs, scraped off the surface rust and oiled the chain and brakes. Then it was 'Look out, Bradley Wiggins!' Mad Max was on the road. He hadn't been back to his office yet – he knew as soon as he went in there and smelled that heady mixture of stale biscuits, paper and the massed effluvium of Mrs B's hoover bag, the last seven months would just disappear. So instead, he had headed straight to the Hall, to see how the results were being received by His Own. Heads of Sixth Form, he knew, were supposed to look across the board, at *all* the subject results of Year 13, looking for balance, width, improvement, differentials. Bollocks to that; he went straight to the History list.

He was still chuckling to himself as he swept into the Hall through a throng of milling hopefuls, all in jeans and scruffy t-shirts, much the same as they had worn for the last two years, really. He took in the room with its squeaky floors and long, faded curtains. Nothing had changed. Nothing at all. The same spider that had been building its web last Christmas still sat there in the far corner at the centre of the biggest Arachno Condo Maxwell had ever seen, a small piece of tinsel caught at the edge, the spider version of archaeological evidence. Then he smiled again because nowhere did he see a sign that read This Is A Drug Free School. He felt good about that.

'McSween, you old shit!' The Head of Sixth Form was selective with his expletives. Tom McSween was eighteen going on forty. Apart from the hair, which was Justin Bieber meets Cher, he could have been at school with Maxwell himself in the great days of yore. 'Well done. Brasenose?'

'Yes, sir,' the boy beamed, feeling a surge of pride as his Head of Sixth Form gripped his hand.

'Bad luck,' Maxwell commiserated. 'If you ever see sense and want to go to a real university, I still have a few friends at Jesus. *Cambridge*, that is,' and he winked. 'Geoffrey, you dark horse. B, eh? Well done, well done.'

'It's all thanks to you, Mr Maxwell,' Geoffrey grinned goofily.

'Flatterer,' Maxwell laughed. 'But I think Mr Moss and Mr Gold had something of a hand in your success, didn't they?'

'Ah, it was the groundwork, sir,' the happy lad assured him, 'in Year 12. Before you went to . . .'

'Abroad, lad,' Maxwell finished the sentence for him. 'It's a bloody place, believe me.'

Then he was glad-handing with all of them and commiserating with the few. Time was that he would have been there as they collected the dreaded brown envelopes, watched for the falling of crests and the crises of confidence. He would have put his arm round the distressed, taken them down the pub and put their worlds to rights. Not any more. Over half of them had their results already, the day before, online. Only the successes came in to get results these days. To jog a lap of honour, to laugh and cry with happiness . . . and to take a last look at the school they had called home for seven years and would never see again until their own children went there. And anyway, putting an arm around a student these days was equivalent to signing up to Gary Glitter's gang or enrolling in Yewtree. What a sad indictment of the times.

And, talking of sad indictments, where was that excuse for a headmaster, Legs Diamond? If anyone knew anything about Bernard Ryan, surely he would.

James Diamond was having the worst summer of his life. He was one of nature's worriers anyway, but he usually had Bernard Ryan on hand to take the flak. He had always thought that Bernard Ryan didn't have an emotion in his body but he had seen the man crumble, albeit briefly, when the police had taken him away. The fear in his eyes only flashed there for a second, but it had been enough to make the smoke that Diamond knew was never there without fire. And now . . .

The tap on his door made him sit up straight, every hair on his neck tingling. Although he didn't know it, he was briefly at one with the rodentia of Columbine. No one, *no one* tapped at a door quite like that. He thought he wouldn't be back for weeks. And yet, here he was, outside his door. The headteacher cleared his throat. He had learned that when you were dealing with Peter Maxwell, you had to be careful to show no weakness. The man could smell fear.

'Come!'

Outside the door, Maxwell mouthed 'in'. How much breath did you save in an average life by not saying that tiny word? He would have to ask the Maths Department. He pushed open the door and went into Diamond's office. There was no reason for the room to have changed, but somehow there was a subtle difference. Legs looked less assured, the desk was certainly fuller and there was an air of desolation, of loss that Maxwell thought he understood.

'Did you miss me, headmaster?' he asked, flinging himself into a chair.

Diamond pinned a smile on his face as best he could. 'Of course, Max. Welcome back. We . . . we weren't expecting you just yet. We thought you might be enjoying the Californian sun for a while longer.'

'Over-rated,' Maxwell said shortly. 'And you seem to be having sun here, anyway. Without the smog and the wind.'

Diamond was not a geographer, but that didn't sound right to him. 'You can't have both, can you?' he asked.

'You'd think not,' Maxwell remarked then, leaning forward, 'What are you doing about Bernard?'

For a horrible moment that turned his bowels to water, Diamond thought that Maxwell was offering to be his Deputy and swallowed hard. When he didn't answer, Maxwell filled the silence with words that brought relief.

'I don't mean as a deputy head. I imagine you've already got something sorted on that score. Mmmm,' he looked at the ceiling briefly, thinking. 'It's Jane Taylor, I would imagine. IT.' He looked at the headteacher and smiled. 'Am I right?'

'Yes,' Diamond said. 'But . . . I only rang her yesterday. I told her not to tell anyone.'

'She didn't. I worked it out. She is the obvious choice, especially since she has been doing the timetabling for years.'

Diamond's eyebrows shot up.

Maxwell held up a calming hand. 'Don't worry, it's not common knowledge by any means. But she is a nice woman and no one hates her.' He almost added the 'yet' but managed to restrain himself. 'Good choice.'

'Well, thank you.' Diamond settled his ruffled feathers. 'It's just a temporary measure, of course. Until Bernard . . .' he narrowed his eyes at Maxwell. 'How much do you know about Bernard and his troubles, by the way?'

The answer obviously was a lot more than you, headmaster, but again, the Head of Sixth Form forebore to say what was in his mind. 'Not much, headmaster. I was away when it all began.'

'Your wife . . .?' Legs knew how many beans made five. But only approximately.

Maxwell shrugged, an elaborate gesture that took in his entire body, from his barbed-wire hair to the cycle-clip indents at the bottom of his trouser-leg. 'She was away as well, if you remember.'

Diamond was not convinced, but the need to share was overwhelming and although Maxwell was the reason for almost every one of his grey hairs, for at least fifty percent of his ulcer and all of his nervous tics, he had experience in this kind of thing. Too much experience, in Diamond's opinion, but needs must when the devil drives.

'It was last term,' he began and Maxwell settled his features into an expression of interest. He would get nowhere by bursting out with the proper version of events, the Matthews Version; Diamond could spin for England but Maxwell would have to play a waiting game. On one balmy evening, sitting out in what he had learned to call the yard, he, Jacquie and Nolan had watched a gecko stalking a locust, each movement tiny, slow and controlled so as not to lose its prey. He decided to take a leaf out of its book and he all but disappeared into the chair. Gordon (as they had inevitably named the creature) would have been proud.

'It was last term. Bernard hadn't spoken to me, but he had had concerns about a girl he was tutoring. I haven't had all of the facts, but it seems the long and the short of it is that Bernard may have been the last person to see her alive.'

Maxwell may have been in gecko-mode, but he had to speak. 'The next to last person, surely,' he said.

'What?' Diamond blinked. 'What?'

'Her murderer would be the last person, surely?' he said, with a small smile.

'Yes, yes.' Diamond was cross with himself. He shouldn't have fallen into that trap – it looked bad. 'Yes, as you say. There were . . . certain factors that made the police come and take Bernard in for questioning.' He took off his glasses and peered short-sightedly across his desk at Maxwell. 'Only questioning, mind you. There was no arrest.'

Maxwell inclined his head, reptile-style.

'I did ask Bernard later how things had gone and he told me that he had declined to give an alibi. That's the actual word he used, Max. *Declined.* So, of course, I had no option but to ask him to accept suspension from his post. I told him he could have a union representative with him, or a friend from the staff, but he said no, there was no point.' Diamond managed a wintry smile. 'In fact, he said with you not around, there was no one he would choose.'

'Me?' Maxwell was staggered. He had exchanged few words with Bernard Ryan that could not be classed as frankly hostile, as far as his innate public-schoolboy manners would allow. If he was the nearest thing to a friend that Ryan could summon up, it was a sorry state of affairs to be sure.

'I don't think as a friend, so much, as someone who knew what the score was. You have been . . . in trouble,' the headteacher had the grace to look a little shamefaced, 'yourself and of course you do have your links with the police.'

'Well, my wife is a detective inspector,' Maxwell conceded.

Diamond looked at the man. He was no less exasperating now than when he had seen him last. He would never help you out of a hole if he could throw more earth in instead. He let it go. 'Quite so. Anyway, Bernard took his suspension and he is still off, as you already know. I suppose you also know he has been taken in by the police a second time.'

Maxwell could not use a five and a half thousand mile distance as an excuse this time and decided to give the sucker an even break. 'Yes, I did hear something about that.'

'Do you know why?'

This wasn't right. He was in here to ask Diamond the questions, not the other way around. He toyed briefly with swivelling the headmaster's lamp into his eyes and rapping out something from *The Untouchables*, but he knew that Legs Diamond had no sense of humour at all. 'I got a tiny gist, but I can't really . . .'

'I do understand, Max. I shouldn't have asked.'

Diamond the humble was not something you saw very often and Maxwell felt the earth tremble slightly beneath his feet. 'If it's any comfort,' he said, 'Jacquie is sure there is nothing in it. It was simply the police exploring every avenue.'

Diamond perked up a little, as far as he ever perked. He gave a nervous laugh. 'I thought it was probably something like that. So he'll be back soon, you think?'

Maxwell had heard that tone before. When Nolan's goldfish had died, he had asked when it would wake up in exactly the same way.

'It's not for me to say,' Maxwell said, 'but in his shoes I think I would wait a while longer until he was sure that he wouldn't be pulled in again. It wouldn't look too good, would it, if the police . . .'

Diamond shied like a startled filly. 'Oh, no, no, you're right. I'll tell him to not even think of coming back until . . .

well, until . . .' He had picked up the phone and stabbed a fast dial code. He waited, receiver to ear, smiling vaguely at Maxwell. The sound of the phone ringing at the other end oozed through his head and into the room. After a moment or so he put the receiver down. 'Not in,' he said. 'I wonder where he might be.'

Maxwell pressed his lips together in what in certain circumstances might pass for a smile. He knew where Bernard Ryan was and he wouldn't be in a position to answer the phone. He decided to try to find out at least a little more than he knew already. 'Any idea why Bernard wouldn't give an alibi?' he asked. 'It would have prevented all of this, right from the start.'

Diamond spread his arms out wide. 'I have no idea. I think I always assumed that he didn't have one. That he was out for a walk, at the cinema, something like that; somewhere anonymous.'

'But that isn't declining to give an alibi, is it?' Maxwell persisted. 'That's just having a rubbish alibi. No, Bernard must have something to hide. But what?' He waited expectantly.

Diamond leaned forward and briefly looked almost human. 'Don't think I haven't thought about this, Max, because a day hasn't gone by since the police took him away that I haven't thought about it. You have no idea how awful it was. They didn't bother to be even slightly subtle. They used handcuffs! On Bernard!'

'I'm sorry Jacquie and I weren't here,' Maxwell said, and meant it. 'I'm sure she could have . . . well, she just doesn't do handcuffs unless there is no option.'

'Of course, the students loved it. It was all I could do to make them put their mobile phones away. Bernard isn't popular, as you may know.' Diamond made the last statement sound like news and Maxwell felt for the man; that he could be so unaware of other people was almost a talent. 'Bernard behaved with a lot of dignity but he was very short with me when we spoke on the phone a few days later. I got the impression he had someone with him, and of course . . .' he looked left and right and then dropped his voice, 'I couldn't help *thinking* if you know what I mean?'

'Indeed, headmaster,' Maxwell said, getting up abruptly. For a moment there, he had felt sorry for the man. But he was clearly an arse. 'I must go. I'm on Nolan duty until we start term. His mother is back at work, as you know, so I must be away. Mrs Troubridge isn't getting any younger and Nole's a bit young yet to be calling ambulances. I'll see you at the start of term.' And he turned on his heel and was gone. He sighed. He had hoped to sort things out here, but the horse's mouth it would have to be. And, after a brief word with morning Thingie, who asked if he'd met Brad Pitt, he and White Surrey were purring through the highways and byeways of Leighford, Columbine-bound.

Maxwell rapped on Mrs Troubridge's door with his usual élan and waited patiently for her to answer. He and Jacquie had realised long ago that they and Mrs Troubridge saw a completely different thing when they looked at Nolan. They saw a feisty child, slightly on the stocky side, with hair that would lie down sometimes for as many as three minutes together, with the heart of a lion, with a mouth on him that would get him into serious trouble one day and the brain of a rather sophisticated thirty year old. She saw a delicate creature, put on earth to be wrapped in velvet with a protective layer of bubble wrap for safety, with a fragile ego that could be crushed like an eggshell by the smallest slight, a creature of air and cobwebs who she, Mrs Troubridge, must guard to her last breath. Therefore, when he was on the Troubridge side of the door, he was not allowed to hurtle down the stairs to open it, for fear of broken bones on the way down and potential shock forward slash abduction when he got there. Maxwell heard the tell-tale signs of Mrs Troubridge's careful steps underscored by Nolan's cry of 'We're on our way, Dads!'

'It might not be your father, dear,' he heard his neighbour say, her voice now clearly just the other side of the door. 'Let me look through the letterbox to see before we open the door.'

Maxwell always felt faintly embarrassed as Mrs Troubridge's critical gaze examined his general crotch area and he never knew what to do with his hands. But whatever it was she used as criteria clearly passed muster this time and she opened the door, sliding bolts and chains until it was free.

'Mr Maxwell!' she said, amazed that he should be there of all places, at the previously appointed time. She looked over her shoulder. 'It's your father, Nolan.'

'Yes,' Nolan said, wriggling to the front of the unlikely duo. 'Dads, we're in the middle of a film. Can I come round when it's finished?'

'Well . . .?' Maxwell raised an interrogative eyebrow at Mrs Troubridge, aka Mary Poppins.

'I'd be delighted,' she said. 'Besides, That Woman is next door cleaning, so it wouldn't be suitable for Nolan.' She clutched him to her side, to protect him from Mrs B, in absentia though she was.

'Mrs B?' Maxwell asked. 'I wasn't sure she would be coming any more. I understand that Hector . . .'

'Mr Gold is *most* fastidious,' Mrs Troubridge said smugly. 'He couldn't contemplate That Woman's slapdash ways.'

'But I thought you and Mrs B were friends these days,' Maxwell remarked.

'Not *friends*, Mr Maxwell,' Mrs Troubridge hissed. 'I don't think you could call us *friends*.'

Maxwell smiled and looked down at Nolan, who was starting to squirm a little in Mrs Troubridge's iron grip. For a little old lady, she had a lot of core strength. 'Well, in that case, Mrs Troubridge, if Nolan could stay a while, that would be wonderful. I do have an errand to run, possibly, so . . .'

'Any time,' Mrs Troubridge twittered. 'His bed is made up, as always, so don't worry. He can always go to bed here if you and Jacquie are going to be late.'

'And Metternich?' Maxwell loved to wind his neighbour up on the subject of the cat and just let her go till the clockwork wore down.

'You know my views,' Mrs Troubridge said, bridling. She looked like a very tiny, very wizened Les Dawson. 'But I have some sachets to hand, of course. If he calls.'

Metternich could smell a sachet of cat food, opened or unopened, at an as yet undetermined distance and so Maxwell knew he would be fine. All he need do now was to track down Bernard Ryan and the next stage could commence. He tipped his hat to Mrs Troubridge, kissed Nolan on the top of the head and went down one path, up another and opened his own front door, to the distant whine of the hoover.

It was clear from the first second that Mrs B, 'that woman', who cleaned up at the school and chez Maxwell, had not changed in the seven months since Maxwell had seen her last. He did not mean that in the underwear sense, of course, if only because underwear and Mrs B were such non-sequiturs it didn't bear thinking about. No, it was as if she had been poised there, Dyson in hand at the end of the hallway, just waiting for this golden moment.

'Hello, Mr M,' she roared over the machine, as if she had forgotten how to switch it off. 'Ain't you brown? Bet the old lungs are full of smog, though, eh? Did you meet Brad Pitt at all? Ooh, and what about that Mr Ryan, up at the school? There's more than that to meet the eye. But it's really nice to have you back.'

Maxwell had missed the staccato rattle of Mrs B's conversations; she was a one-woman Gatling gun. But he could match her, bullet point for bullet. 'Yes, I suppose I am. Yes, smog is a Californian problem, but, as you see, I have survived. Sadly, Bradley was out when we called. What about Mr Ryan indeed? Yes, there always is. And it's nice to *be* back, Mrs B and to gaze upon your radiant features.'

'Whatever,' Mrs B said, and gave the skirting board an extra hard whack, to hide her confusion.

The Leighford Nick desk sergeant had become quite complacent while the Maxwell family had been in California. He had got quite used to answering the phone without his adrenalin flooding his system, even though he knew that news of fresh disasters might even so be on the other end. At least it wouldn't be Maxwell. But now, here he was again and his visit to the good old U S of A hadn't changed him a bit. With no attempt at conversation, the desk man merely pushed the button for Jacquie's extension and put the phone down. He only forebore to wipe his hand down the side of his trousers because he was in the middle of dealing with one of Leighford's madder old biddies, here to report a missing cat; she had forgotten, for the eighth time that week, that Tiddles had gone to that great litterbox in the sky when that nice Mr Brown had been at Number Ten.

'DI Carpenter-Maxwell.'

'I love the way that rolls out,' Maxwell was doing his very best Wile. E. Coyote.

'Hello, Max,' she said, with a hint of suspicion and a soupcon of having someone in the room with her. 'Is everything all right?'

'Indeed,' he said. 'Results surprisingly good, Nolan and Mrs Troubridge like two little birds in their nest and Mrs B is wielding a handy hoover. All well with you?' He hoped the question was loaded with innuendo.

She got the subliminal message and dropped her voice a tone. 'All is well at this end,' she said. 'Everyone's back at home where they may not be for long, but apart from that, it's all hunky dory.'

'Wonderful!' he exclaimed. 'Er . . . I may be out when you get back. Nole is with Mrs T and your dinner is in the lodger. 'Bye.' And he hung up quickly. If she asked no questions, she would hear no lies and that was the best way all round.

'Max!' she hissed down the phone but knew she was too late. He was too far away for her to reach the house before he was long gone, but she had a way of checking his destination. She glanced round at Jason Briggs, who was trying not to look as if he were eavesdropping at the far side of the room. 'Excuse me, Jason, I must just make a call. Child care. Such a problem.' She flashed him a sweet smile and went out onto the landing and dialled a familiar number.

'Leighford High School.' Thingie One hated results day. Lots of irate parents who couldn't believe their little geese had failed everything, wanting to speak to Diamond just drove her crazy, but the worst was over now.

'It's Mrs Maxwell here,' Jacquie said, cutting the preamble. 'I assume Mr Maxwell had left, has he?'

'Oooh, Mrs Maxwell,' Thingie One burbled, trying to decide whether she should ask the woman if *she* had met Brad Pitt. 'He's looking ever so well, we thought. The sunshine must have suited him.'

'Yes, it did.' Jacquie knew it was easier to go through the motions and she forced a smile into her voice. 'He's gone though, has he?'

'Oooh, yes. A while ago. We were saying, he's still got his bike, then.'

'Oh, yes, you won't part Mr Maxwell from his bike.' Jacquie managed a chuckle. Perhaps going home would have been quicker. 'Did he say where he was going?'

'No,' Thingie One thought for a moment. 'Home, I think. Oh, no, wait a minute. He asked me where Mr Ryan lived.'

Gotchya, thought Jacquie. Did she know this man or what? 'Oh, right.'

'It's ever such a shame, we were all saying this morning. Well, I know Mr Ryan . . .'

'Yes. So, he's going to see Mr Ryan, is he?' she asked.

'Well, he didn't say so, no. We thought perhaps he was going to send a card, or something. You know, kind of sympathy.'

The picture that that conjured up almost rendered Jacquie speechless, but she managed to say goodbye before hanging up the phone. She would need to finish her de-brief with Jason and then she would be on her way. Maxwell would have to arrange transport, so that gave her a while in hand. She couldn't stop him before he got to Ryan's house, but she could nip it more or less in the bud. She turned and pushed open the door.

'Well, Jason, sorry about that. So, your views on Bernard Ryan?'

'Well, he clearly did it, ma'am. We just need to pin it on the sick bastard, don't we?'

So, she thought with a sigh, the old adage of innocent until proven guilty was clearly alive and well and living in Leighford Nick.

Not.

Chapter Six

The girl looked up from her meal, the milk moustache making her look younger than her fourteen years. She was beginning to get a bit bored and was ready to go home. What had started out as fun had now become just like being at home, with rules and regulations, don't do this, do do that all the time. The flattery, the presents, everything had stopped pretty much. Except the sex. That was still very much on the menu. And, she had to admit, enough was as good as a feast in that department, too. The first time it had been magical. He had taken her out to dinner. Proper dinner, not just some fast food rubbish like the boys at school might spring for. He had brought her some clothes to wear, proper clothes that made her look years older than she was, that fitted her like a glove. Then, he had taken her back to his hotel, not behind some church hall leaning against a skip. The room had been like fairyland; low lights, the curtains drawn back from the huge picture window, the lights of the marina bobbing far below. There had been rose petals, actual *rose petals* on the bed and when she had started to undress herself ready to get it over with like she generally did, he had stopped her and slowly done it for her, only loosening his own clothes gradually so that, in the end, they both were naked at the last minute together. So, this was why they called it lovemaking, she had thought, as she sank onto the bed, drunk with bliss. This wasn't sex. This was love. And that had lasted for a week or two. And, even now, it could be spectacular if he was in the mood. But normally these days it was as if he wasn't thinking of her at all. As if he were thinking of someone else entirely.

'I think I'd like to go home now,' she said. 'If I'm away much longer, my mum will start to get suspicious. And school will be starting soon as well. If I'm not back for then, they'll look for me.' She wasn't at all sure that was true, but she hoped it might be.

He looked at her and seemed to consider. 'All right, then,' he said. 'Off you go.' He turned back to the newspaper he was reading. 'I expect you're right. You don't want her to get suspicious, do you?'

She looked at him, her milk and sandwich forgotten. She hadn't wanted him to agree; she had wanted him to beg her to stay, tell her he could never love anyone like her. All the stuff he had told her a few weeks ago when they had met along the beach, when they had just walked and walked for miles, talking. The friends she was walking with had stared at him. He was so handsome. He was old, of course, she knew that. He had to be . . . thirty? Forty? Well, she'd never been any good with ages. At school, in the history lessons, the mad bastard she had had in Year Seven, he'd asked them all how old they thought he was. She had put eighty, but loads of the others had put even more. She knew he wasn't eighty, she just wanted to wind him up. But he'd just laughed.

And now, she was being told to go. This wasn't right. She was his soulmate. He'd told her so, often. He couldn't just let her go back home. 'I . . . I don't mean I'd *like* to go home,' she said. 'I just thought you might want me to.'

He put the paper down now, folding it in half and sticking it down the side of his chair. He got up and walked over to her, lifting her chin in his hand so she was looking up into his eyes. He reached across with his thumb and wiped a crumb from a corner of her mouth. She smiled up and him and he smiled down at her. He reached around behind her and picked up a towel, left on the back of the chair, ready to go in the wash. Still smiling, he wrapped the towel around her neck. Her smile became puzzled but he blotted it out by kissing her gently on the lips.

She didn't start to struggle until the towel started to get quite tight. He was pulling and pulling, with his mouth pressing harder on hers, so her head was pushed right back. She could feel her teeth digging in to the soft skin inside her mouth and she tasted blood. She tried to raise her arms, but she felt somehow tired and weak. Her feet drummed on the floor and everything started to go dark, although her eyes were wide and staring. From somewhere, and she was quite certain it was from outside her head, a bell was ringing. Then there was some banging. And then, like a miracle, the pressure on her throat stopped and he stepped away from her. He dropped the towel, first using it to wipe his mouth where her blood had stained his lips.

'Stay there,' he grated. 'You'll enjoy that the next time. It's time you started the next stage.' He tried a smile, but it didn't quite work. 'You'll love it. I do it because I love you.'

Stuck in the chair like a rabbit in the headlights, she heard the noise continue. The bell was ringing and someone was also banging on the door. Faintly, she could hear someone calling. It was a woman's voice, and it was starting to sound a bit annoyed. He wiped his mouth again and went into the hall, closing the kitchen door behind him.

'All right, all right,' she heard him call. 'I'm on my way.'

She heard the door open and a woman's voice, slightly petulant but also upset-sounding, came through the closed kitchen door. 'Where were you? We've got things to discuss.'

'Have we?' she heard him say. 'Like what?'

The woman started to cry and it went quiet, out in the hall. Somehow, the woman's tears galvanized the girl and she slid silently out of the chair and over to the back door. Sometimes it was locked, but not today. There was a ten pound note on the side, ready for when the milkman called. He didn't like tradesmen waiting at the door, he had explained to her. They might see his little princess and he didn't want them talking. People wouldn't understand. They would want to part them. She got used to hiding, ducking, diving. But that was over now. She pocketed the tenner and was away, sprinting up the passage at the side of the house and away up the road. She didn't know where she was, but she knew where she wanted to be. And that place was Somewhere Else.

Jacquie had never known a de-brief take so long. If Jason Briggs had been deliberately slowing things up, he could not have made a better job of it. He fumbled through his notebook, lost himself in the tape of the interview and generally didn't seem to know his arse from a hole in the ground. Jacquie was at a distinct disadvantage. Ninety nine percent of her knew that Bernard Ryan was innocent. That her husband, Mr Body Language, had worked with the bloke for years and couldn't believe he had done it was almost all she needed to know. Add to the mix the fact that Ryan was quietly adamant that he didn't know Mollie, despite the fact that there was a tenuous link with Josie Blakemore via St Olave's and her gut reaction became stronger. But then, there was the problem of the alibi. It always came down to that alibi. And he wouldn't budge on it. Even so, in the end they had had no choice but to bundle him into a police car and send him home, with instructions not to leave the country. He had volunteered his passport and that, for now, was that. Jason wanted to beat him to a pulp. Jacquie wanted him to climb down off his high horse and tell them where he had been. Somewhere between the two lay closure on this case. Finally they talked themselves to a standstill and she had grabbed her bag and made for the car park and the world beyond the Dam.

   Maxwell had found things just as difficult to get going. Ringing for a cab had sounded easy and the ringing part had certainly not presented a problem. Finding one that would take him out of town for less than the national debt of a small emergent nation was altogether another, but finally he had struck lucky with a driver who was kicking his heels before picking up a fare from Gatwick, so going out over the Dam was on the way for him and they came to an arrangement, involving driving past and pausing at an ATM. He felt slightly guilty as he walked down the path and got into the cab when he noticed Mrs Troubridge's door open a crack and Metternich slither in. Whether Mrs Troubridge liked it or not, there wasn't a bolt that could keep Nolan in or the Count out; they made him proud.

Maxwell's Return

All the way to Bernard Ryan's house his phone was making the small wurbling noises he had learned to ignore. He had promised Jacquie years ago that he would always carry it. He had even agreed to be sure it had battery. But there was nothing she could do to make him answer it and he didn't feel bad – she knew the score. She should know to quit while she was ahead. He tucked it deeper into his pocket and tried to ignore his vibrating leg.

'Somebody wants to get hold of you, mate,' the cab driver observed eventually. Why didn't the mad old git answer the thing? That ringtone was beginning to get on his wick.

'Hmm?' Maxwell decided to act dumb.

'Your phone.' The driver spoke louder. 'Somebody's ringing you a lot. It might be urgent. Should you answer it?'

'No,' Maxwell said with a beatific smile. 'It will just be my fan club secretary. They just won't leave me alone.' He sat back, looking at the passing countryside with a slight smile on his face, his hands calmly folded in his lap.

The driver turned his rearview mirror slightly, to get a better view. 'Fan club?' he asked.

Maxwell caught his eye in the mirror. 'Oh, yes. A necessary evil in my position, sadly.' Then he looked out of the window again.

'So, you're famous, then?'

'For my sins.' Maxwell looked rueful.

'Would I have . . . seen you in anything?'

'Ha ha,' Maxwell gave a theatrical laugh. 'Possibly.' The man could luvvie for England.

The driver was racking his brain. Now he came to think about it, the geezer did look a bit familiar. A quiz show, perhaps? Or comedy, with that hair. 'Are you on the telly or in films?' he asked eventually, swinging around a corner into a rather select estate.

Maxwell extended a hand, rocking it from side to side. 'I go wherever the work is, my dear chap,' he said fruitily, trying to sound like a mixture of Donald Wolfitt and Stephen Fry – actually not as hard a task as he had first expected.

The cab driver checked his sat nav. 'Well, guv, we're here,' he said. ''Ere, who are all those people?'

'Ah,' Maxwell said, a histrionic hand to his brow. 'They have tracked me down again.' He leaned forward with the requisite handful of notes. 'The price of fame,' and he was out of the cab and bounding up the drive to rap on the front door. 'No pictures,' he cried, 'no autographs, I beg.'

The reporters outside Ryan's house were understandably confused, except the one from the *Leighford Advertiser*. 'Mad Max,' the Old Leighford Highena muttered. 'I was wondering when he'd get here.'

Bernard Ryan opened the door the minimum amount and hauled Maxwell though the gap by his lapel almost before his knuckles grazed the wood. The two men stood in the hall looking at each other and Maxwell found himself in unfamiliar territory in more ways than one; he was totally lost for words. Usually when he and Ryan met in a corridor, classroom or meeting they inclined their heads a fraction and muttered a minimal greeting and this time was no exception.

'Max.'

'Bernard.'

After that, it was hard to think of an opening. Finally, Ryan broke the stalemate. 'I was wondering when you would get here,' he said and he sounded so matter of fact that they might have been talking over tea-cups in Leighford's twee-est cafe, about timetables and the length of assemblies.

Maxwell was confused. 'Did you invite me?' he said, puzzled.

'No,' the Deputy Head replied. 'Since when did you need an invitation to a disaster? I thought that if you hadn't caused it yourself, you would at least be the first on the scene.'

Maxwell was affronted and drew himself up accordingly. 'I have no idea what you mean,' he said.

Bernard Ryan drew a deep breath and lifted a hand, finger extended, to begin the list. Maxwell stopped him hurriedly.

'I have possibly been occasionally involved in some unusual situations,' he said, 'but I admit you have hurt my feelings, Bernard. I came to offer my support and commiserations, that's all.'

Ryan snorted and led the way into the sitting room. The curtains at the front were drawn to keep out the more pushy reporters' noses. 'Come off it, Max. Don't forget we go back a long way. You've come to snoop around. Unless I miss my guess, you have already spoken to . . . let me see . . . Sylvia Matthews, Helen Maitland and James, not necessarily in that order. Plus your wife, of course.' Maxwell didn't reply and Ryan persisted. 'Am I wrong?'

Maxwell sat back in his chair, a leather affair that looked as though it was going to be hard but was actually amazingly comfortable. In fact, the house was a surprise all round. Larger than one person would need, stylishly furnished. Very nice. He realised that he had been expecting Bernard to live in his late mother's house, perhaps with his late mother still in the fruit cellar. This was a pleasant surprise. Eventually, he answered.

'No, Bernard, you're not wrong. With one transposition, you've even got the order right. But . . . I haven't come to gloat or snoop. Jacquie doesn't know I'm here.' As he said the words, he knew they weren't strictly true. 'Well, perhaps I should say I haven't *told* her I'm here. On previous showings, she has either sussed me already or soon will. But my point is, I am not here to get things out of you that the police haven't. I'm actually here to tell you that I don't think you did it.'

'Them.'

'You're such a stickler, Bernard,' Maxwell said. 'Them. But I don't see why you won't give yourself an alibi.'

Ryan shrugged and if Maxwell was expecting more, he was doomed to disappointment.

'If I may just speak out of turn for a minute . . .' Maxwell began, to fill the gap, 'Jacquie and the police don't understand why you are being so stubborn. They aren't reporters on a red-top, you know. They won't sell your story to the highest bidder. All they need is a name, a place, just something to convince them that you couldn't have killed Josie Blakemore . . .'

Ryan cut in with a sneer, 'So, you have her name down pat, then?' he said. 'You've committed the whole thing to memory, I expect. Every sordid little detail.'

Maxwell was genuinely surprised. He had always assumed every teacher could remember a child's name after one hearing, but he would have to accept he may be wrong on that score. He didn't take Bernard up on that remark, but on another word. 'Sordid?'

'Yes,' Ryan said. 'Sordid. The clothes, the . . . signs. All that.'

'I don't think I know any of that,' Maxwell muttered. 'All I heard was that a girl who you tutored was found dead on the beach, having come to you for help over a family issue.'

Ryan looked at him doubtfully. 'So, your wife told you nothing about the way she was found? Dressed like a hooker and left on the beach. Signs of . . .'

'Sex?' Maxwell leaned forward to look into the man's eyes.

'Yes. Well, that wasn't a surprise to me, she had after all hinted that someone was behaving inappropriately. But the clothes didn't make sense. She had been wearing her school uniform when I saw her last. I told them that, the police. And to be honest, she didn't seem the sort of girl who would be off on the dunes with somebody.'

'You think that's what it was?'

Ryan shrugged. 'It looks like that to me,' he said.

'Don't men who molest girls usually do it rather more clandestinely than that?' Maxwell asked. 'Not that I'm an expert, but I don't see a man who has been grooming a girl in the bosom of the family suddenly going out on the dunes. From what I hear as I wander the corridors of Leighford High, those dunes can be as busy as Cabot Cove on a balmy summer's evening.'

'Perhaps it wasn't him. Perhaps it was some spotty oik from school.'

'St Olave's?' Maxwell was sceptical. For a start, it was an all-girls establishment and from what he had ever heard of it, the students were kept on a pretty tight leash, even the day girls.

'Well, you know, they find the boys somehow.'

'The main thing is, though, Bernard, we need to prove it wasn't you, don't we?'

'We?'

Maxwell flung himself back in frustration. 'The royal we, Bernard. The "we" as in people who think you are being totally stupid. Where were you, for God's sake? With a prostitute? A married woman? At the dogs?' Maxwell's eyebrows rose. 'Dog fighting? Dogging? What?'

Bernard Ryan took a long, shuddering breath and sat forward in his seat, his hands pressed together, fingers interlaced. He was white around his mouth and his eyes were closed. He looked rather like a picture of one of the more minor saints about to be torn limb from limb or pecked by ravens or whatever form of torture was to be his lot. Maxwell didn't stir. Gordon had trained him well. Finally, the Deputy Head looked up and Maxwell realised he had never really looked the man in the eyes before. They were a deep brown, with golden flecks in them; he could briefly see why Sylvia Matthews had said he was not unattractive. Then, the eyes dropped again. The voice when it finally came through his dry lips had little resemblance to his usual hectoring tone.

'I have come to a decision, Max,' he said. 'Since this all happened, many options have been open to me and most of them would shock people who know me. I have been contemplating suicide.' He held up his hand before Maxwell could speak. 'I know, no answer. I do know that. And I didn't want to hurt . . . anyone. I thought of resigning and moving away, but that would be tantamount to admitting my guilt, and I am not guilty. And anyway, I like the way I live. I'm not sure I would want to manage on less money.' He gave a dry chuckle. 'That's why I do the tutoring, in case you wondered. I really do like money. It's as simple as that. So, anyway, I had come to the end of my options, all bar one, and that was to tell the police my alibi.'

Maxwell thought carefully then decided not to speak. This was a moment where masterly inactivity was key.

'But I decided not to. That oik of a sergeant would promise me secrecy and then would make sure it was plastered over every report and ultimately newspaper and I couldn't do that. I wouldn't want to . . .'

Maxwell couldn't help himself. 'Hurt anyone?'

Ryan nodded, still looking down at the floor between his knees. 'Yes. I wouldn't want to hurt anyone.'

'And how does anyone feel about this?' Maxwell asked gently.

'Anyone says I should tell the police,' Ryan smiled. 'Some people trust the police. I don't. Unless you have been arrested – as you have been, I know, Max – when you haven't done anything, you can't understand how it feels.'

'Tell Jacquie,' Maxwell said. 'You know you can trust her.'

'She has a job to do, just like all the rest,' Ryan said.

'But if your alibi checks out?' Maxwell said, raising his hands and letting them fall with a slap on his knees.

'It's only one person,' Ryan said. 'Why should the police give it any more credibility than when it is just my word?'

'Well, it's twice as many people, for one thing,' Maxwell said. How could the man be so dim?

'So, anyway,' Ryan said, sitting up straight and putting his hands on the arms of his chair and tossing his head to get rid of a lock of hair in his eyes. He looked not unlike the statue of Abraham Lincoln, sitting forever gazing into the reflecting pool – but all he was gazing into were Peter Maxwell's eyes, as deep as any pool, and kinder. 'So, anyway, I have decided to tell you.' He raised a finger. 'Don't speak. Listen. I will only say this once.'

Maxwell fought down a picture of Michelle Dubois assuring René that he would not be hearing the instructions again. Memories of TV comedy classics could threaten the most serious of moments.

'I do have an alibi,' Bernard Ryan said, quietly. 'I was with my lover all night. I only came home to change for school. I shouldn't have left Josie. She was clearly distressed but I was selfish. We don't get together very often. Joe doesn't live here, you see. It's only when there is business locally that we get to meet.'

'Jo doesn't come here, then?' Maxwell checked.

'Oh, no.' Ryan gave a little laugh. 'Married.'

Maxwell tipped his head and smiled. 'You wouldn't be the only one to be having an affair with someone married to someone else,' he said. 'Nor the last, I daresay.'

'We both have a lot to lose,' Ryan said. 'I have my position to consider and Joe also . . . well, the press would be all over it.'

'So, Jo is famous, then?'

Bernard Ryan could not resist a small smile. 'TV,' he said. 'Business correspondent for satellite news.'

'Wow!' A little bit of LA crept in to Maxwell's mouth. Well, it was the shock. 'I can't say that I am that familiar with satellite news channels. What does she look like? She's not that amazing blonde, is she? The one with the . . .'

'Jumping to conclusions, Max,' Ryan said. 'No, Joe isn't the amazing blonde, although it is true in certain lights his hair has got some golden tints. Joe is the one with the sharp suit and the taste in rather crazy ties. His eyes are green in some lights, blue in another. He has a little stutter sometimes, when the Dow is doing exciting stuff.' He paused and looked at Maxwell, smiling with relief now it was out in the open. 'Got him, now?'

Maxwell nodded. 'Got him,' he said.

'So,' Ryan relaxed into his chair. 'Now you know. We were in a rather nice hotel tucked away in the countryside out beyond Billingshurst. Joe's company have a suite there for when their correspondents have news to chase outside of London. Joe has *rather* a lot of news to chase outside London.'

Maxwell was still pretty much speechless. Bernard Ryan, one-dimensional, boring, pernickety Bernard Ryan, had not only a secret life but a really *interesting* secret life. Had he been asked, Maxwell would have said that the nearest the man came to a secret passion was perhaps midnight snacks of left-over trifle, about which he would agonize for days. But no – he was having a crazy affair with a TV personality. The Bart Simpson which was never far beneath Maxwell's surface came bubbling to the top. 'Cool!' he said.

'Cool?' Ryan was expecting any number of reactions, but not that.

'Perhaps cool is the wrong word,' Maxwell said, sitting up straight and running a hand through his barbed wire hair. 'I think what I really meant was that it was cool that you are so clearly in love with this man. I hope he deserves you.'

'Max!' Maxwell was disconcerted to see tears in Ryan's eyes. 'I don't think anyone has ever said anything as nice as that to me.'

'Joe does, surely,' Maxwell twinkled.

Ryan blushed like a girl. 'Well . . . yes. But none of this changes the fact that he is married with two young children. I know these are modern times, but his career will nosedive if this comes out; he is on the shortlist to front the news programme when the anchor leaves after Christmas. He loves his wife. He adores his children.'

'Who said you can have it all?' Maxwell asked, rhetorically.

'Well, yes. Quite. So, because I have less to lose, I have decided to keep quiet. He's furious, but I won't change my mind. So now perhaps you see why I can't tell the police.'

'Let me call Jacquie . . .'

'No!'

'She . . .' The doorbell rang, followed quickly by a knock on the door. 'There seems to be someone outside.'

'It will be one of those vultures from the Press. Max, can you open it?' Ryan seemed to have put his faith in Mad Max. Who would ever have thought it?

'All right. If you're sure.'

The knocking got more insistent and was joined by a voice, coming loud and clear through the letterbox.

'Max! Peter Maxwell! Open this door. I know you're in there!'

Ah, Maxwell thought as he moved more quickly to open the door as ordered. No need to call the police when the police could be relied upon to call on you.

Chapter Seven

'Heart!' Maxwell said, flinging open the door. 'Fancy meeting you here.'

'Fancy,' Jacquie said shortly, shouldering past him and into the sitting room. She left the paparazzi speculating wildly in her wake. For a moment, Maxwell was surprised but then remembered she had been here before.

'DI Maxwell,' Ryan said, half-rising.

'Please, don't get up,' the policewoman said, plonking herself down in the chair still warm from her husband's bum. 'It wasn't really you I came to see, Bernard. I just came to reclaim some lost property.'

'Jacquie, I . . .'

'Just don't get me started, Bernard,' she interrupted him. 'I'll take him out of your hair now. He had no right to come and bother you.' She stopped, looking from one man to another. 'Am I missing something?'

Maxwell cocked an eyebrow at Bernard Ryan, who sighed and nodded. 'Just her, though, Max. It isn't to go any further.'

'I promise,' the Head of Sixth Form said. 'Do you have a card, something so that we . . . er, Jacquie can check the details.'

'Oh, yes, of course, how stupid of me.' Ryan fished out his mobile and looked at Maxwell. 'What's your number? I'll text it to you.' Then he caught Jacquie's eye and smiled. 'What was I thinking. Jacquie, what is Max's phone number?'

She reeled it off, and Maxwell was amazed all over again. Ryan punched some numbers and there was a faint wurble deep in Maxwell's trousers.

'You are carrying it, then?' she said.

'Of course,' he said, bridling. Then he reached over and shook Ryan's hand. 'It's been fun, Bernard. See you at the chalk face next week, then?'

The Deputy Head looked at Jacquie. 'It will depend a lot on your wife,' he said, 'but hopefully, yes.'

'See you then, then,' he said and left the room.

The DI looked at her main, indeed her only, suspect with a questioning tilt of the head.

'He knows,' Ryan sighed. 'We've had quite an interesting afternoon. It will be a shame to get back to normal.'

'You won't be giving him an easy time over cover, then?' she asked, knowing the answer.

'Of course not!' He smiled at her and unexpectedly leaned over and kissed her cheek. 'It's a shame things weren't different. Max and I could have been friends, perhaps . . .'

Maxwell, in the hall, gave an all-over shudder. Over his dead body. Or someone's at any rate.

The paparazzi at the roadside were agog. The bloke they thought must be famous had now come out of the house with that DI, the one they had seen here before. And he looked to be in big trouble. They muttered into their iPhones, tapped on their tablets and got themselves very excited. All except the man from the *Leighford Advertiser*, of course, who just laughed up his sleeve.

The paps were right in one respect, though. Peter Maxwell was in big trouble. *Very* big trouble.

'So,' Jacquie said finally, after some intentionally hair-raising turns. 'You went there because?'

'Because?' Maxwell said, wounded. 'Because you knew I would go. Otherwise, why did you come to find me? I was just checking on Bernard. On a colleague, as you do.'

'As *you* do, certainly,' she snapped.

'Legs said that Bernard has spoken very highly of me. Said he would have chosen me to be his teacher's friend if he had had a tribunal.'

'That was easy to say, seeing as how you were in California at the time.'

Maxwell was silent. Somehow he could tell her heart wasn't in this. He could keep it going, but what would be the point in the long run? He cut straight to the chase. 'I know where he was,' he remarked, his voice as flat as a board.

'Proof?' she said.

'Well, there is only one person involved, but presumably that is the case with alibis as often as not. How many of us go around getting alibis from hundreds of people – unless we need one, of course?'

'Okay, I'll buy it. Who is it?'

Maxwell chuckled. 'That's the problem. I have no idea. He's famous, I gather. Name of Joe and on some satellite news programme. Business correspondent.'

'Like Robert Peston?'

'Presumably not like Robert Peston, no, as he has hair that has golden tints in the sun and eyes that are neither green nor blue.'

'Oh. *Oh!* I see. So Bernard has a famous boyfriend. I won't pretend my gob isn't smacked, but why all the drama?'

'Bernard has a *married* famous boyfriend. He was being fine and noble.'

'And a pillock.'

'Naturally. And a pillock.' Normal service seemed to have been resumed, to Maxwell's relief.

'So . . . we can ring this chap, can we?'

'You can. I promised Bernard you would deal with it yourself.'

'You can't go around making that kind of promise, Max. You know that.' She spoke gruffly, but he knew he had been forgiven. The ride home became less white knuckle and eventually she gave his leg a little pat and all was well.

Suddenly, the world was taken over by Last Week-itis. Not last week of the world, as such, but last week of the school holidays; which, for some, amounted to the same thing. Nolan's feet seemed to have grown beyond all reason in the last month and so the search was on for a new pair of shoes that would please Mrs Whatmough's Footwear Stasi and also Nolan's almost ludicrously well-developed sense of his own street-cred. Jacquie had calculated that there might be one such pair in the entire town and after an exhausting two days, Maxwell could vouch that this was indeed true. He had ended up in an unseemly scuffle in an unbelievably expensive shoe-shop but finally, the search was over. The uniform had been checked for size and found wanting on almost every level so that was another two days of his life that Maxwell would never get back again. And so, Friday dawned. Having been in LaLaLand had been disorienting for a while, but now, with All Hell Day on the horizon, Maxwell felt he had never been away. Nolan, kitting out thereof, had taken so much of the week he was only just starting to take on board the fact that he might or might not meet Bernard Ryan on Monday as they both strode the corridors of power – actual power in Maxwell's case, assumed in Ryan's. He thought it was time to grill the Mem again, just so that he was up to speed. Just as soon as she got back from work, assuming she did during the thinking hours; work had taken her over again as softly, surely and completely as an avalanche of custard flowing down over their life. He gave himself a shake – he was doing too much cooking these days. It was making him use edible metaphors, always a bad sign.

He wondered whether a call to the Nick might start the ball rolling, but, with his hand on the phone he changed his mind. Better not interrupt her; forewarned would be forearmed and he certainly didn't need that disadvantage. He hadn't even asked whether Bernard's alibi had checked out – oops, been corroborated – and if she had noticed the time they spent these days watching satellite news channels, she had said nothing. But he would renew the campaign over the weekend and by Monday morning would, if everything went to plan, know all she did and a little more. He just managed to prevent himself from rubbing his hands together and emitting an evil chuckle and went into the kitchen. He suddenly fancied some custard.

Jacquie was not thinking about custard although she wouldn't have said no to something sweet and sticky just to raise her spirits. A sludge coffee and a limp ginger nut just weren't quite doing it for her. She had been at her desk finishing off the paperwork on finally removing Bernard Ryan from the suspect list of one when Henry Hall stuck his head around her door.

'Hello?'

She looked up and welcomed him in with a smile.

'Jacquie, can I ask a big favour?' he said.

'As always, it depends on the favour,' she said. 'I am always suspicious when the words "big" and "favour" crop up together.'

He walked across and sat opposite her, sprawling in the chair a little more casually than was his wont. 'I wouldn't ask you this as a rule, but I am starting to feel a bit as though I am going down for the third time,' he said. 'Just keeping everything ticking over is taking me all day. Sometimes I ask myself what I'm still working for. When you were away, I applied for a sabbatical, you know.'

Jacquie stopped breathing and didn't look up. She needed Henry to keep it professional. There had been a close call while she had been in Los Angeles when one of the Assistant DAs had found it hard to believe that she and Maxwell were very happy together and it had sharpened her antennae.

'It wasn't the same without you,' he went on. He made the noise that in Henry Hall passed for a chuckle. 'Don't worry,' he said. 'This isn't what it sounds like. It's just that after all these years, it's hard to come to terms with other people, people who don't know how many sugars I take, when the kids' birthdays are. God, Jacquie, you even know when my wedding anniversary is!'

She gave a little, one-shouldered deprecatory shrug.

'Anyway, the sabbatical was turned down. Because you were away, ironically enough. But I could do with a break.'

Jacquie's Renée Zellweger needed work, but she did it anyway. 'You had me at hello.'

Henry Hall took them both by surprise and smiled. 'That's what I'm talking about,' They both took the Fats Waller impersonation as read.

'So,' she said. 'This favour.'

'Josie Blakemore's family are in the main interview suite.'

'And?' Just because she intended to help him didn't mean she should make it easy.

'And it would be a huge favour if you went and spoke to them. Jason isn't really a people person . . . no, that's not fair. He isn't a grieving parent person. They were interviewed at the time, of course, but with Ryan's alibi checking out . . . well, it was time for another chat. And they deserved an update.'

'They don't know me, though, guv,' Jacquie pointed out. 'Might they think they're being fobbed off?'

'On to a DI? Why should they? I just think a fresh eye on this might be helpful as well as the fact that since then there has been one more murder. You interviewed the family then, so you might be able to make a few more links. Give it a try, anyway. Please?'

Jacquie put down her pen and stood up. 'No problem,' she said. 'It might put a few things to bed from the Molly Adamson case. There was something about the sister that I can't quite put my finger on.' She came out from behind the desk and Henry Hall stood up to leave with her. 'And as for missing me, guv . . .'

'Yes?' They were standing very close together. In a TV cop show, he would have kissed her roughly.

'The feeling was entirely mutual. And that, you may be surprised to learn, goes for Max as well.'

Henry Hall looked at her with his blank glasses and then turned and opened the door. 'After you,' he said and ushered her out. There was simply no answer to that.

After the rather abrasive experience with Molly Adamson's sister, Jacquie was ready for anything. She had met some very strange people when she was working with the police in California, where money seemed to immediately bring out the worst in people. These parents had sent their daughter to an exclusive private girls' school, so she was expecting groomed, she was expecting coiffed, she was expecting to be told they were personal friends of the Chief Constable. In almost every way, she was wrong. The father was well turned out in suit and immaculate white shirt. The mother was a mess. Her clothes were expensive but she seemed to have dressed in the dark and there were dribbles of something – was it gravy? – down her cashmere sweater. Her eyes were hollow and haunted. She had been a tiny little thing to start with, but now she looked as though she might blow away like thistledown. The father stood up as soon as Jacquie came in; she waved him back into his seat and settled herself opposite him, the file on her knee. She liked the informality of this interview room, with its option of low sofas as opposed to hard, chipped formica table and chairs screwed down to the floor. At last, Leighford Police had accepted that not everyone with something to tell was a homicidal maniac.

'Mr and Mrs Blakemore,' she began, 'I am Detective Inspector Carpenter-Maxwell. I was not on duty when your daughter died but . . .'

'Murdered.' The woman had scarcely opened her lips to say the word.

'I beg your pardon?' Jacquie smiled slightly at her.

'Murdered.' This time it was louder and held a tinge of hysteria. 'My daughter didn't die. She was murdered. Horribly murdered and then . . . desecrated.' Mrs Blakemore brought out a handkerchief and scrubbed at her nose. 'Tell her,' she moaned to her husband. 'Tell her.'

Brian Blakemore took a deep, shuddering breath. Jacquie could see how it was at their house. His wife had lost *her* daughter. He was not allowed to be upset. He couldn't cry. But he had lost more than a daughter. He had lost a wife as well. She gave the marriage another six months, tops. It was nothing she hadn't seen before, many times. 'My wife and I feel that perhaps . . .' he looked down at the woman and there was not much love left in the look. 'My wife and I,' he began again, 'feel that the police perhaps haven't been taking things very seriously. Because of . . . well, because of how it looked. The clothes. The . . .' He ran out of words but his wife found more.

'Because she was dressed up like a tart. A common tart,' she spat. 'And because of the sex.' She shouted the word as though it took every ounce of strength to get it past her lips. 'My Josie didn't dress like that. She didn't have sex with people. She was a child. She . . . she never dreamed of that kind of thing until she went to that school.'

'St Olave's?' Jacquie checked.

'Yes. There. We sent her because we wanted to give her the best. The best education. And look what happened.'

'Do you think that someone at the school had something to do with this?' Jacquie asked quickly. Mollie Adamson had gone to St Olave's, albeit briefly.

'No.' Brian Blakemore cut in quickly. 'The school has nothing to do with it, I'm sure. It's just that some of the girls there are quite . . . sophisticated for their age. Cynthia thinks that it might have been their influence, but you can't go around saying that kind of thing.' At his shoulder, his wife snorted. 'Well, you can't,' he said to her. Then, to Jacquie, 'We've had solicitors' letters. From a couple of the girls' parents. I'm afraid that Cynthia has been . . . rather outspoken.'

'That doesn't matter in here,' Jacquie was quick to reassure him. 'Anything you tell me here won't go any further unless we think that it will help our investigation. And then we won't say where our intelligence came from.'

Blakemore looked dubious.

'I can guarantee it, Mr Blakemore,' she said, crossing her fingers to counteract the white lie.

Cynthia Blakemore sat forward on the sofa and began to speak, quietly and calmly at first, but her voice kept rising to a hysterical scream and her husband stopped her with a hand on her shoulder until she calmed again. 'Josie went to St Olave's for nearly a year before she was murdered.' That word again, but Jacquie let it go because it seemed to bring a perverse comfort. 'She had gone to the local school before that, but she was just sinking in the numbers, she wasn't the kind of girl to push herself forward, she was very shy. Then she started talking of bullying and we knew we had to do something. So we got her into St Olave's.'

'Did you have friends with daughters there?' Jacquie asked, getting ready to make notes in a pad inside the file.

Cynthia Blakemore looked at her husband. 'I suppose . . . who was it we used to know?' In the end, she shook her head. 'No, not really. We just went by the reputation.'

Jacquie nodded her head and the woman carried on.

'She flourished from the start. Small classes. Teachers who were not just chasing stupid initiatives, government guidelines, all that nonsense. She got some good teaching from good teachers. After-school clubs, everything we used to take for granted at our own school. We didn't ask for more. Then at Christmas, she went to some parties; well, you can't keep your children in a bubble, can you?'

Jacquie wanted to say you could have a darned good try, but forebore.

'She stayed out too late a couple of times, but we soon clamped down on that and she soon stopped all that. She was our little Josie again.'

'So she had . . . shall we say, pushed the envelope?' Jacquie asked.

'Do you have children, DI Carpenter-Maxwell?' Brian Blakemore asked, waspishly.

'Yes,' Jacquie said. 'Yes, one boy.'

'Then consider yourself lucky,' the man said. 'The boys make the trouble, they don't get into it. You mark my words.'

'Well, mine is a little young as yet,' Jacquie said, placatingly. 'Are you saying there was a boy on the scene? Only, I don't seem to remember seeing that in the file.' She flicked the pages as though the fact would spring to the top.

'No,' Blakemore said. Then, specifically to his wife, 'No, Cynthia. There was no boy. Just thoughts of boys. She was fourteen,' he said, spreading his hands. 'What girl doesn't think of boys at that age?'

Jacquie cast her mind back and almost blushed.

'Around about April,' the mother took up the tale, 'she started to get quite secretive. There was nothing much to hide, of course. She went to a few classes after school, but we always collected her from those, one or the other of us did, and so we knew she wasn't going anywhere else and lying about it.'

Jacquie felt more sorry for the child now than she had before. It sounded as though her life was like a prison with everyone snooping and spying, suspecting her before, during and after the fact.

'She was always quite sporty and she liked dance. She did theatre club on a Saturday. She sang in the church choir on a Sunday and of course there was practice on a Friday night. She had her tutoring sessions as well – well, you know about *those*.'

'With Mr Ryan?' Jacquie checked.

'Bernard, yes,' Brian Blakemore said. 'We know him socially. Friends of friends, you know the kind of thing.'

'Yes,' Jacquie said and left them to carry on. Cynthia Blakemore had narrowed her eyes at her husband. Jacquie had seen it written down before but had never actually seen it done. 'Is there something, Mrs Blakemore?'

'Bernard Ryan,' she said. 'He had no alibi, I understand.'

'I don't know why you might understand that, Mrs Blakemore,' Jacquie said, perhaps a little more frostily that she intended. 'Mr Ryan's alibi has been thoroughly checked and we know he could not have hurt Josie.'

The woman looked at Jacquie like a basilisk. 'And now there's been another one,' she said.

'We are looking at a similar death, yes,' Jacquie said blandly. With a pair of blank glasses, she and Henry Hall could pass for twins in some lights.

For a moment, the room rang with the silence, then Cynthia Blakemore took up her monologue again. 'As April went on, she went very quiet. She started to lock the bathroom door as well and she wasn't so . . . cuddly. She wouldn't kiss us goodbye in the morning, or goodnight at bedtime. She was very . . .' she seemed to be searching for the word, 'reserved. That's it. She got very reserved.'

'Mr Ryan suggested that perhaps she was having problems with someone in the family circle. Or a family friend, perhaps.' Jacquie put the fact out there to see who took it up and ran with it. Inevitably, it was Josie's mother.

'Rubbish!' she shouted. 'Who would it be? We don't have a large extended family, there's only us and her grandmothers left. No uncles. No cousins. Just us. And now . . .' her voice raised itself to a howl, 'and now there isn't even Josie!' She scrubbed at her nose again. 'So, Ryan is talking nonsense. He just said it to be spiteful.'

Jacquie could see why they had had solicitors' letters. 'What about the parents of her friends?' she asked, carefully. 'Perhaps she would have referred to them as family friends to Mr Ryan.'

'You've got their names in there,' Brian Blakemore pointed at the file. 'I assume you've checked them out?'

'Yes,' Jacquie said. 'Everyone has been carefully checked. I was wondering if perhaps you might have thought of anyone else.'

'No.' The woman's mouth snapped shut like a turtle's. It was definitely not a good look.

Brian Blakemore edged a little way away from his wife on the sofa. Peter Maxwell would have rubbed his hands with delight had he been there. The body language was superb and Jacquie noted it on her pad. Then, in a voice that sounded unlike his own, he said, 'There is a name that isn't in your file.'

Jacquie raised an eyebrow and looked expectant but he said no more. 'May I ask whose?' he said.

'Ask her,' he said, with a toss of the head at his wife.

'How do I know whose name is missing?' she said but there was an odd note to her speech. 'Everyone is missing, if you look at it like that.'

'True,' her husband agreed. 'But more precisely, the name of your fancy man is missing. The one that Josie knew about and told me about just before she died.'

The room went so still that for a moment Jacquie thought she had gone deaf. Then, it exploded with sound.

'My *fancy man?*' the woman screamed. 'How *dare* you? My daughter is dead and you accuse me of having a *fancy man?*'

Here it comes, Jacquie thought. The straw that was going to break this marriage's back had just started to float down through the air. In a moment, you would hear the first crack. Brian Blakemore was quiet, almost too quiet. This was a man who had been carrying a load for a while and had chosen here, chosen now to put it down. Jacquie heard her husband's voice in her head, quoting Kipling as he did from time to time. 'They have cast their burden upon the Lord, and – the Lord, He lays it on Martha's Sons!' She had never felt more like a Martha's son than she did at that moment.

'Detective Inspector,' he said, 'I want you to know that I don't think my wife hurt our daughter. If she had known that Josie had told me about her bit of rough, she would have brazened it out. Just like she always has done in the past. That's not what I'm saying.' He didn't look at his wife at all, who had turned in her seat so her back was to him and was screwing her handkerchief round and round. 'No, I mean that this *man* might well know something about Josie's death. No, Cynthia is right, let's keep calling it murder.' He swallowed hard and went on. 'Usually Cynthia's little peccadilloes have been with her friend's husbands. That's why we have such a very small social circle. Even the friend who introduced us to Bernard Ryan has gone, driven away by Cynthia's constant need for validation, if that is what I can call her screwing every man who so much as looks at her.'

Cynthia Blakemore reacted to this by turning and thumping her husband on the chest, but in a very ineffectual way, designed to make herself look like the little woman, sore oppressed. Jacquie was not convinced and gestured with her pen for Blakemore to continue.

'But this time, she reached outside the family circle. To the builder working on the house, no less. A cliché, I know, but one she has avoided thus far.'

The woman dropped her head into her hands.

He looked at her with a sneer. 'She does that,' he said to Jacquie, 'because she knows what's coming next. One day, back in March, Josie was sent home from school. There was a bug going round and any day girl feeling poorly was sent home by taxi. Josie came in and assumed that her mother was out as the house seemed empty, but it seems as though this was not the case.'

Jacquie spoke to the woman, 'Do you have anything to add, Mrs Blakemore?' but she just shook her head.

'I will keep the details to the point and brief,' Brian Blakemore said, 'and you can decide how to interpret them, Detective Inspector. When Josie went up to her room, she heard noises from our bedroom so she poked her head round the door. Who should be in there but my wife and Michael Harrison, Bespoke Builder, No Job Too Small.'

'She must have found that very upsetting.' Jacquie found that she was addressing the room in general.

'Upsetting.' Brian Blakemore repeated the word without inflexion. 'Yes, that's right. Upsetting. They were quite engrossed and they didn't notice her. Did you, Cynthia?' he turned to his wife who shook her head. 'What were you doing, Cynthia?' he asked. 'No, we don't need to know that. What were you wearing, Cynthia?'

The woman mumbled into her hands.

'Sorry,' her husband shouted, leaning down so he was yelling into her face. 'I don't think the Detective Inspector quite caught that. What were you *wearing*, Cynthia?'

She stood up, making him jump back to avoid being nutted in the face and then she ran to the door. She wrenched it open and then turned in the doorway. As a histrionic gesture, it was second to none, but for keeping the story just between the three of them, it was not the best plan as the door opened out into the corridor of the Nick and was full of people about their business, who all stopped to listen. 'I was wearing her school uniform,' she shouted. 'Her spare one. Her knickers, her blouse, her tie, her socks. Okay. He liked me to dress like a schoolgirl. Satisfied now?' and she stormed out. One by one and in stilted movements, the corridor came to life again in a snapshot as the door swung shut behind her, leaving Jacquie and her husband looking at each other across the coffee table that suddenly seemed as big as a continent.

Before the silence could get so long that it was embarrassing, Jacquie spoke. 'Why did you not tell us this before?' she said.

Blakemore shrugged. 'I was ashamed to, if I am to tell the truth, Detective Inspector. I have got used to being laughed at behind my back by everyone who knows what she's like. If she wasn't having knee tremblers between courses at formal dinners, she was at it like a weasel on the golf course. I thought it was the thrill of discovery that turned her on. Then this builder came along and she seemed to go into overdrive. This dressing up thing is new for her as far as I know, but in her own daughter's clothes . . . it has made me sick just to think of it. But when Josie was found dressed, if anything, like someone years older than her years, I put it aside. But I can't. I can't put it aside. As far as I know, Cynthia is still seeing this Harrison person, but obviously, what with . . . what's happened, she has lost a lot of her sparkle. He's still around. Perhaps he loves her.' He sounded incredulous. 'Perhaps he is keeping her close, so she doesn't speak out.'

'We'll need his name and address, Mr Blakemore,' Jacquie said, poising her pen.

He got out his wallet and riffled through some business cards and handed one across.

'Thank you.' Jacquie wondered briefly how many men carried the card of their wife's lover and their daughter's possible killer in their wallet and thought that it was likely to be very few. 'Would you like to stay here for a while? A cup of tea?'

The man nodded, sagging back on the sofa, his chin on his chest. As she went out to arrange the drink and to write up her notes, she paused behind him for a second, then patted him on the shoulder. As she closed the door, she heard him sob. Just once, but it had all the sorrow in the world in it. Another Martha's son, if ever there was one.

Chapter Eight

After she had seen Brian Blakemore off the premises, Jacquie went along the corridor and up the stairs to Henry Hall's office. Cynthia Blakemore seemed to have disappeared without trace and she was rather concerned by that because she might be a witness. Other than that, she didn't care if Cynthia Blakemore was abducted by aliens.

Henry Hall looked up as she stuck her head around his door. 'Jacquie,' he said. 'Come in and tell me all about it. That was some show she put on, wasn't it? The WI on their yearly look at how their tax penny is spent will dine out on that for ever, if I'm any judge.'

'Tell me you're joking,' Jacquie said, plonking heavily into a chair.

'Do I ever joke?' he asked, with a straight face.

'No . . . but I hope there's a first time for everything,' she said.

'Yes, as it happens,' he said. 'It was only police personnel and if it hadn't been, she had no one but herself to blame. We'll need to interview her later.'

'I don't know where she went,' Jacquie started to explain.

'Don't worry,' Hall comforted her. 'Jason took her home. I gather she wanted to collect some things and then she was going to the boyfriend's place. I hope he knows what he's in for.'

'We'll need to speak to him, of course.'

'Yes, indeed. I gather Jason was hoping to kill two birds with one stone. He's rather stuck for a number one suspect now that Ryan's alibi has panned out.'

'Is that confirmed for definite?' Jacquie heard herself and winced. Maxwell had been known to hang kids up by their earlobes for lesser crimes against grammar than that.

'Yes. We rang the private number on the card you got from Ryan – good work on that, by the way.'

She gave him a tight-lipped nod and in doing so confirmed his suspicion that the hand of Peter Maxwell was in the mix.

'Yes, we caught him on his own, so he was able to speak freely. Obviously, we would have kept trying if necessary, but we got it all with one call.'

'Are we following it up?' Jacquie asked. It wasn't like Henry Hall to cut any corners.

'We have his address now and we'll check up if we have to, but I never had Ryan in the frame from the beginning. I know you came to this late, but there was just something about his story which rang true. And we had a quick word with Sylvia Matthews up at the school . . .'

'Sylvia couldn't tell a lie to save her life,' Jacquie said.

'That's the impression we got. So, although we had to go through the motions, I never really had any doubts. But now we have at least one more lead.'

'Harrison?'

Hall nodded. 'It's possible that Josie would refer to him as a family friend for lack of another phrase,' he said. 'And he clearly has a thing for schoolgirls.'

'Does that really gel, though?' Jacquie asked. 'Cynthia Blakemore is a very skinny woman but she is a *woman*. Having her dress up as a schoolgirl isn't the same as an *actual* girl, surely?'

Hall shrugged. 'Best he could get, perhaps?'

'Are we going to pull in his previous partners? Wife? Blakemore didn't know much about him.'

'He's been married twice. Two divorces. One we've tracked down, the other seems to have disappeared. She isn't in Brighton or here, but that leaves a lot of the country unaccounted for.'

Jacquie went quiet and the icy feeling in her diaphragm that meant that two pieces of information were about to come together struck her and took her breath away. She went white.

Hall looked across his desk at her, concern etched on his face. 'Jacquie? Are you all right? You look like you've seen a ghost.'

'I'm not sure what it is,' she said. 'Just listen and tell me what you think. Mollie Adamson's half sister's mother was married to a man named Mike, who she divorced.'

Hall's glasses flashed as he nodded his head.

'Mike is the only one of several of Caroline Morton's stepfathers who keeps in touch. So . . .'

'If Michael Harrison is that same Mike . . .?'

'He would have known Mollie, yes.'

Hall set his mouth in a grim line. 'Lots of people called Mike, Jacquie.'

'Two girls dead,' she riposted. 'And we don't believe in coincidence, do we, guv?'

Hall tapped his pen on the desk. 'No, we don't. Can you ring Caroline Morton? Find out a bit more about this stepfather. Let me get this straight, though – he isn't *Mollie's* stepfather?'

'The family tree has more branches than Sainsburys,' Jacquie said. 'I'll jot it down for you when I confirm about Harrison.'

'That would be a help. Thanks. Meanwhile, I'll call Jason. Make sure he doesn't tip Harrison off that we're interested. Less he knows about how we're thinking at this stage, the better.' Hall looked up at the clock. 'Once you've rung Mrs Morton, get off home. You're not even supposed to be back until next week and here you are at all hours.' He paused. 'Is Max glad to be back?' The question was delivered blandly as usual, but there were more layers in it than Nolan's breakfast pancake stack.

'Well, he's not really back until next week,' she hedged.

'But he's been in touch, of course.' Again, the flat delivery, but there was no mistaking the question.

'Of course. Sylvia and he go back years. And Helen, of course.'

'And Bernard Ryan.'

'Um . . . I'm not sure . . .'

'Come on, Jacquie. Max must think he's died and gone to heaven. Not back in Leighford five minutes and he discovers a colleague is a murder suspect. I assume you haven't told him any details.' How often, Hall wondered, had he heard himself saying *that*? 'It could make it very difficult for him at work. Is Ryan going back, do we know?'

'I don't know.' That was the truth. Alibi or no alibi, Jacquie wasn't sure whether Bernard Ryan could brazen it out or not. 'I expect Max will tell me on Monday evening. He'll know by then, of course.'

'But that's all he'll know, hopefully.' Hall took off his glasses and polished them carefully before replacing them. 'Jacquie?'

'Oh, sorry, guv. I didn't know that was a question.'

There was a pause, prickling in the silence of the office.

'So?'

'Of course, guv. That's all he'll know.' She also glanced at the clock. 'I'll see if I can catch Caroline Morton at the office, then I'll be off if that's all right with you,' she said a little stiffly. 'I'll drop you an e about Harrison.'

'Fine.' Hall could do terse. It was one of his only two emotions. 'See you Monday.'

'Yes. See you Monday,' and Jacquie left, trying hard not to slam the door. She couldn't work out where the row had come from. One minute they had been pulling together and the next they seemed to be at the opposite ends of the universe. As always, the catalyst was Maxwell and as always, she promised herself she wouldn't tell him about the latest developments. Ryan was off the hook and that was all he needed to know.

Back in her office, Jacquie took a few deep breaths and picked up the phone. Checking in the file, she dialled the number of Morton and Morton, Solicitors. A secretary answered and for once was both efficient and pleasant. In her current mood, Jacquie needed that. She was put through to Caroline Morton.

'Detective Inspector,' the solicitor said. 'How may I help you?'

'Something has come up in our investigations and I wonder if you could just confirm something for me. You mentioned when we spoke at the hospital that you were still in touch occasionally with your stepfather. Mike, I think you said his name was.'

'That's right.' Caroline Morton's voice was guarded and Jacquie was reminded again that the woman was a solicitor.

'Could you give me a little more detail? Surname. Address, perhaps.'

'I don't know where he lives right at the moment,' she said. 'He is a builder and tends to live in houses short term while he does them up prior to selling them on.' Jacquie smiled and put a tick on her notepad. 'His surname is Harrison but, look, Detective Inspector, what has this to do with anything? Why are you looking into Mike? He hardly ever met Mollie, if that's where this is going?'

'We just have to check every avenue, Mrs Morton,' Jacquie said, adding another lavish tick to her page.

'Yes,' the woman persisted. 'But why is Mike an avenue?'

'His name cropped up in another investigation,' Jacquie said, keeping her voice neutral. 'You of all people must realise, Mrs Morton, that I can't tell you more. Thank you for your help. If you remember Mr Harrison's current address, could you let me know? You can leave a voicemail here or my email address is . . .'

'Don't worry, Detective Inspector Carpenter-Maxwell,' the solicitor said crisply, giving equal weight to every single syllable. 'I know your email address. And that of your immediate superior. And that of his, if you catch my drift.' And with that, the phone went down with a loud click.

Jacquie put her phone down more slowly, and wiggled her mouse to bring her computer out of hibernation. She logged on and sent a brief email to Henry Hall. 'Michael Harrison checks out – he is the stepfather. See you Monday. Jacquie.' After a pause, she added, 'Sorry.' After another pause she erased the last word and clicked send. She logged out, switched the computer off, grabbed her car keys and was gone, before anyone changed her mind.

'Smells good.'

Peter Maxwell turned round from a basting session and saw his wife lounging in the kitchen doorway. 'Hello, heart of darkness,' he said. 'You're early. Nole and I were going to eat and run – he rather fancies a session with the scooter.'

'Oh, has the box arrived?' Jacquie looked around aimlessly, having forgotten what was in it and whether anything should be in the kitchen.

'Yup. Nothing broken as far as we could see. All unpacked and stashed.'

'The box?' Jacquie knew the answer to this one.

'In the garage, currently doing duty as Camelot.'

'And King Arthur?'

'Merlin, *if* you please!' Maxwell said, affronted. 'Why be just a king when you can be a magician?'

'He can't wander off, can he?' Jacquie said, looking over her shoulder down the stairs to where the garage door was situated. 'You did lock the door?'

Maxwell bent to put his chicken back in the oven and then crossed to his wife and tucked her into the crook of his arm, where she fitted so well. 'You're getting confused, sweetness,' he muttered. 'It's other people's children who are lost, stolen or strayed. Ours is in the garage, or should I say in Lyonesse, where I believe the potatoes come from or have I got that wrong? Anyway, he's away with the fairies, locked in the garage.' He looked round into her face. 'Don't let the thought police hear that – I expect locking a kid in the garage is probably a Bad Thing. And there must be a Court of Human Rights issue in there somewhere. Anyway,' he gave her a squeeze and let her go, 'I've already lost one baby.' There was a pause while he collected himself. 'I have no intention of losing another.' He kissed the top of her head and moved away. 'Now, piss off, dearest, while I create culinary magic.'

Jacquie stood there, arms by her sides. 'Max, I . . .'

'I know you didn't,' he said, not turning round. He gestured with one shoulder to the work surface under the window. 'See that bath sheet?'

'Yes.'

'It's Taliesin's cloak of invisibility. You can have a lot of fun under that.'

She picked it up and went out onto the landing, looking back at her husband over her shoulder. They rarely talked of the time before. Before she and Nolan had come along to patch the hole left by Maxwell's wife and child, dead on a wet road years before. It was easy for her to forget sometimes that they were only just beneath the topmost layer of his skin and also, simultaneously, tucked beneath his heart. 'Any special incantations,' she said lightly, 'spells, things of that nature?'

'How about, "Merlin, come out of that castle or I'll bite your bum"? That should do it.' He turned round and smiled. 'I'm all right. Really. Off you go. I'm doing sweetcorn fritters and bacon and spinach salad. If it sounds like a strange combination . . .'

'And it does.'

'. . . take it up with Merlin.'

'Will do,' and, swirling the rival magician's cloak of invisibility around her shoulders, she swept down the stairs. Maxwell went to the door of the kitchen and heard her call out and Nolan's shriek of delight. He shook his head and went back to the cooker. Everything he loved was under his feet, fighting for Camelot, aka a very tattered cardboard box. Metternich had done grudging service as the Beast Glatisant but was now sulking in the attic. There was only so much a cat could take.

Later that evening, with Merlin safely bedded down for the night, washing up stowed in the dishwasher and Metternich coaxed down with chicken skin and similar subterfuge, Detective Inspector Carpenter-Maxwell and Head of Sixth Form Peter Maxwell sat opposite each other in the sitting room. They may have looked like Mr and Mrs Not Totally Average but in fact the atmosphere was similar to that reported a few minutes before the Earps destroyed the Clantons and McLowerys in a hail of lead down by the Corral. Jacquie had the sofa and therefore the cat – Metternich had gone through his usual evening routine of pressing with his feet on the arm and his head against the leg of whoever was trying to share the furniture with him. The plan was that the person in question would end up on the floor, leaving the cat in sole possession but Jacquie was in no mood to pander tonight and Metternich had given in gracefully. He was now curled up with his nose up his bum; a comfortable position enough, for those who were up to it. Maxwell had a glass of Southern Comfort in one hand and the TV remote in the other. He was flicking through the channels one by one, staying long enough to hear a few words and then moving on.

'Motion to suppress . . .'

'See ya downa Vic . . .'

'At the High Court . . .'

'*There* goes Jensen Button . . .'

'. . . to spend more time with his family.'

Finally, Jacquie had had enough. She reached over and knocked the remote from his hand, leaving them on a rerun of *Countryfile*. She switched the television off at the wall and turned to face him.

'Are we going to sit like this all night?'

Maxwell glanced at the clock. 'For another hour or so, I imagine,' he said calmly, and foraged for a book stashed down the side of the chair for just this eventuality.

'I know you want to talk about Bernard Bloody Ryan!' she said, flinging herself back down on the sofa, narrowly missing the cat. 'Sorry, Count.' The apology was automatic. Without it, one could easily lose an arm.

'I would quite like to,' Maxwell said, with infuriating calm. 'But I don't expect you can, so I'll just read my book. Look, why don't you go and have a nice hot bath? Some of your nice aromatherapy stuff in it? I'll light you some candles, if you like. Wine? Glass of wine? Cadbury's Flake?'

She looked over at him and could have screamed. The casual observer would have seen a concerned husband, trying to help his wife over the stresses of her job. He had cooked dinner. He had played their child into docile exhaustion. He had read the bedtime story – naturally, *The Once and Future King* which probably no other father in the land would have had to hand on the day Camelot was rebuilt in a cardboard box in the garage. He was perfect. But behind that face, the eyes of a basilisk looked out and she suddenly felt an affinity with the thousands of voles who had come to an untimely end in the back gardens of Columbine.

'Has anyone ever told you how alike you and the Count are?' she asked, trying to keep it light.

'Oh, yes. I've often been told I look like a large black and white cat,' he smiled.

'It's something about the eyes,' she said.

'Mm hm,' he said, his eyes already back on the book.

She gave him a few minutes to re-engage and then gave in. 'Bernard's in the clear.'

'I think I knew that,' he said, looking up.

'Yes, but he really is. We've checked the alibi and it all makes sense. His boyfriend even has receipts. He scanned them and emailed them over.'

'And you're accepting that?'

'The guy's got too much to lose. He could easily have denied it. He seems genuinely fond of Bernard.'

'Nice for Bernard.'

'Max . . .'

'Yes?' He folded the book around one finger and looked at her. 'What?'

'Henry had a word today. The usual word. You know the score. I can't talk to you about this case.'

'Of course not. It isn't fair of me to expect it.'

She bounced on the sofa in frustration. 'But you *do* expect it!'

He stuffed the book down the side of his chair. He had been reading it upside down anyway. It was the only way to make sense of Isaiah Berlin. 'You know it won't go any further. And it helps to talk, you know it does.'

'I've got Jason . . . and Henry.'

He raised an eyebrow.

'I won't be able to give you any details.'

'Naturally not.' He wriggled down into his chair so as to give her his full attention.

She blew down her nose like a racehorse. 'Max, please don't accidentally on purpose tell Bernard any of this, will you?'

'Not a word, heart. He will hate me again as soon as he is reinstated. Do you know anything about that, by the way?'

'That's nothing to do with us. It's Legs' call, I would imagine. Or Legs and the governors.'

'Right. Legs will go the way of least resistance, whichever that turns out to be. But you were saying.'

'Without going into every detail . . .'

A few nerve endings in Maxwell's brain all simultaneously signalled 'Damn'.

'I had an interview with the parents of the first girl today.'

'That would be Josie Blakemore, Bernard's tutee.'

'Correct. They came in and, well, let's just say that things in the Blakemore home were not quite as they at first appeared.'

'Homes are never quite as they first appear,' Maxwell pointed out. 'Many people, for instance, think that we are a perfectly normal family.'

'Many?'

'Some. A few.'

'It turns out that Mrs Blakemore was having an affair with a rather dodgy character who also has a link to our second girl.'

'Mollie Adamson.'

'Again, correct. I had to have a word with her half-sister . . .'

'Mrs Blakemore's half-sister?' He was just checking.

'No, Mollie's. Anyway, it turned out that Mrs Blakemore's bit of rough, as her husband pleasantly called him at one point, was once married to her mother.'

'Too many pronouns. Whose mother?'

'Caroline Morton, Mollie's half-sister.'

Maxwell took a deep breath. He was no watcher of soaps, but assumed this was the kind of level of complication that millions of viewers coped with every day. How hard could it be? 'So, to get this right, and for the last time, Josie's mother is having an affair with the ex-stepfather of the half-sister of Mollie. Yes?'

Jacquie looked at the ceiling and ran through it, using her fingers to keep track. Finally, she said, 'Yes.'

'That's quite tenuous, you know.'

'It is quite, but Caroline Morton said that the stepfather . . .'

'Has he got a name?'

'Yes. The stepfather,' she looked under her eyebrows at Maxwell who knew better than to push it, 'sometimes visited the house where Mollie was living. Perhaps I should have said, Mollie's own mother was dead and she was living with her half-sister.'

'Not so tenuous, then.'

'No. Details that Josie's father passed on show that Mi . . . the stepfather may have a predilection for young girls.'

'Ah.'

'Anyway, it may be nothing, but we're checking it out. Nothing to Bernard now, though. Do you hear?'

'My lips are sealed, dear one,' Maxwell said, zipping them ostentatiously, like the Red Team always do on *Bargain Hunt* (or so he'd been told). 'He won't hear anything from me.'

'Well, I hope not.' Jacquie smiled at Maxwell. 'I do feel better, you're right. I don't know how you do it, you know, day in, day out.'

'What, specifically?' Maxwell could think of a thousand things he did on a daily basis that most people wouldn't touch with a long pole. In the days before Political Correctness he would put his arm around crying girls and boys, pour cold water over writhing couples at the Sixth Form Prom, pile into the school minibus, Helen Maitland at the wheel, with lads off their faces on drink and see them safely home. He would shout, he would whisper, he would stare – all in a day's work at the Chalk Face as was. Secretly, he was glad he had never taught infants – your own infant's sick and poo was all in a day's work; but somebody else's? Euww!

'Dealing with kids,' Jacquie was thinking along similar lines, but at a distance. 'Meeting the parents, seeing the mess they're making.'

'They fuck you up, your mum and dad. They may not mean to, but they do. It's not often that Philip Larkin and I can be said to be at one, but with that I totally agree. All we can do is try to make the sow's ear back into a silk purse.'

'That's what I mean. You can see what these kids could have been, before their parents got their hands on them.' She looked across at him. 'What were your parents like?'

Maxwell put his hands behind his head. 'I don't know. I was just a kid.'

'You must have memories of them.'

'My mother was always cooking. And when she wasn't she was washing. Ironing. Telling me to wear a vest. I had almost left home before Sandie started kicking up; I know my mother agonised about that, but she was just being a girl. I think I brought myself up, by and large.'

'And your dad?'

'Father. Not Dad. He was always at work. He would come home, sit down, eat his tea – it was always called tea, whatever time he eventually got to eat it – and then either read the paper or go out. He hardly spoke to me as I recall. Not sulking. Just had nothing to say.'

'They were clever, though?'

'I suspect that my father was a deeply stupid man who had managed to convince the powers that be that he could do his job. My mother was very bright but decided early on to take the path of least resistance.' He lapsed into silence for a moment. Then, 'You?'

'My mother . . . well, you know what she's like. Dad was a bit like yours, a deep voice above my head and then, suddenly, with nothing in between, someone to ignore.' She stroked the cat absentmindedly. 'Max . . .?'

'You are an excellent mother. I hope I am an all right father. Metternich is the perfect pet. So was the goldfish, of blessed memory.' He smiled across at her. 'No one will hurt Nolan. He will never have this conversation with his significant other. He will say, when asked by a passing psychologist examining him for his post as President of the World, "Problems with my parents? No, I love my parents and they love me." And he'll be right.' Her bottom lip began to tremble, and he held out his arms. 'Hot bath?' A nod. 'Wine?' Two nods. 'Coming right up.' And he put her gently back on the sofa and went off to light the candles.

Chapter Nine

As usual, he met them in the Library. As usual, they faced a brave new world together.

'This,' he threw his arms wide, 'is the library. For the past five years you have all known it as a place where they keep computers and quirky little angular bits of furniture that are ideal resting places for your recently departed wads of chewing gum. Now, in your time here, during those five years, you may have noticed rectangular things lining the shelves. They are called books and they will be an indispensable aid to your next two years. A and AS levels will be impossible without them. And the member of my Sixth Form who so much as whispers the word Wickedpedia will be on the Eastern Front by morning.'

Maxwell had fought his way through All-Hell Day countless times before. This was the day that he and Helen Maitland, the Fridge, admitted hopefuls to Year 12. This was the day they signed on for another two years at what was once the Chalk Face and what was now the Whiteboard Jungle. The historian in Peter Maxwell couldn't help thinking back to his own time. When he was sixteen, Maxwell, P. joined Lower Classical and Modern VI X (no one knew what the X stood for, but it must have been a factor) and one of his shoulders was already slightly higher than the other. This was not out of deference to his hero the late King Richard III but because he had been hauling around a heavy satchel full of books since he was eight. Today, he could have got his old school on charges of child abuse. Then again, the historian in Peter Maxwell knew that when Edward the Black Prince was sixteen, he was commanding the wing of an army at a little punch-up called Crecy. God, how the Old Order had changed.

'Here,' he was still addressing the troops who all looked a little uncomfortable now that they didn't have to wear uniform any more, 'are the entry forms. Fill 'em in, dears. Name, d.o.b., inside leg and above all, GCSE results – Mrs Maitland and I don't have time today to look them up. You'll notice four columns – A,B,C,D – and a list of subjects under each one. On no account can you choose two from the same column because they are timetabled at the same time and not even I can be in two places at once. Fill 'em in and do your best with the long words. If you can't manage that, perhaps you shouldn't be here in the first place and you can just trust to luck like that great role model Mr Cowell.'

He half bowed as they swarmed forward to collect the paperwork. 'No pen, Doris?' he hissed to a lanky ginger-haired lad to his left. 'That doesn't bode well.' Maxwell and Maitland, collectively known as the M & Ms, marched along the corridor and up the mezzanine to their respective offices, adjacent as they were.

'Was I a little too elitist, do you think?' he asked her.

'Mr Gove would be proud of you,' she smiled. 'Who's turn is it for coffee?'

Maxwell liked Helen Maitland. There were four women who held Leighford High School together. One was Sylvia Matthews, who had nursed with Nightingale, she of the soft shoulder and morning-after pills. Numbers Two and Three were the Thingees, who womanned the switchboards mornings and afternoons and took all the flak that should have gone Legs Diamond's way. And the fourth was the large, blonde woman who stood alongside Maxwell now. Nothing ever ruffled Helen Maitland. Maxwell had never seen her cry or even blush. She did both of those things of course but never in the presence of Mad Max.

'Coffee?' he frowned. 'That'll be me. Still like it hot and black, Hel, baby?'

Helen Maitland *did* remember *Shaft,* but she wasn't giving Peter Maxwell the satisfaction. They disappeared into their respective offices to await the hordes demanding their right to continue in full-time education. Maxwell looked around his office, the one he hadn't seen for seven months and more. Mrs B. had done him proud here. The old coffee stains had gone, the spider plant was still alive and the film posters that were so much part of his life still adorned the walls. He had treated himself to a new set on a day out in Hollywood, but for now he was happy to lock eyes with dear old Boris Karloff in *The Body Snatcher*, to take seriously Robert Ryan's warning to *Beware My Lovely* and to watch the sun sink into the sands of the Normandy beaches at the end of Daryl F. Zanuck's *The Longest Day*.

Then . . . 'Mrs Maitland!' Maxwell's roar had been known to shatter glass and his assistant came running.

'Max,' she said, seeing him standing there, pointing wordlessly at the wall. 'Whatever's the matter?'

'Would you like to tell me what *that* is?' he managed, through gritted teeth.

Helen Maitland laughed. 'It's a poster, Max,' she said. 'Mel Gibson in *The Patriot*. Apparently, it's all about the War of American Independence. It's a present from Hector Gold; he said you'd love it.'

'Oh, I do, I do,' Maxwell nodded with a rictus grin on his face, 'but not as much as Hector will when I post it back to him with instructions to the postman to stick it up Mr Gold's . . . back again, Doris?'

The lanky lad stood in Maxwell's doorway.

'Sorry, Mr Maxwell, have you got a pen?'

'Yes, thanks,' Maxwell said. 'Oh, I see. You want to borrow one. Here. Don't say I never give you anything.'

The Head of Sixth Form threw a biro at the lad who caught it expertly. 'That's the First Eleven for you, my lad,' he smiled. 'Assuming we still had a cricket team, of course. Eleanor.'

A surly, spotty girl stood at Doris's elbow, form in hand.

'Radiant as ever. Who do you want? Me or Mrs Maitland?'

'Mrs Maitland,' the girl surlied.

'Naturally. Well, enjoy, Mrs Maitland. I'll get the coffee underway.'

And so it went on for the rest of the morning. The early ones were the easiest (apart from Eleanor) – the A* and the As, whose greatest shame was a B in Social and Religious Studies. All Hell Day it may have been, but there was a certain satisfaction for Maxwell in passing the buck. He was not going to take the rap for enrolling a student onto Further Maths when he/she only had a D at GCSE – better go and see Mr Leadbetter, the Head of Maths; it was his call.

'I'm having second thoughts about French,' David Walker was saying, tapping the relevant place on the form.

'Aren't we all?' Maxwell nodded. There was a sharp knock on the door and a slightly frazzled Bernard Ryan popped his head around it. If Maxwell had worn glasses he would have looked over their rims at the visitor. 'I have to say you are a *little* on the elderly side for Year 12, sir,' he said.

David Walker laughed, but Bernard Ryan didn't. 'Can I have a word, Mr Maxwell?' the reinstated Deputy said.

'Of course, Mr Ryan,' Maxwell said graciously. 'David, pop next door and chat to Mrs Maitland, will you? If you're not happy about a subject at this early stage, we don't want to shoehorn you into it for the sake of it. What were you thinking of doing instead?'

'History,' the lad said.

'There you are, you see,' Maxwell said, clapping him on the shoulder. 'Go and get that done. *What* a wise choice! Off you bugger now, there's a good lad.'

He ushered the Deputy Head in and closed the door behind them. He felt the kettle – it was still warm enough to dissolve the odd granule. 'Coffee, Bernard?' he asked.

The Deputy shook his head. 'I can't stay,' he said. 'James has decided to keep Jane Taylor on to shadow me for a while and I have to bring her up to speed.' He caught the look in Maxwell's eye. 'I can't blame him, Max. He can't be sure . . .'

'Can't be sure that you won't be found to have nothing to do with a murder of a young girl again? Surely, it goes without saying. I don't know what he's thinking, Bernard. What kind of message does it send?' Maxwell found himself in the unusual position of being on Bernard Ryan's side.

'His hands are tied,' Ryan said, sitting down. 'Do you know, I think I will have that coffee. Jane Taylor can wait.'

'Well said,' Maxwell nodded, and to show solidarity actually switched on the kettle to re-boil. 'This calls for some proper coffee. Hector left me his stash.' Only Bernard Ryan would find no double entendre there.

'He was a good teacher, Max,' Ryan said. 'He'll be missed.'

'I was glad to leave the historians in good hands. And our house has never been so tidy.' The kettle rumbled to the boil and Maxwell poured the water into the cafetiere. The elephant circled the room, trumpeting softly under its breath.

Ryan cleared his throat. 'I wonder if you could pass on my thanks to Jacquie?' he said. 'Joe said that the whole thing was done very discreetly. He . . . well, he was over last night and he said it was all right.'

With relief, the elephant packed its trunk and said goodbye to the office.

'Over?' Maxwell pressed the handle down and the coffee smell filled the room. 'I thought it was strictly hotels with you two?' He glanced round and saw that Ryan was looking down at his hands, blushing slightly.

'He came over to my house last night. He . . . he's moving in.'

'That's a bit of a turn up, isn't it?' Maxwell asked, handing the man a mug. Anything to stop him twiddling his fingers and blushing like an adolescent on his first date. 'What about his wife? His job?'

Ryan took a sip and burned his tongue. 'Ouch,' he said. 'Hot. It turned out his wife had known for ages. Not about me. Just about Joe being gay. Wives can tell, I guess.'

Maxwell thought of Mrs Wilde and shrugged.

'And work have just adopted a diversity initiative. I suppose they will be glad to have the token gay without having to advertise.' He risked a smile. 'Is it stupid to say I'm happy, Max?'

'It's never stupid to be happy, Bernard,' Maxwell pointed out.

'I suppose not. It's just that it's a bit new for me. I . . . only came out to Joe. I'd always hidden my sexuality before. Oh, on holiday. With the odd waiter, that kind of thing . . .'

Maxwell held up his hand. 'Bernard,' he said. 'I'd love to share, I know you believe me when I say that, but let's not forget you will be yelling at me before the week is out for not covering a lesson you had me down for. Let's not say things we may regret.'

Ryan looked at him and blinked, like someone waking up suddenly. 'You're right, Max,' he conceded. 'It's just that . . .'

'You're happy. Yes. Marvellous.'

There was a tap on the door and Maxwell flung himself at it as a starving man will leap on a crust.

'Sounds like someone needs my words of wisdom, Bernard,' he said. 'And don't forget you've got to share your happy news with the headmaster yet.' He ushered the man out and grabbed the new visitor by the shoulder, hauling them into his office. Ryan looked stricken as the enormity of his next task dawned on him but Maxwell put him out of his mind by the simple expedient of closing the door on him.

He turned into the room, speaking as he did so. 'Now, David, how did . . . You're not David.' This was clearly the case, as a woman of about thirty one or two stood in front of him. 'No, hang on, don't tell me. I know who you are. You're . . . tip of tongue . . . Yes. You're Lindsey Summers, oh, God . . . what year, though?' He smiled at her, waiting for her to fill in the missing figure.

'A long time ago, Mr Maxwell,' she said. 'And I never did my A levels. I got pregnant, if you remember?'

'So you did,' he said, softly. 'I remember now. You were a damned good mathematician, if memory serves.'

'Yes, well, it comes in handy working in Asda,' she said, but with no bitterness in her voice. 'I had April and for a while her dad and I were happy. But you know how it is – we were just kids.'

All this talk of happiness today, Maxwell thought. There's a lot of it about, one way and another. 'So it's just you and April, is it, these days?'

The woman smiled. 'No. I've got two others, little ones, you know. And another on the way.' She cupped her stomach protectively. 'But I always worry most about April. Her dad was a wild one. That was the attraction, I suppose.'

'I don't remember who . . .'

'He wasn't from Leighford High,' she said. 'He lived up on the Barlichway in a squat. He was only my age, mind you, but he'd left home. He was a rebel.' Her face softened as she looked back down the years.

Maxwell kept his smile pinned on. He wasn't quite sure why she was here, on the busiest day of his year.

'Anyway, when April was about six months old, he just cleared off one night. I woke up and he was gone. I went back to my mother's for a while but she was all I told you so and all the rest. I moved out and met Phil and we've been together ever since. But I left April with my mother while I went to work. Then when I had my Robbie, I had her back, but she didn't settle. She lives where she wants, with us, with my mum.'

Maxwell felt it was time to move things on. 'And now she's at Leighford?' he asked.

'No. She came in Year Seven, but it wasn't handy for my mum's. When she's with us, Phil takes her to school, but Mum hasn't got a car. Makes sense she goes to school there.'

'So,' Maxwell thought he'd try another tack, but couldn't think of one. 'You're here because . . .'

'Sorry, Mr Maxwell. I'm not thinking straight. I've been over and over this in my head and so I think everybody knows. April's got a bed at ours and over at my mum's. For most of August, I thought she was there . . .'

'And your mum thought she was with you.'

'Right. That's right, Mr Maxwell. She won't tell us where she was, but she keeps crying and she doesn't want to go out. She'll only set foot outside if Phil goes with her. She's been back for over a week and she isn't getting any better. I remember how kind you were when I . . . well, when I fell for April. I just wanted to talk it over with someone other than Phil and my mum.'

'Phil, he doesn't hit you or April, does he?' Maxwell had to ask.

'God, no. He's a softie, but he is getting a bit fed up. My mum just shouts. Tells her to pull herself together. Anyway, I just thought she'd been off with some lad, you know how girls are.'

He did indeed. 'How old is she?' he checked.

'Fourteen. Fifteen in April.'

'I see. So just fourteen, then.'

'Yes.'

'And you weren't surprised to think she was off with some lad?' he asked, a little more sharply than he intended.

'Don't you shout at me, Mr Maxwell,' she said, her chin trembling. 'I don't know where else to go. Children's services will probably take the other kids as well as April. I don't know what to do.'

'But, Lindsey,' Maxwell said, putting a hand on her arm. 'She's back now.'

'Yes, she is,' the woman said, shaking his hand off and stepping back a pace. 'She is back, and she's not the same. This was no lad she was with. I don't pretend I'm a perfect mother, Mr Maxwell. I've got three kids, four soon and not enough money. I work all the time just to keep us fed. I can't watch her all the time. Where we live, the kids see things they shouldn't see. I don't want to draw you a picture, Mr Maxwell, but you've got no idea. April was off with lads as soon as she could be and I know they weren't playing Scrabble. But she's always been all right before. You know, afterwards. A bit of a row, a scrap and she'd be back home telling us how rubbish he was, things like that. But this time is different. She'd gone quiet. Until this morning.'

'And this morning?' Maxwell gently piloted her round to a chair and sat her down. He sat opposite and leaned forward. 'What happened this morning?'

'I found her in the bathroom, doing a pregnancy test.'

'And?'

'Positive.' The woman shrugged. 'It happens,' she said, with a lopsided smile. 'It wasn't that. When she saw me there, she looked at me and she just crumbled. She asked me . . . she said, will he love me *now*? I said to her, boys, they don't stay around when a baby's on the way. And she said, *boys* don't. *Men* do. I went cold, Mr Maxwell. Cold. Where's she been? Who's been at my baby?'

Maxwell sat back and looked at the woman opposite him. He could remember her when she was the brightest star in his Sixth Form. Her grasp of figures was innate, the Maths department had stars in their eyes and all she had had in hers was a layabout in a squat. But, as he knew too well, she wasn't the first and she would not be the last. Two dead girls rose up behind the woman and looked into his eyes. 'Lindsey, did she tell you anything else?'

'We talked for a while. She didn't know his full name, or where he lived. She knows the area, but not the road. She went there in the dark and she said when she got away from him . . .'

'Got away?' Maxwell felt his scalp crawl.

'Yes, she said . . . well, he tried to strangle her, she said. I thought she was probably making that bit up. You know, so I wouldn't be cross, about the baby.'

'Lindsey,' Maxwell said, getting up but extending an arm to keep her in her seat. 'I think you need to talk to my wife.'

'Your wife? All the kids used to say you were gay.' Even in her distress, Lindsey could be gobsmacked.

'So, my subterfuge worked,' Maxwell muttered, reaching for the phone and punching a number. 'Thingee, dear one. Could you get me Mrs Maxwell please? On the phone or here. Here for preference. Mm. Yes. Thank you. How are you keeping, by the way? And congratulations. Yes. You're welcome.'

Maxwell turned back to the woman who was looking as though she might be planning to leave.

'Lindsey, don't worry. I haven't gone mad. My wife is a Detective Inspector and she's investigating a couple of murders. No, don't panic . . .' The woman had jumped up and was looking set for flight. 'Is April with someone?'

'Yes, she's at Mum's.'

'You're sure?'

'Oh, yes. I took her myself. She knows better than to cross me again.'

'Good. Ring your mother from here. Don't worry her. Just make sure she keeps April with her. When my wife gets here, you can go together and interview April. She is a very rare thing.'

'What's that?'

'A live murder victim.'

In the end, a police car had swept up to the main doors of Leighford High School. Staff sitting near windows overlooking the front of the building turned blasé eyes back to their lesson preparation and gave a mental shrug. Bernard Ryan. Up to whatever it was he was doing *again*. Been there. Done that. Bernard Ryan himself was crossing the foyer and, as he related to Joe later that evening, almost crapped himself with shock. But Jacquie, in full DI mode, swept past him without a glance and was through the door and up the steps to the Sixth Form mezzanine without a pause. Thingee carried on pecking away at a keyboard. She was spending rather a lot of time looking on mother and baby websites these days. Especially those which dealt with subjects like 'Sex in pregnancy – how to keep your man happy'. She looked at Jacquie, then back to the screen and sighed.

Maxwell was sitting talking to Lindsey Summers, trying to keep her calm. Every now and again she would jerk and almost get up, like someone dreaming of falling. And in a way, she was falling. She just wasn't dreaming at the same time. She had rung her mother and been told that April was on her bed, reading. She had been a bit sick – had she eaten something that had disagreed with her? Or was the silly little tart up the spout? Mrs Summers senior was not the most sensitive of women. The Head of Sixth Form turned at the sound of the tap on the door. The queue of Year 12 wannabees had shifted a few feet to the left to stand outside Helen Maitland's office. Would it, they wondered, always be like this?

'Dear heart,' Maxwell said, leaping to his feet with almost indecent enthusiasm. 'This is Lindsey . . . Miss Summers, I should say. It's her daughter April . . .'

'Thank you, Mr Maxwell,' Jacquie said, formally. She stepped forward and extended a hand to the woman, who was standing waiting, with almost the same expression on her face as fifteen years ago when she had told Maxwell she was leaving the Sixth Form. 'Miss Summers, I am Detective Inspector Carpenter-Maxwell and I understand you are concerned about your daughter, April.'

'Yes, that's right. But . . .' Suddenly it all seemed a bit big and formal. Lindsey had a feeling that she had just rolled a snowball off an Alp and there was no telling how big it might be by the time it reached the bottom. Nor how many bodies it would contain. 'I may be over-reacting.'

'That's possible,' Jacquie said brightly. 'But let's go and have a word with April, shall we, then we'll see. If you would just go down to the car with the constable here, I just need a word with Mr Maxwell.' She ushered the woman out of the door and then turned to face her husband. 'Thank you,' she said, planting a kiss on his mouth. 'That is a very good call.'

'Just doing ma job, ma'am,' Maxwell drawled, an amalgam of every old timer ever seen on screen; Gabby Hayes meets Arthur Hunnicut. Then, in what passed for normal, 'It seemed to me that this girl may hold the key.'

'Did she say anything specific?'

He shook his head. 'You've still got a hunt and a half on your hands. The kid was in lurve and in the dark when they arrived, panic-stricken when she left so she has no real idea where the guy lives. He's older, but we don't know by how much and of course kids are useless at ages as we know. Lindsey thinks he could be as much as mid-thirties, but can't be sure. The girl says he's handsome, but have you seen the latest Dr Who heartthrob? He looks as though he has been hit in the face with a frying pan, so who knows what handsome means to a kid. So the world is still, I am afraid, light of my being, the crustacean of your choice.'

'Never mind. We're nearer than we were. And she's still alive. That's the main thing.'

'No,' he said, seriously. 'The main thing is that she's alive and also hopefully the last.'

'True.' She wiggled her fingers at him at the door. 'Are you okay for Nole?'

'He's at Plocker's. His mum is bringing him home around six.'

'Wonderful. I don't know when I'll be home – soz.'

'Soz indeed. We'll see you when we see you.' And he wiggled his fingers back at her and then crossed to the window, wondering how a woman who still looked amazing foreshortened as she was from three storeys up, could possibly be his wife. But he was heartily glad she was. Then he turned back to the Day Job, hauling open his door and yelling, 'Right, you 'orrible little men – and women, of course – step this way for the Rest of Your Lives.'

'Dads?'

'Son?'

'When I'm big enough to come to your school . . .'

'Oh, mate! Let's not go there.'

'Well, I will be big enough, one day.'

'Granted. All right then, when you're big enough to come to my school . . .'

'What things do you think I'll be good at?'

'What things are you good at now?'

'Maffs. Stories. Singing.' Nolan tried a few tra-las for good measure. 'Recorder. Drawing. Colouring. *Dance*.' Maxwell hoped the emphasis on the last word was because his son was running out of subjects rather than that hopping and skipping was where he saw his future lying. Ghastly images of *Billy Elliot* floated in his brain. 'Did I say stories?'

'Yes, you did.'

'Well, any of those. I like them all and Mrs Whatmough says I am promising.' He lifted his chin and looked at his father through ridiculously long eyelashes. 'I don't member promising her anything, but you can't tell with Mrs Whatmough.'

Maxwell could believe it. 'Well, Nole, you have a while before you have to choose. And by then, who knows? When Dads was a lad, the exams were known as O Levels and if you were very clever, you got a One. Then they brought in some things they called CSE and in those you had to get a One or it didn't count but if you got a One it was an O Level. Then there were GCSEs and if you are clever you get an A star and if you get a D that doesn't count either. Soon, they are going to be called something cockamamie like . . . ooh, I don't know . . . MMQ.'

'What does that stand for?' Nolan wanted to know.

'Mickey Mouse Qualification, or a Gove for short. With those, we're back to numbers but a One isn't good any more, a Nine is good and a One is bad.'

'*Nine?*' Even Nolan could see that was stupid. 'Why nine?'

Maxwell sighed and ruffled his son's hair. 'Who knows?' he said. 'Who knows? Quick game of Snap before bedtime?'

'Can we play Scrabble?' Nolan was already out of the chair and halfway across the landing heading for the games cupboard.

'All right,' Maxwell said. 'But be gentle with me. You know you always win.'

Nolan stopped and turned. 'Do you *let* me win, Dads?' he asked.

Maxwell slumped and shook his head. 'I did that once, when you were about two,' he said. 'Since then, it's been a fair fight.'

Nolan pulled out the box and opened the lid. He looked up at his father and winked at the cat, stretched out on the sofa, possession being nine points of the law. 'Best of three?'

Later that night, bloody but unbowed, Maxwell tucked the Scrabble King into bed and went one floor up into the attic to start work on another member of the Light Brigade, Private Charles Cooper of the 11th Prince Albert's Own. Not much was known about this man. He had been a plumber beforehand and was killed in the Charge, so Maxwell could use a little licence. He thought he might make him look like Bernard Ryan and then, in years to come, he would be able to work back to when he was made. He was an historian. He couldn't help it. He began by carefully gluing Cooper's legs together and then the legs to the torso. The angle of the head was always a problem.

The moment Maxwell had chosen to depict was the one when Louis Nolan (no relation to his son) had ridden up to Cardigan with the fateful order that would do for men like Trooper Cooper in the next twenty minutes. The Brigade were just sitting their horses, waiting. Now, for a challenge, he'd give the ex-plumber a boiled egg to eat, as some of the real men had. So, he head would be . . . he checked it through his modelling lens . . . like so.

He looked over his shoulder at the purring mound of cat on top of the old linen basket which, over the years, had taken on the shape of the animal's body. 'Awake, Count?' he asked.

The purring changed tone and he took it for a 'Yes.'

'I wonder how the Mem is getting on with young April?' he said. 'I can't think she is still with her, can you? It's . . . ' he squinted over into the gloom beyond his lamplight, '. . . can you see the clock from there, Count? No? Well, let's just call it late, then. Perhaps she's out making an arrest, eh? That *would* be a bit of a result.'

He carried on positioning Cooper's arms for a moment or two, bringing the plastic hands together as though shelling an egg and then leaned over and prodded the cat in a particularly portly part with his brush.

'I said, that *would* be a bit of a result.' The cat turned over with a grunt and Maxwell nodded. 'Exactly. The poor kid is still pregnant, though. Just another statistic, you might say and before you were Done I daresay you were responsible for many such. But you didn't prey on kittens, did you, unless you fancied a snack, presumably. This is an adult, not a kid who opens his flies and his brains fall out. He knows better. It's a choice and it's a choice we've got to prevent him making again.'

There was a pause, totally silent apart from a slight creak from the linen basket.

'Yes,' Maxwell said, gesturing at the cat. 'I did say "we". After all, it was me who got Bernard's alibi, it was me to whom Lindsey came with her little problem . . . No, I don't know why. Race memory, I suppose. So, yes, the bottom line, my feline friend, my companion of a vole, "we" I said and "we" I mean. Let's talk serial killers, Count.'

Maxwell set the 54mm ex-plumber aside to dry and stared up at the stars beginning to come out beyond his skylight. 'Since you are one, I expect your input to be pithy and precise. As I understand it, we left 74% of them behind when we left the dear ol' US of A. So all we have to worry about are the remaining 86% who live here in Leighford. Sorry.' He caught the cat's steely gaze. 'A *little* flippant perhaps, bearing in mind the subject matter. Let's look at the victims first of all. Two dead girls, both mid-teens and a possible third – attempted. Did they know each other? Josie went to St Olave's – most kids meet via school unless they're neighbours. Molly went there too, but only for a few days, tasters for this coming term. Lindsey's girl was at Leighford for a while – yes, of course, Count,' he heard the animal's disapproving inrush of breath. 'I'll be checking with her Year Head tomorrow; although . . . Year Seven, that's Angie 'Airhead' Skillington, so my hopes are not of the highest.'

He was twirling the paintbrush in his fingers. 'Of course, they could have met at a disco, nightclub, wherever girlies go after dark. School may be a red herring,' and he winked at Metternich. 'Makes your mouth water, doesn't it, me ol' piscavore? One type of serial killer is disorganised. He's driven by forces he can't control, so he's an opportunist. He'll launch a blitz attack one night and he's brought no murder weapon with him. In this case, the cause of death is strangulation so the weapon of choice is a ligature of some kind or his bare hands. He leaves the body where it is and does a runner . . .'

Maxwell sighed and rubbed his eyes. He was getting too old for this. Close-focus modelling *and* crime-solving, all at the end of a day's work. Where was the light at the end of the tunnel?

'But that's not his MO, is it, Count?' he said, picking up the two halves of Private Cooper's horse, minus, for the moment, head and tail. 'Chummy doesn't leap on people out of the shadows. He selects them, grooms them. Hell, if Lindsey's girl's bloke is our man, he lives with them. Sex, presumably, is consensual, so that's not likely to be the motive. But power, you see, Count, power. Robbie Coltrane in *Cracker* used to do it well, didn't he? Remember?'

The cat didn't.

Maxwell lapsed into Lowland Scots. 'He's won the girl away from her family, her friends. She's his plaything now. She belongs to him.' He dropped the Coltrane suddenly, and became what passed for himself again. 'The Home Secretary assures us that domestic slavery is all too common in this great country of ours. Subservients brought up in confined spaces, locked into some ghastly Stockholm Syndrome relationship with their captors. Is that what we're talking about here? And does the captor suddenly have no more use – or no more space – for these girls? So he discards them, like so much recyclable waste?'

He frowned at the black and white beast coiled in front of him. 'Talking of which,' he sighed, 'Isn't it about time you began your cycle of killing? I'm sure there's a rodent out there somewhere with your name on it – if you'll excuse the unlikely idiom for a moment. Off you bugger – I think I just heard the Mem draw up outside and she'll want a bite to eat.'

Chapter Ten

The Head of Sixth Form's ears had not misled him and he met Jacquie on the landing, she at the top of the stairs, he at the bottom. She smiled weakly at him and mimed a cup of tea and a sandwich as she headed for the sitting room where he heard her bag land with a thump on the floor. This was standard practice for his wife who, although clean, could never be accused of being tidy. The floor for her was just one enormous shelf and she used it to its maximum. The house was still Hector Gold clean – which meant very clean indeed – but things were beginning to gather in the corners, including a new civilization of socks in the corner of the bedroom. Never mind, Maxwell smiled and looked back over his shoulder to where Jacquie's shadow danced on the wall between the windows overlooking the street, he wouldn't have her any other way.

When he joined her in the sitting room, cup of tea steaming and the sandwich a tempting round of her favourite ham and hummus, he found her relaxed back in her favourite chair and her feet up on a stool. She held out a hand wordlessly for the tray and took a swig and a mouthful, in that order. She chewed with her eyes closed and then sighed. 'You have no idea how much I was looking forward to that,' she said, looking up at him. 'Your ex-star mathematician might be bright but she's not much of a hostess.'

'A lot on her plate,' Maxwell suggested.

'Hmm.' She took another bite of her sandwich and nodded. 'She does have a houseful. But I don't know if it is going to get much bigger after all.'

'Oh?' If Maxwell was surprised at the level of sharing, he didn't show it.

'I'm telling you this because I have no doubt Lindsey will be round tomorrow telling nice Mr Maxwell all about it, how his nasty wife asked her April all sorts of things that are rude and unnecessary. She has suddenly decided to pretend that April is as innocent as a babe unborn – is that a quote? It sounds like one. Anyway, I think someone, her mother perhaps or a friend, has told her that if she admits that April has been at it like a weasel since she left Junior School, the Social will be round to take the kids, including her own unborn one. So we had a bit of an uphill struggle, to say the least. I kicked the mother out from the first – she really does call a spade a spade. Some of the words she used for having sex I'm going to have to look up later. Lindsey isn't foul mouthed, but she seems totally . . . unsurprised, is the word, I think. When she remembered, that is.'

'She did take me aback a bit, being so casual about the promiscuity.' Maxwell had thought he knew it all, but he had to admit that Lindsey took lax parenting to a new level.

'Yes, well, in the end, we had to get her to leave the room as well. We could hear the two of them at it hammer and tongs in the kitchen. Blaming each other, I suppose. Fortunately, one of our appropriate adults had just come in with her expenses sheet as I was leaving the Nick and I nabbed her to come with me.'

'Ah, you had your precognition turned on all right,' Maxwell smiled.

'I certainly did. For some reason, the kid really took to her. Most of the time she does the appropriate bit with some real low-lives so she came into her own when dealing with basically a very nice, very scared little girl.'

'You mentioned the family not getting bigger . . .'

'Yes,' Jacquie frowned and put her hand on her own stomach, reminiscently. 'I think April may be planning a termination. She isn't very far along and she certainly fits all the criteria for getting one quickly. And . . .' she paused, struggling for words. Since having Nolan, it was sometimes hard to be hard. She swallowed and took another run at it. 'It will be easier for us to extract DNA. From the foetus, you know, rather than by amniocentesis.'

'Yes, I know,' he said softly.

'Anyway, she's seeing a social worker tomorrow. I personally think that is the only way out, but it has to be her decision, in the end.'

'Does it make any difference the baby being the result of sexual assault?' Maxwell checked.

'Is it?' Jacquie said, suddenly remembering her sandwich and taking another bite. 'There was no assault as far as I could tell. This bloke . . .'

'Do we have a name? We can't keep calling him "this bloke" can we?'

'Bearing in mind that you shouldn't be calling him anything at all,' she reminded him.

'Always bearing that in mind, dearest, of course,' he said. 'So, name?'

'No, and funny you should call me "dearest" at that point, because apparently, he told her that names were only labels, that they were no longer who they had once been before they met and so they only used endearments.'

Maxwell whistled through his teeth. 'What a very, *very* clever predator you have to catch, Detective Inspector Jacqueline Bind-their-kings-in-chains-and-their-nobles-with-links-of-iron Carpenter-Maxwell, to give you your full title.'

'Now, that *is* a quote!'

'Macaulay, well spotted, yes. But that is just what I would do, if I wanted to trap and discard someone. Disorient them by taking away their identity, whilst making them think that losing their name is a good thing and *meanwhile* making sure they don't know who you are. Genius!' Maxwell tried not to grin – this man was a monster and had to be stopped. But still . . . it was damned clever.

'We asked her if she had any seen any post, had anyone rung and overheard him answer with his name, all that; but the answer was no – he never slipped, not once. And of course, using random endearments makes it foolproof in bed. None of this accidentally murmuring the wrong name.'

'Indeed, Mousehabit,' he said. 'It does. This bloke . . . oh, for heavens' sake,' he said, 'you must have a name for him. The Vole or something.'

'The case has been assigned a random name, yes, just for filing and reference, but it came out as Umbrella. The next one copped Viking which would have been easier to use without laughing, but that went to someone who has been widdling in other people's wheelie bins. Quite impressive range, by all accounts.' She finished her tea in one gulp and put her tray to one side, brushing random crumbs from her lap. 'Delicious, thank you,' she smiled.

Maxwell was delighted, however. 'Umbrella man!' he said. 'From the Zapruder film.' He looked at her before her went on.

'Yes, yes,' she said, flapping a hand. 'Grassy knoll, all that. Okay, Umbrella Man he is. However, may I point out that this is no help at all, except for convenience. We can't search the electoral roll for Mr U Man, can we?'

'No, but it helps him seem more real, rather than a nebulous "bloke". Next, address?'

'Absolutely no help. She ran out in a blind panic, was driven home by what she describes as a nice lady, she thinks she might be foreign because she was sitting on the wrong side of the car.'

'Tourist.' Maxwell slumped in his seat.

'Indeed. Tourist. And she could be anywhere in Europe by now. We'll have to leave that strand as something to follow when all else fails. In any case, April thinks she may have run as much as half a mile before getting picked up.'

'Umm, what else is there?' Maxwell held up a wagging finger.

'Well, description, I suppose. Sadly, she was looking through the eyes of love.'

'Uh oh! Let me guess. In the old days it would have been Sean Connery. Who is it now?'

'Well, this is where I was surprised. Daniel Craig, so same franchise. I took this to mean that he really is that type. Daniel Craig rather than Daniel Radcliffe. So we have settled on medium height, up to six foot. Lightish hair rather than dark. Thirties rather than twenties . . .'

'Mr Craig would be delighted,' Maxwell observed. 'But I also assume this lets out the stepfather, the boyfriend, the builder . . . I don't quite know what label to use for the man, lacking, as I do, his name.'

He smiled encouragingly at her but she just smiled right on back.

'I don't know why I assume stepfathers have to be older . . .' he hinted.

'Yes, it does let him out. For this one, at least. We are not anxious to put all our eggs in one basket just yet. But, anyway, if I can interrupt myself,' Jacquie said, 'we did ask her about age and got some photos out, just the usual suspects, you know, the equivalent of a quick identity parade. She immediately threw out everyone over around thirty five as an old git, so we decided that he is in his thirties.'

'So, thirties, blondish, tallish . . . build?'

Jacquie almost blushed. 'I don't think you want to know the details. But apparently he does strip off quite well.'

Maxwell chuckled. It wasn't often his wife was discomfited. 'Any distinguishing marks or features?'

'May I refer you to my previous answer?' she said, 'or I will have to take the Fifth.'

'He has five of them?' Maxwell said, throwing up his hands in horror.

'To hear April, he would need every one. I think she was trying to shock me and Viv – the appropriate adult – but she gave up after a while. She got quite tearful, poor little soul. All she wanted was someone to love her.'

'I wonder how he finds these girls?' Maxwell mused, tapping a forefinger on his chin.

'Just prowls, I assume. He certainly picked April up on the Esplanade.'

'*Leighford* Esplanade?'

'No. Brighton. But he lives in Leighford. We know that for sure.'

'So the fact that the other girls come from Brighton way is not a red herring?' He didn't usually use the same phrase twice in one evening if he could help it, but sometimes it had to be done.

'We don't know. Because we don't know where he met them, how he got into conversation with them . . . in fact, without having the perp in custody, we really don't know much.' She stopped for a moment and ran the sentence back. She smiled across at Maxwell, who had raised a sardonic eyebrow. 'Sorry about the perp thing. Umbrella Man, I mean.'

Maxwell decided to turn the conversation from its current cul de sac. 'Do you think the DNA will help, however you get it?'

She shrugged. 'I doubt it, except as proof later. I just don't get the impression that this bl . . . Umbrella Man is on our books. His methods don't really fit the pattern of a large-scale sexual predator. He has taken at least one girl back to his house. He doesn't like having sex anywhere but inside, according to April, so he isn't likely to be the sort to jump out at girls and drag them into the bushes. They are the ones that tend to get caught. The impulsive attackers. The flashers. That kind of thing.'

Maxwell looked across at her, noting the shadows under her eyes, the way one bit of hair stood up at one side of her head where she had run exasperated fingers through it. 'Early night?' he asked.

'Is it still early enough to count as early?' she asked, squinting at the clock on the DVD player.

'It depends on where you are,' he said. 'It's pretty early in LA. In fact, it's positively afternoon. Call it a siesta, and it will seem early. What do you say?'

'I say I think that sounds like a plan,' she said. 'I'll just look in on Nole and then hit the hay.'

'If he's smiling, don't be surprised,' Maxwell said.

She cocked her head and put her arms around him, leaning briefly on his shoulder. 'Scrabble?' she said, indistinctly.

'I couldn't possible comment,' he said, rubbing her back then giving her a decisive pat. 'Come on, bed for you, woman. Tomorrow it will be another day, another collar.'

'Hopefully,' she said and made for the stairs.

Down on the seafront at Leighford, there was a fin de siècle air abroad, as all the schoolchildren from the town made the most of the last of the late nights. Back to school tomorrow, back to scratchy jumpers, shiny-bummed trousers, new, squeaky shoes. Back to looking like a kid, instead of anything upwards of twenty. There were a handful of boys there, leaning in gangs on the railings, shouting half-hearted insults at the girls as they tottered past in too high heels and too-tight jeans. They looked like baby colts, all legs and knees, eyelashes out to here, looking for love. Umbrella Man leaned in the shadows of a beach-goods hut, closed now that the season was over. The shutters over the serving hatch made a small niche of the doorway and he could hide in there without looking like a lurking pervert. Because he *wasn't* a pervert. Of that much he was sure. He just had sex with these girls quite normally, nothing perverted, just a bit rough sometimes. They liked it really. And sometimes things could get . . . complicated. He felt his erection growing and pressed it with his palm in his specially adapted pocket, the one with no lining. Get down, he muttered. No good approaching his quarry with a hard on. These girls looked for that. Her mates would all laugh and he wouldn't be able to peel her off from the herd. That's how he thought of himself, a leopard, sinewy and lithe, a pretty face with a black, carnivorous heart. He leaned forward slightly as he heard the clack of a clique of girls heading his way. He carefully searched every face, looking for the right one. And, yes, what he had been hoping for, the laggard, the weakling, the runt of the litter, a few steps behind, looking a bit sulky, a bit left out. Pretty enough, though. He had his standards. He stepped forward and she turned to him, her little peachy cheek just asking to be stroked, her lips, jammy with gloss, parted in an unspoken question.

'Hello,' he said. 'What's your name?'

Caroline Morton was in bed, but sleepless. She had gone to bed early, being bone tired, deeply exhausted as only weeks of lying awake can make a person. Her world had been turned upside down. A year ago, she had had everything. A loving husband. A loving father, stepmother, sister. Now, she had nothing. A self-pitying tear squeezed out of the corner of her eye to run down and join the others soaking into her pillow. She reached out for her phone, never far from her because she always seemed to be on call these days, always working. Working and crying, that was her life now. She ran her thumb around the edge of the phone and then punched two keys. She waited as the signal bounced from tower to tower until she heard the ringing sound. To her, it sounded like a standard ring. At the other end, she knew, it sounded like *Stairway to Heaven* played on the spoons in a bucket. Another tear squeezed out, ran down, soaked in.

'Yes. Morton.'

'Darling,' she sobbed. 'It's me.'

'Caroline.' It wasn't a greeting. Just a remark.

'Darling . . . I . . . I'm asking you to come home. The house is so empty without you.'

There was a silence at the other end of the phone.

'Well, it would be, of course, with Mollie gone.'

The tears were flowing now and she turned on her side so she didn't choke. 'Don't be cruel, darling . . .' she said. 'It's killing me having to act as though everything is all right all day at the office and then to come back here by myself. Darling?'

'Sorry, what?'

She sat up and heard her own voice grow shrill, taking on the fishwife tone he hated so much. 'Who's there? Who have you got there? I can hear her. There's someone . . .'

'Caroline,' he said, 'I don't think you can hear yourself. You ring me to beg me to come back to you and then you start accusing me of . . . well, whatever it is you're accusing me of this time. Let me think, who has it been so far? Secretaries; well, of course. Our office has the ugliest lot of staff of any law firm in the country.

Colleagues; naturally. Sadly, you can't insist that the courts only ever use plain prosecutors. Neighbours; goes without saying. But Mollie, Caroline? That took the biscuit and as far as I am concerned all bets are off. I intend to wait a while so I don't look a total bastard and then I'm divorcing you. I wasn't going to be so blunt, but you came to me, remember?'

'But,' and this time she did choke on her tears, 'you love me!'

'Did, Caro, did.' His voice softened. 'Look, are you going to be all right? I can come round if you like, but you must understand, it's over. It really is.'

She blew her nose and gave a determined sniff. She patted her hair into place as though he were next to her in the enormous, empty bed. 'I don't want to interrupt your evening,' she whispered.

'You're not interrupting anything,' he said. 'Look, give me half an hour. I just want to wake up properly and have a shower or something. Freshen up. I'll . . .'

'Thank you,' she said, almost inaudible. 'Thank you, darling.'

'I'm just talking to Caroline,' she heard him say.

'Who are you talking to?' she screamed.

'If you must know,' he said, 'I was talking to Suzanne. From the judges' office, you know her I think.'

'Why are you talking to Suzanne?' she asked, wiping her nose with the back of her hand.

'Because before you rang, you mad bitch,' a woman's voice sounded in her ear, 'he was screwing the arse off me. So thanks for ruining what was working up to a perfect evening.' In the background, she heard her husband's voice raised in mild protest. 'Well, it's time she was told,' the woman snapped and the line went dead.

Caroline Morton bent over in pain, just as agonizing for not being real. She screamed soundlessly, jamming her knuckles into her mouth until she almost broke the skin. A cracked groan escaped her and she drummed her feet on the mattress, like a child having a tantrum. Then, with a sudden, convulsive movement, she sat up, wiped her eyes and took up the phone again. Scrolling through her contacts she chose one and waited as the call connected. She tucked a lock of hair behind her ear and cleared her throat, ready for when it answered.

'Hello?' a sleepy voice said. 'Can I help you?'

'Detective Inspector Carpenter-Maxwell?' she said, crisply. 'It's Caroline Morton here. I would like to give you some information about the death of my sister. I believe I know who her murderer is.'

Chapter Eleven

Jacquie Carpenter-Maxwell lay on her face, her arm dangling over the side of the bed, her fingers slowly relaxing so that the phone dropped to the floor. Through the pillow, Maxwell could just hear her muttering 'No, no and hell no!' Could it be that bad if she was attempting a take-off of Will Smith in *Men in Black*? He risked a question.

'Anyone I know?' He leaned back, ready for the reply but she was too tired to rise to it.

'Mollie Adamson's half sister. Apparently, she knows who the murderer is.' It took him a moment to translate, the whole being filtered through the pillow, but he was pretty sure that was the gist.

'That's good.' The question hovered at the end of the sentence.

She nodded her head, face still down in the pillow.

'Is she likely to be right, do you think?'

This time the head circled. 'No. Yes. I have no idea.' She sat up and turned to face him. 'What time is it?' she asked and he screwed round to look at the clock behind him on the bedside table.

'Half past one.' He groaned. 'Why did she wait until now?'

'If it was anyone other than her, I would say she has an axe to grind. Most people who come in or ring in the middle of the night do it on the back of a row. But she wouldn't row. She would pontificate. That's her style. Oh, I won't deny she was upset about her sister, but . . .' she flicked the bedclothes back with a sigh, '. . . she wants to meet me at the Nick. I suppose I'd better go.'

Maxwell stopped her with an arm across her chest. 'I don't often do this,' he said. 'In fact, thinking back, I don't think I have ever done this before. But I am doing it now. I am forbidding you to go in.'

'Pardon?' Shock made her eyes wide. 'You're doing what?'

'Forbidding you. You are exhausted. You haven't seen your son awake for days. You've hardly seen *me* awake, and I'm allowed to stay up late. Leave it to someone who is already up and at the Nick. Surely, they still have night shifts, don't they, or has that nice Mrs May dispensed with those while your back is turned?'

'Most police stations are daytime only . . . well, skeleton staff, you know. But Leighford Nick still has a proper night staff. Processing all the bingers.' She flopped back on the bed and turned her head to look up at him. 'Are you really forbidding me?'

'Yup.'

'Okay,' she turned over and groped for the phone. 'I'll just tell the desk to take her statement. She won't be happy.'

He patted her on the bum. 'You know,' he said, 'you put me in mind of the Rokeby Venus in that position.'

'I'll take that as a compliment,' she said, then, into the phone, 'Yes, hello, who's that? It's DI Carpenter-Maxwell here. Yes, hello. I have someone coming in shortly, a Mrs Caroline Morton. Could you just take a statement and tell her I will get back to her tomorrow? No, sorry, something's come up. Be discreet – she can be a bit. . . Oh, right, at court. Yes. You'll know what she's like then. Thanks. Yes, tomorrow. Lovely, thanks.' She pressed with her thumb to disconnect and then switched off the light. 'I never liked him,' she said.

'Who?'

'That desk man. So I'm glad it's him who will have to deal with Caroline Morton. She's going to be pissed.'

'Oh, you think that's why she rang? Been drinking?'

'No, American pissed, not English pissed.'

'Oh, *American* pissed.' He paused, then patted her bum. 'I forgive you,' he said. 'It was clearly just a slip of the tongue.'

But DI Jacquie Carpenter-Maxwell was already asleep.

'I beg your pardon?' Although the words were polite enough they lost their sweetness when delivered through lips stiff with anger.

'I'm afraid that the Detective Inspector is unable to see you right now,' the desk man said. He was enjoying this. This cow had put him through the mill in court more than once and it was good to have the whip hand for once. 'Something came up.' Mind you, he had no time for Detective Inspector Jacquie Carpenter-Maxwell either, so this was two birds with one stone time.

'Something came up?' the woman screeched. '*I* came up. All the way here, to be precise. How dare she?'

'I can arrange for someone to take your statement, ma'am,' the desk man said blandly. 'If you would just like to take a seat over there for a moment . . . ?'

'No, I would *not* like to take a seat over there, you moron,' the woman spat. Now he came to look at her, the desk man could see she was in a bit of a state. Been crying, for sure. He couldn't smell drink but who knew, these days. She could easily be on something else. He took another surreptitious sniff. Not weed. Something else, then. She narrowed her eyes at him. 'Did you just *sniff* me?' she shrieked. 'Did you just bloody *sniff* me? You pond life. How dare you? I want to speak to your superior.'

'Well . . .' the desk man took his time. This couldn't last much longer and he wanted to make the most of it. 'I'm afraid my actual line manager is off sick at the moment, ma'am,' he said. 'Stress, or so I believe. Would you like to speak to someone else?'

'Yes,' she hissed, through gritted teeth.

'Let me just look through my sheet, please, ma'am,' he said. 'Protocol, I'm sure you understand.' He turned his back on her and started leafing through a file, checking the hierarchy. What he found pleased him more than anything had pleased him for months. Very slowly, he put the file back in the right place on the shelf and turned back to the now incandescent woman. 'I can make you an appointment to speak to my next available line manager, ma'am,' he said, placing both hands on the desk in the time honoured manner and leaning forward with a friendly smile. 'I'm sorry it can't be now, but I'm afraid that Detective Inspector Carpenter-Maxwell isn't here right now. Something has come up, apparently.'

And it wasn't until that moment that Caroline Morton hit him, but she gave it all she had and he went down like a pole-axed steer, files and shelves cascading down over his prone body. In a cacophony of sirens and alarms, the night staff came running, one overzealous policewoman rugby tackling the solicitor to the ground where she lay, unprotesting.

'Can I see DI Carpenter-Maxwell now?' she asked, from under thirteen stone of policeness.

But it was morning before she finally got her wish.

'Toast?'

'And peanut butter? And jelly?' Nolan was still in American breakfast mode. He had stopped using American words when he remembered, but American breakfasts, as far as he was concerned, were here to stay. 'Are we having pancakes?'

'Not today, Nole,' his mother said. 'Back to school today, remember?'

The boy looked down at his bare knees, below new and rather stiff shorts. He felt the weight of the new shoes on his feet, saw through the kitchen door the new Mrs Whatmough-issue duffle coat hanging on the hook. 'Yes,' he sighed. 'Can't we ever have pancakes again?' He turned his eyes to look into his mother's face, pleading.

She planted a kiss on his nose. 'Weekends,' she assured him.

'And holidays?'

'Of course.'

'Birthdays?'

'Don't push it.'

There was a sudden scuffling noise and a stifled curse as Maxwell fell over the cat at the foot of the stairs and then he was in the kitchen, looking over his shoulder at a black and white streak heading off and out as fast as he could. 'I will swing for that animal,' he said, taking his seat and looking round. 'No pancakes?'

'Don't start,' said his wife.

'Weekends, holidays and birthdays,' Nolan told him, bringing him up to speed.

'That sounds fair,' Maxwell agreed. 'Toast it is, then.' Jacquie rescued a piece from the toaster and sat down.

'Thank you for letting me sleep last night,' she said. 'I was exhausted.'

'You're welcome,' the Head of Sixth Form said. He too was kitted out for school, in a jacket that had begun to long for better days and his pre-cycle-clip-creased trousers. The Jesus scarf would not kick in until after half term. 'Are you feeling a little more rested now, Sleeping Beauty?'

Nolan rocked in his chair in silent laughter. 'Dads, you called Mummy Sleeping Beauty.'

'Indeed I did,' Maxwell agreed. 'But now she's awake, perhaps just Beauty would be better.' He raised an eyebrow at his son, but he needed no hints.

'Yes,' Nolan said and his smile was smeared with peanut butter. 'You look beautiful, Mummy.' Then, compliment forgotten, he bent to his toast.

Jacquie looked at them, her men, like two peas in a pod in some lights and muttered a little thank you to the sky, just for luck. She glanced at the clock and jumped to her feet. 'Oh, chaps!' she said. 'Look at the time. I must be off.' Nolan puckered up and she planted a kiss on a peanut butter-free area. To Maxwell, she sent a kiss through the air. 'I'll see you tonight,' and in a flurry of bags and coat, she was gone.

The two sat in silence for a moment, then Nolan broke it.

'Wasn't Mummy taking me to school this morning?' he asked, a touch plaintively.

'Well, I thought so, mate,' Maxwell agreed. 'She seems to have forgotten. Never mind, perhaps we . . .'

There was a thundering of feet on the stairs and Jacquie barrelled back into the kitchen.

'Sorry, Nole,' she panted. 'Can you get your coat on, sweetness? I'm dropping you at school, aren't I?' She wiped the peanut butter off his face and partly into his ear. Phlegmatic child that he was, he poked it out for himself and wiped it surreptitiously on the lining of her coat. 'Got everything? Kiss Dads. 'Bye then. Let's try this again,' and the two of them went down the stairs, a little more carefully this time. It wouldn't look good to deliver Nolan on Day One to Mrs Whatmough in a bent condition.

When the door had slammed, Peter Maxwell sat still for another couple of seconds, just listening to the house stop shuddering, then gave a little chuckle and got up to put the dishes in the washer. He wouldn't go back to having a silent house for a million pounds. He had lived in one of those for long enough. But, he thought to himself, with a start like this morning's, the rest of the day had better go smoothly, that's all!

Henry Hall was at the coffee machine as Jacquie approached her office. He gave her a quizzical look. 'I believe we have a friend of yours down in the cells,' he said, with no preamble.

'A friend of mine?' she asked, puzzled.

'Caroline Morton,' he said.

'In the cells?' Jacquie tried to think what she could possibly have said on the phone to come up with that result.

'She laid out Sid Lewis last night. Right uppercut, by all accounts. He's in hospital with his neck in traction. So she's in the cells.'

Jacquie looked sheepish. 'That might be my fault, guv,' she said. 'I agreed to meet her, but then . . . well, I was just so tired. I rang in and asked them to get a statement.'

'Sid isn't one of nature's gentlefolk,' Hall said. 'He probably looked at her funny.'

'Even so . . .'

'And, it gets stranger than that.'

'It does?' She was pressed as to see how.

'She asked for a solicitor, and when the next one on the list came, it was her old man.'

'Odd. He must have known she was here, surely?'

'It seems not. They have been separated for around six months, if her screams through the door have been accurately noted. I've got the night staff's report in here, if you'll just come through.' He pushed open the door to his office and ushered her in. He picked up the night file from his desk and riffled through the pages. 'Bla bla, hmm . . . No, here it is. "Mrs Morton was placed in Interview Room Three and charged with assaulting a police officer. She asked for a solicitor and . . ." hmm, where is it? Yes. This. "Mr Morton was shown in and Mrs Morton threw her handbag at him, saying that the bastard had left her for some slag from the Crown Court and he could . . ." oh, yes, well I'm sure you get the drift.'

'She didn't say they were separated when we spoke at the hospital.'

'No?'

'Now I think of it, she didn't say they weren't, but I just assumed they were together, from the way she spoke. Anyway, I suppose I had better go down and see her. She says she has information that may lead to Mollie's . . . oh, hang on. She's fingering the husband, isn't she?'

Henry Hall closed the file with a soft snap and looked ruefully at Jacquie. 'I'm afraid so. Good guess, by the way.'

She ran her fingers through her hair. 'I knew as soon as I forgot Nolan this morning that today wouldn't go well.'

'You *forgot* Nolan? You've had him a while, now, Jacquie. Surely you're used to him by now.'

From anyone else, that would have been a joke. But as it came from Henry Hall, Jacquie knew it wasn't. Shaking her head, she made for the cells, leaving him to smile to himself as he sat down. He only smiled when he was alone, and even then, they were strictly rationed, so there would be no more for a week or two.

There was no need to ask which cell Caroline Morton was in, because the noise carried right along the corridor. Tired from screaming, she had settled for pounding rhythmically on the door. The flick of the grille stopped her and she raised a tear-stained face to look into Jacquie's eyes.

'Oh, so you're here,' she said, in a lacklustre voice. 'Been busy?'

Jacquie spoke crisply and without emphasis. 'Mrs Morton, do I need help to get you to an interview room, or will you be all right to come with me without an escort?'

The woman shrugged and stepped back to let Jacquie open the door. 'I'll come quietly,' she said, then gave a mad little laugh. 'Do you know, I've often seen that written down, but I've never had the need to say it myself. Silly phrase, really.'

Jacquie looked at the woman in front of her, a shadow of the person she had last seen at the hospital, weeping decorously into a handkerchief after identifying her sister's body. She was wild-haired and wild-eyed, barefoot and dressed in jeans and a sweat-shirt, both looking the worst for a night in the cells. Her right hand was bandaged but was clearly swollen. She had really socked Sid Lewis good and proper, which was the best thing that could be said for the whole night's work. Jacquie held out a hand and took her by the arm, piloting her gently towards the interview room.

'Did they tell you my bloody husband turned up last night?' she said. 'On bloody call.' She gave another of her crazy laughs. 'That put a spoke in his wheel. Him and his bloody tart.' She turned to Jacquie and the tears began again. 'He's left me, you know,' she said, her voice breaking. 'I thought we were just giving things a rest, you know, before we got back together again. We see each other every day at the office. He's never said. I expect everyone knows but me.'

Jacquie thought she was probably right, but she needed to get to the bottom of things, so shook her head. 'You're tired,' she said. 'Things are out of proportion. Let me get you a drink. Coffee – black, isn't it?'

She nodded. 'You remember,' she said. 'More than that dick ever does.'

Jacquie put her head out of the door and hailed a passing secretary who was only too glad of an excuse to have a few seconds in the room with the nutter who had given Sid Lewis his comeuppance and went off to get the drinks.

Jacquie clicked the switch on the recorder and made sure that the CCTV camera was aligned. 'Mrs Morton,' she said, 'I'm sure you know that I must record everything in this room because you have been charged with assaulting a police officer, but this is not the reason for this conversation. I would like to discuss with you the subject you mentioned on the phone last night.'

'Who killed Mollie, yes,' she said, rummaging in her pockets and coming up empty. Jacquie reached into a drawer and pulled out a pack of tissues which she pushed across.

'That's right. You said you knew who had done it.'

'Yes, that's it. I do.'

'Would you like to tell me now?'

The woman shrugged and blew her nose, crumpling the tissue and stuffing it up her sleeve. 'It's no secret. My husband. He did it.'

Jacquie felt like getting up and walking out, but resisted the urge and continued speaking in a gentle, even tone. She had seen the Assistant DA in Los Angeles question a drug dealer for four hours without ever raising his voice and if he could do it in the room with a man later convicted of killing nine people, she could do it with this troubled woman.

'Do you have proof, Mrs Morton, or is it just a suspicion?'

'Proof? Well, I didn't see him do it, if that's what you mean. But he did it, I'm certain.'

'There must have been something, though?'

'Yes. He kept . . . looking at her. They would watch TV on the settee and if it was a comedy, well . . . they would laugh.'

'Isn't that the plan?' Jacquie could see this keeping her cool thing might prove tricky.

'Yes, but, you know what I mean. He would slap his hand on her leg, she would nudge him in the ribs. Touching, you know.'

Jacquie sat back and looked her woman in the eye. 'May I ask how long your husband had known Mollie, Mrs Morton?'

'All her life, more or less.'

'So, could it be that he considered himself, well, a brother? A father figure, even? Sex isn't the only relationship between two people, you know.'

'I do *know* that,' the solicitor snapped. 'I do, it's just that . . . having her in the house. It was a strain on us all and them being so friendly . . . Anyway, in the end, I asked him to give us a break. That Mollie needed to settle. He got a flat in town, but he still came round for meals. They would still laugh, joke. He would kiss and cuddle her . . . it wasn't right.'

Jacquie pulled a piece of paper towards her and clicked her pen. 'Could I have your husband's name, please, Mrs Morton. Morton, obviously, but his first name, if you would. And his mobile number.'

The woman took a deep breath. 'John,' she said. 'John Morton. Everyone calls him Jack. I can't remember his mobile number. But he'll be at the office this morning. They'll be busy without . . . without me.'

Jacquie jotted down the details and looked over her shoulder, hoping to see the drinks miraculously appearing. But there was no one.

'Mrs Morton, do you have any *other* reason to suppose that Mollie and your husband had a relationship other than a family one?'

Caroline Morton snorted. 'I knew you wouldn't believe me,' she said. 'That's why I didn't come to you sooner. And look what's happened now? My marriage in ruins. And my career – I hit a policeman because of you. It's all your fault.'

Suddenly, Jacquie could see why Mollie went out at nights. If she was looking for love, she wouldn't have got it from this woman. She stood up. 'I'll just go and get our drinks,' she said, 'I can't think where they are. Excuse me.' She slipped through the door into the corridor and it was as though she had gone down the rabbit hole. The usual buzz and hum was missing. It was as though all her colleagues had disappeared since she went into the interview room. She couldn't help sneaking a look at her watch, but only about fifteen minutes had elapsed. She walked along the corridor to the conference room and pushed open the door.

Everyone was sitting in solemn rows and Henry Hall, his glasses gleaming, looked up as she went in.

'Ah, Jacquie,' he said. 'I was about to rescue you. I need you in here now, I'm afraid.' He read her unspoken question. 'Yes, there's been another one.'

She looked at him, hardly understanding what he was saying for a moment and he walked to the door and ushered her into the corridor.

'Another murder?' she asked eventually.

'Almost. The girl was lucky. They were interrupted. By a courting couple, of all people. Their hearts clearly weren't in it – they heard scuffling in the bushes that they weren't causing and went in search. He had his hands around her throat and did a runner when he saw them. The girl's in Leighford General now. The couple are coming in later this morning but by all accounts, they are not the world's best witnesses.'

Jacquie half turned to where she had left Caroline Morton in the interview room. 'I'd better tell Mrs Morton she can go . . . oh, I suppose not. Has she been processed for the assault?'

'Let her go and get her to report locally when she gets home. I don't think I can handle a bolshie solicitor today and nor can you. Hurry up and join us. I was about to begin.'

She nodded and went back the interview room and went in, not sitting down at the table. Caroline Morton was looking more waspish even than usual.

'Something come up?' she said, with a sneer.

'As it happens, yes,' Jacquie said. 'You are free to go but we would ask you to call in at your local police station when you get home. We will send details of your assault on a police officer over to them and they will progress the case.'

'But my husband . . . ?'

'Has an alibi,' Jacquie said drily. She ushered the woman out of the room and closed the door. 'Please report to the desk and they will return your things. Thank you for coming in, Mrs Morton.' And the DI went into the conference room, letting the door swing closed on the sound of Henry Hall's voice.

Chapter Twelve

'Bernard's back,' Paul Moss muttered to no one in particular, sitting near him in the staff room.

'What's the matter with it?' Gerry Tranter's stand-up patter left a little to be desired.

'I thought *I* did the jokes around here.' Peter Maxwell squeezed past on his way to a chair. There were general 'Hellos' and 'About times' and 'What are you doing heres' from old colleagues who had secretly missed the man. Only Ben Holton went far enough back with Maxwell to risk going further – 'Glad to see the old extradition treaty still works.'

'Oh, it does.' Maxwell reached across heads to shake the man's hand. 'I just told them, "I am now and I have always been a member of the Communist Party."' He held his right hand over his heart. 'So help me Rhonda.'

Anyone who had been in on All Hell Day would have seen Bernard Ryan, but those who hadn't nodded or raised an eyebrow, depending on their level of sophistication. Only the two NQTs at the front looked on as the Dauntless Three took their positions at the front of the room. All they saw was the headteacher who had interviewed them both last June, a rather nervous looking bloke they assumed was his deputy. And a token woman. A similar scene was being enacted in schools up and down the country at that moment.

'Welcome back, everyone.' Legs Diamond began talking as usual while a murmuring hubbub was going on. Maxwell tutted and rolled his eyes; the man had no classroom skills at all. 'I trust you all had a good break and are ready for the challenges of the new term.'

The old joke rattled through Maxwell's head, of the keen Westpointers' stock response to such an oration – 'Yarc, Yarc; You're Absolutely Right, Commander.' Then he looked around him; there were so few good men. What happened next impressed him, though. As if nothing odd had occurred during the summer; as if the deputy head had not been handcuffed and taken away in irons; as if girls had not died in a sleepy seaside town; as if there was not a madman at large, Legs Diamond cleared his throat. 'First, Bernard. Could you talk us through the exam results, please?'

And Bernard did. He was nervous at first, halting, deferential even. But by the time he was into his stride with predictions and differentials and bar charts and spread sheets, it was as though he had never been away. Was it only Mad Max, the film buff, who nevertheless saw something of the maniacal Tod Slaughter in Bernard Ryan's face, eerily lit by the powerpoint's glow?

When he had finished, Diamond made the annual mistake he always made at this time of year; he asked if there were any questions. Paul Moss braced himself, grinning like an idiot, because he knew what was coming. Gerry Tranter did too and wished he'd got his tape recorder for moments such as these. Ben Holton sighed and folded his arms; he knew what he'd be doing for the next twenty minutes and closed his eyes. Only the NQTs sat upright, craning round to look at the bow-tied old geezer with the mad hair who looked as though he was about to make a point. It was the equivalent of 'Can I Do You Now, Sir?', 'The Day War Broke Out', 'And It's Goodnight From Me.' Peter Maxwell leaned forward, speaking as he did for the common teacher and for common sense – 'With respect, Headmaster . . .'

When the agony was over, it was time for the ecstasy. Peter Maxwell went into his office and shut the door with care. He walked over to the shelf space in the corner dedicated to coffee and comfort biscuits and indulged in that First Day pleasure of making a hot drink without having to scour the mug out first. He was still standing there, wondering how he would manage the remaining seventy working days until the Christmas holidays began. Retirement had often crossed his mind in previous years, but now it was tending to cross his mind, sit down halfway and start a crossword. Being a househusband might be fun. He drifted off into a little reverie which was, as all his reveries of any size were, interrupted by a tap on the door.

'Come in,' he carolled. He always made tappers sound welcome even before he knew who they were. That way, he could take them by surprise when he subsequently kicked them out unceremoniously five seconds later. Paul Moss stuck his head around the door.

'Max,' he said, 'I was going to pop in for a quick meeting, you know, before the hordes arrive to start making the place look untidy, but I met this lady in the corridor, looking for you so I thought we might meet later. She seems a little,' and he dropped his voice and enunciated the word silently and extravagantly, 'upset.'

Maxwell poured the water on his coffee and stirred it thoughtfully. One day in and already there was an upset woman outside his door. Never mind, start as you mean to go on. 'Show her in, Paul,' he said. 'We'll talk later.'

Moss nodded and withdrew his head, then the door opened and Lindsey Summers walked in, head down and her hand cupped over her stomach in a familiar gesture, protecting her baby while she could, before the world intervened. 'Mr Maxwell,' she said. 'I'm sorry to bother you again, but . . . well, your wife was lovely with my April, but I had to talk to you again.'

'Always welcome, Lindsey, of course. How are you all? April . . .?'

'She's at home now. My mum isn't the easiest woman at the best of times and she really hasn't been helping. Her stepdad is with her – he'll make sure she doesn't go off.' Her lip trembled. 'It isn't easy for me, Mr Maxwell, to talk about this sort of thing with you, but . . .'

He put an arm around her shoulders and led her to a seat. It was so much easier, he couldn't help thinking, when you could touch a person you were supposed to be comforting, and talk to them on their own without the door open. It was always like that before the

Molestation Movement gathered momentum. Heady days. 'Here, sit down and tell me all about it.'

'I expect your wife told you all about her talk with April.'

'Heavens, no!' Maxwell managed to sound convincing. 'Not allowed.'

'No, sorry, of course not. I . . . well, she talked to April and got a few details, but I don't think it will be any help, not in the long run. I'm sorry she couldn't be more use, Mr Maxwell. I don't like to think of this pervert running round Leighford, taking girls off the streets.'

'Nor do I, Lindsey, nor do I. But he seems to have a wider range even than Leighford. My wife is working with other police stations, all over the county, really. Still, she's good at what she does. She'll catch him if anyone can.' He smiled and hoped it looked better than it felt.

'Well, what I came to say was that my April's decided to have an abortion. A termination, you know, get rid of the baby.' Her voice was harsh and Maxwell couldn't tell whether it was in agreement with her daughter's decision or sadness.

'Perhaps it's for the best,' he said, gently. 'It's no start for a child, is it?'

'No,' the woman sighed. 'But . . . it's a lot to have on your shoulders, Mr Maxwell. When you're only a kid yourself. You can't put the clock back if you regret it later.'

'True,' he agreed. 'But you can't undo a baby either, when it's here. April will be getting counselling, won't she? She won't make this decision on her own.'

'We're taking her to the GP tomorrow,' the girl's mother said. 'I spoke to him on the phone this morning and there shouldn't be any problem. It seems that in cases of . . .' she foraged in her sleeve for a hankie and brought out a sodden rag on which she blew her nose, '. . . sexual abuse, there isn't usually any problem.' She leaned sideways until she was on Maxwell's shoulder and there, cushioned by ancient tweed and encircled by his arm, she cried, for the lost childhood of herself, her daughter and all the little girls out there whom even Maxwell couldn't protect from harm. He leaned his cheek on the top of her head and let her weep, absently patting her arm and shushing her as though she were a child.

Eventually she had cried herself to a standstill and had sat up, wiped her eyes, sipped some coffee and left. Maxwell looked at the clock and stifled a curse. Just where had the day gone? He had a new lot of Year Sevens to terrify and they would be waiting for him downstairs in the Hall for a re-enactment of the Battle of Bosworth. Just the thing to banish the baby blues. He picked up the phone and punched the zero.

'Reception'

'Thingee old thing . . .' Puzzled, he looked at the clock. Something was wrong. 'Thingee?' he asked. 'Is that you?'

The girl had worked at Leighford High for a while and before that was a Leighford Highena. She understood Mad Max as well as she understood herself.

'Charlotte isn't in today, Mr Maxwell,' she said. 'It's me, Thingee One. Sarah.'

'I thought it was,' Maxwell said, proudly. 'Nothing serious, is it? Thingee's absence?'

Sarah's voice was solemn. 'We're not sure, Mr Maxwell,' she said, dropping the volume so no one else could hear. 'She's afraid she might be . . . well, there may be a problem with the baby.'

Babies again. It was the theme today and no mistake. 'I'm sorry to hear that,' Maxwell said and meant it. 'I hope it's all a false alarm. Is . . . is Mr Baines with her?'

There was a puzzled silence, then the penny dropped. 'Oh, no, I'm not sure they're . . . it's very complicated, Mr Maxwell.'

'Oh dear, well, much as I would love to chat, I rang to say I am on my way down to the Hall for the Year Seven induction lesson but I am running a bit behind. Can you pop your head round the door and tell the other staff in there I won't be long and can they make a preliminary division into two armies for me. If someone stands out as Richard III, they can make a choice but ask them not to choose anyone too . . . obvious. Remember the fuss last year.'

Thingee did. The law suit had only just been averted.

'Thank you, Thingee. Tell them five minutes. Ten at the outside.' Maxwell didn't replace the phone, but pressed the rest and then punched a number. It answered on the first ring.

'Sylvia Matthews.'

'Sylv, dear heart, it's me.'

'Max. How's your day going?'

'Not well, but better than many, I can't help thinking. Have you got time for a bit of a chat at the end of the day today?'

'If it's short.'

'Yes, I'm not over-endowed with time myself. But I have a bit of a trend developing and I want to talk it through with you. Will you come up here?'

'No, not with your coffee. Come down here and I'll make you a decent cup.'

'Excellent woman. I'll see you then.'

'Everything's all right, Max, isn't it?' Sylvia Matthews may well have a man of her own and know that Maxwell was more than adequately looked after himself, but she still couldn't help worrying. His vulnerable side was well and truly hidden, but she had seen it peeping out sometimes and she would do anything to keep any more sorrow from those eyes.

'Sylv, don't fret all afternoon, now. We're all on great form; it's two other people I'm worrying about. See you later.'

She smiled at the phone. 'In a while,' she said and replaced the receiver. She turned to the boy standing in the doorway. 'Now, then,' she said. 'You've caught what in where, did you say?'

The Form Tutors had done the roll-calls and handled the tours of the school bit. Two hundred and thirty eight eleven year olds already had no idea where they were or who anybody was. *And* they had just had Maths and Double Science. So, as usual, it was left to the master to bring them back to the keen, bright-eyed questers for knowledge they had been only four hours ago by giving them an experience they would never forget.

Maxwell hurtled across the stage, dragging his left leg behind him. He carried a ruler in his hand and his right shoulder was hunched. 'A horse!' he shrieked in his finest Larry Olivier, 'A horse! My kingdom for a horse!' His glittering eyes lashed his audience. For hundred and seventy six eyes stared back at him, wide in disbelieving horror. Who was this maniac and where had he escaped from?

Maxwell drew himself up to his full height, dropped the shoulder and smiled. 'That,' he said, in his normal voice, 'was how William Shakespeare thought King Richard III looked, sounded and behaved. Alas, he was wrong on all counts. I know, because when I was your age, I met the king. And in the years to come at Leighford High, when your English teachers try to explain Shakespeare to you, you can tell them that Mr Maxwell knows all about it.' He then undid centuries of good work and stood St Francis of Assisi on his head – 'Where there is harmony, let me sow discord. It might not be politically correct, children, but it will make you think.'

The minions had not stirred. Not dared even to look at each other. Some of them had older siblings at this school. Some of them had mums and dads who had gone here. And one or two of them had mentioned Mad Max. But none of the two hundred and thirty eight that day had reckoned on madness as extreme as this.

'Where's Bosworth?' Maxwell asked a spotty kid in the front row. Nothing.

'Leicester?' he asked somebody else. Nothing again.

'Don't feel embarrassed,' he smiled. 'Geography Departments all over the country have been short-changing you people for years. But get them on climate-change and there's no stopping them. What's White Surrey?'

The ginger girl with the teeth had no idea.

'A halberd?'

The lad with the train-tracks didn't know that either. Maxwell was toying with asking what a beavor was, but he couldn't risk the loss of pension and left that sort of thing to the Science Department.

'Right,' he sighed. 'We've got a lot of work to do.' He looked out through the newly-cleaned windows to the green of the playing fields. 'It's a lovely day. Who wants to go outside?'

Most of the hands shot skywards, some because they thought they might be able to escape from this lunatic.

'We're going to pretend, boys and girls,' he said, 'that it is August 22nd, 1485. And we're going to restage a battle.'

The lads laughed and cuffed each other. They were with him already. The girls were less sure. 'And if you think History is all about boys,' Maxwell called above the excitement, 'you're right. It is. But there *are* exceptions. Boudicca, Cleopatra, Eleanor of Aquitaine, Joan of Arc – all women. And all of them put the frighteners on thousands of men.'

Now it was the girls' turn to laugh. And once again, Mad Max had the whole of Year 7 in the palm of his hand.

There were no bruises at the end of the day, no bad tempers or hurt feelings. Just two hundred and thirty eight kids who went home to tell their mums or dads or both about the amazing Mr Maxwell and how they knew how to handle a halberd. And an arquebus. And a crossbow. The rest of the day? It was all right.

Peter Maxwell pushed open the outer door to Sylvia Matthews' domain and inhaled the comforting smell of cotton wool, Savlon and general warm cleanliness. It was here that every child and most teachers in the school came with scratches, bumps, rashes and collywobbles, with worries large or small and went away comforted. He had been gravitating here himself for years and if he didn't know how much she loved him, he was probably the only one. The smell was now overlaid with freshly brewed coffee with a slight hint of Hobnob.

'Sylv?' He never liked to broach her inner sanctum without warning. Heaven only knew where she might be sticking a plaster at that very moment.

'Come through,' she called back. 'There's no one here . . .'

'Except us chickens,' he completed the old joke, so old they had almost forgotten the rest. He flopped down in the corner chair and let his head rest on the back. 'Bosworth doesn't get any easier,' he said.

'Who won this time?' she asked, stirring in the milk.

'It was a nail-biting finish,' he said, 'but History was not rewritten this time.' He took the proffered mug. 'Thanks. How was your day?'

She sat opposite him and smiled. 'The usual mix of minor bumps and the odd meltdown at being in Big School. Other than that, uneventful, except I gather Charlotte . . . oh, that's Thingee Two . . . is off sick.' She leaned forward. 'So, what was it you wanted to talk about?'

'That, partly,' he said. 'I had Lindsey Summers in this morning . . . you remember her?'

Sylvia Matthews had an almost computerlike recall of all the girls who had come to her sobbing about being pregnant, despite the fact that they had 'done it' standing up, with their feet in cold water and all the other old wives' tales. Lindsey Summers stood out as one of the few who had told her calmly that she was pregnant, that she was going to have the baby and give it a life better than her own had panned out to be so far. She nodded her head.

'There have been two girls found dead now, I suppose you know, the one Bernard was in the frame for and another, found in Willow Bay.'

'Don't tell me the other one is Lindsey's!' Sylvia was appalled. It somehow seemed so much worse that she should die young after such a start.

'No, she isn't, but Lindsey's daughter, April, is a victim of the same man, I am convinced. She disappeared over the summer – long story – and it turns out she was living with a man years older, who more or less kept her prisoner. And now, she's pregnant. Except that her mother told me today she is planning a termination.'

'The best thing, surely.' Sylvia didn't believe in storybook endings. 'If this man *is* the killer, he won't be playing mummies and daddies any time soon. But surely, if she was living with him, she can take the police there. Catch him.'

'She ran away in a panic, arrived there in the dark. She doesn't know where it is except in the widest terms and the police can't knock on every door in Leighford hoping to find him. It's worse than a needle in a haystack.'

'DNA?'

'Yes, from the baby. If she goes ahead with the termination, it's easy. If she changes her mind again, there would need to be court hearings, all kinds of hoops to jump through.'

'An amniocentesis does carry risks,' Sylvia agreed. 'It isn't something that should be carried out lightly.'

'Lightly?' Maxwell said. 'It could save lives.'

'Or lose one,' the school nurse said, calmly. 'It's not an easy decision to make. Do you risk one life to save several, when the several are not in immediate danger?'

'We've got off the subject,' Maxwell said, 'and now I can hardly remember what the subject is.'

Sylvia thought she might as well change the subject, as Maxwell had lost track of it so thoroughly. 'You'd heard about Charlotte, then? I thought it was being kept quiet.'

'Thingee One told me. She had no choice, really – she answered the phone to me this afternoon and I asked her why. I think my mind was full of April and then when I heard . . . I suppose I wondered whether she was losing the baby or . . . well, I just wondered.'

'Can anyone keep anything from you, Max?' Sylvia asked.

'No one told me anything,' he said. 'It was a train of thought. Don't blame Sarah.' Somehow, the subject had become too serious to use nicknames.

'You're right,' Sylvia said. 'Charlotte is having a termination. She went into Leighford General last night. She didn't make the decision lightly, but in the end, she couldn't see herself bringing up a baby on her own. They hadn't been together very long and I think it knocked the stuffing out of the relationship as soon as she told him.'

Maxwell's Return

'Do the kids know?'

'That Mr Baines is giving that secretary one?' Sylvia lapsed into the vernacular and the years dropped away. Maxwell smiled to see the teenage girl peeping out through the nurse's world-weary eyes. 'Of *course* they do. Do they know she's pregnant? Possibly not. The news only leaked out at the very end of term and so they have never seen her with a bump. She is only around nine weeks even now. They may have got away with it.'

'I haven't seen him to speak to yet. Not that we have much in common – he's a little hearty for me; all jock-straps and pretending there's such a thing as Sports Science. She's a sweetheart – I'm sorry that it has worked out like this for her.'

'I've seen a bit of her over the holiday. She doesn't have anyone to talk it over with, really. Her parents have moved away and she didn't know how to tell her mother, let alone discuss it with her. She had doubts about the relationship even before she got pregnant. He works all hours, coaching, that kind of thing. I suppose it goes with the territory.'

'As I said – too hearty.'

'Yes, running, PE, cricket, soccer . . . apparently he's never met a game he doesn't like.'

'I don't see how they would ever find anything to attract them in the first place.'

'Christmas party, or so I understand. Something to do with the girls' showers, but I didn't dwell.'

'No, fair enough, Sylv. There is such a thing as too much information. I gather they hadn't got so far as moving in together.'

'That was the clincher, I think. She wanted to move in with him, or at least set up a nursery in both houses, but he wouldn't agree to anything like that. She seemed quite cowed by him, but I suppose that would make sense. He's a good bit older than her and a teacher.'

'A *PE* teacher, Sylv,' Maxwell admonished her.

'Yes, yes,' she flapped her hand at him, 'yes, a PE teacher. But I think the relationship was never very equal, from what she has been saying. I've never liked the man, I have to say. Always a bit slow to send dented kids down to me, for example. Do you remember Nick Hessel? Ginger. Bit gangly.'

'I remember him. Nice lad, despite the ginger.'

'Well, he had a broken arm, got it in PE and Baines wouldn't let him come down and have it looked at. It displaced in the end, lad passed out and it rather got above Baines' remit. I can't believe the parents didn't sue.'

'I suppose Legs headed them off at the Pass.'

'No doubt, but what I'm getting at is that Charlotte is well rid of Baines.'

'Is she leaving?'

'Why should she?' Sylvia asked, a trifle tersely.

'No reason in the world, except that she is a relative kid and he is a thirty something teacher, as I believe you have already mentioned.'

'Sorry, Max.' Sylvia leaned forward and patted his knee. 'It's just that I get a bit hot under the collar when I think about him. I've heard a few things from Charlotte . . . sorry.'

'My fault,' he said, ever the public schoolboy. 'But, is she?'

'Is she . . . ?'

'Leaving.'

'No, but he is. Apparently, he has a job in January, some school along the coast. He missed the resignation day, but they are willing to wait. Apparently, he teaches there already, evening classes, that kind of thing.'

'Keen,' Maxwell observed.

'Mean, more likely,' Sylvia said. 'Apparently, he has never taken Charlotte out. They always met at her place, very occasionally his, but she would do all the catering. He never put his hand in his pocket. That's another reason she has made the decision she has – she said she didn't want to spend the rest of the child's life trying to drag money out of Baines. She has had to grow up fast, poor girl.'

Maxwell drained his cup and put it down, preparing to go.

'Is that it, Max?' Sylvia asked him. 'This conversation seems to have gone off piste rather.'

'No, not really,' he said. 'I just needed to get my head around things. Two women – because April Summers is a woman in this context, despite her age . . .'

'Which is?'

'Fourteen,' he sighed. 'Two women, both taking a big decision, essentially alone. I just needed to talk it through. Find out how hard it must be for them. And I find out it isn't hard; it's next to impossible.'

'Sometimes it's the only way. How likely is it that the DNA will help, do you think?' she asked.

'It depends. Jacquie doesn't seem to think that this man is known to the police. There have been no complaints, no reports. Just two dead girls and one traumatised one. And when I say "just" of course, I don't mean to minimise the importance. I just mean . . .' He ran his hands through his hair. 'It's very strange, Sylvia. The girls don't go to this school, but the links are still so strong. It can only be a matter of time before it is one of our girls. And then it will all hit the fan, what with Bernard having been involved already. I don't know whether he can survive any more.'

'He has Joe,' she remarked.

'Good Lord Above, woman,' he said, getting up. 'Is there *anything* you don't know.'

'Lots,' she smiled. 'I'm always hazy on the date of the Battle of Towton, as you well know.'

'1461,' he said, automatically. '29th March.'

She waited.

'Sunday,' he added, with a smile. 'It was snowing like buggery.'

'I do happen to know about Bernard's domestic arrangements, though,' she said, 'because I have become, by a strange default mechanism, his confessor. It's like having a fourteen year old lad in here, telling me about his first date. I have to rein him in sometimes – as you rightly say, there is such a thing as too much information.'

'Well, if I had some explosive news burning a hole in my tongue, I would come to you as well, Sylv, so the man is showing some sense at least. But . . .'

'He has Joe, whose employers have turned out to be very understanding. Apparently, they are leaving him in the closet for now, ready to produce him if they need to up their cred with the LGBT brigade.'

'The . . .?'

'Lesbian, gay, bisexual and transgender, you old dinosaur. I went on a course. We all had training while you were away, as a matter of fact.'

'In Los Angeles, we had more than training – every day was a practical exam, believe me. I'm glad Bernard is happy but I'll give you my final verdict when I find out how many covers he has given me this week. But I must be off. The Mem is due home early tonight; First Day Debrief with Nole and then a night with our feet up.' He smiled at Sylvia and put a gentle hand on her arm. 'I miss our first day back suppers.'

'Ratatouille,' she said, laying her hand over his.

'With just the right amount of rat,' he agreed and, with a peck on her cheek, he was gone.

Chapter Thirteen

As Maxwell skidded to a halt outside 38 Columbine, he was pleased to see that Jacquie's car was already there and when he opened the front door his son was in full cry.

'And then she made me read it out, Mummy!'

'How did you get on?' he heard his wife say, over the unmistakeable sound and smell of pancake production.

'Weeeellll,' Nolan could prima donna for England, 'I couldn't do *all* the voices, but I think I did quite well. I've never been very good at mouses.' Maxwell smiled as he climbed the stairs. Without the occasional grammatical lapse, it was easy to mistake Nolan for a short and well-preserved octogenarian.

'Ask the Count,' Jacquie said. 'He knows better than anyone how a mouse sounds.'

'That's true,' Nolan agreed. 'I'll ask him later.' He turned his head and a grin split his face. 'Dads! I was just telling Mummy, I had to read out loud today, and I did the voices, except the mouses.'

'That's my boy,' Maxwell said, blowing a raspberry on the boy's cheek and then heading off to do the same to his wife.

'Blow on Mummy!' Nolan egged him on from his place at the table, then thought twice. 'No, don't, Dads. She's doing pancakes.'

'So I see. Yum.' The Head of Sixth Form looked into the face of the Detective Inspector and saw a lot there that had hopefully passed the boy by. 'Have you laid the table? Got the syrup out?'

'No.' The child was scrambling down from the table.

'Spit spot.' Maxwell could do a mean Julie Andrews when the occasion demanded it. With Nolan's back turned, he leaned his head on his wife's shoulder and whispered in her ear. 'Bad day?'

'Not too good. Yours?'

'Unusual. Tell you later.'

'Mmm. Post-pancakes.'

'No better time.' He planted a kiss on her neck and turned to help his son lay the table. 'Nole, you are a left-handed booby, what are you?' He turned the cutlery round the right way.

'A left-handed booby.' Nolan waddled away, hands tucked in and feet spread out, a booby to the life.

'Okay, chaps,' Jacquie turned from the cooker with a pile of pancakes on a plate. 'How many do you have room for? And do you want them with bacon?'

'Loads. Yes.' The child looked at his mother and added, 'Please.'

'Let's go, then.'

And they sat there, the most nuclear of nuclear families, and swapped tales of Mrs Whatmough, Legs Diamond and the old lady who had come in to see Jacquie because she had lost her dog.

'That lady loses her dog a lot, doesn't she?' Nolan remarked. 'She should buy it a lead.'

'Or teach it to say its phone number,' Maxwell added.

'Dogs can't *talk*, Dads.'

Maxwell looked wildly from side to side. 'They can't?' he said, eyes wide. 'Since when?'

Jacquie leaned back. This could go on until bedtime. Or at least, with any luck it could.

Maxwell appeared much later in the sitting room, damp but otherwise unscathed. Jacquie was sitting with a drink already poured, watching something mindless on TV which as far as the Head of Sixth Form could tell was based around people having all their worldly goods repossessed by shaven headed men.

'Good programme?' he asked, blandly.

'Yes, though I don't think "good" is quite the word. Appalling, possibly. But strangely addictive. Tiddler asleep?'

'Unconscious.'

'You have to hand it to Mrs W, she does know how to exhaust a child.'

'So . . . what's up?' He picked up his drink and swirled the melting ice cubes around ruminatively.

'Bad day,' she said. 'Sorry I was miserable at tea time. I was still detoxing.'

'And now?'

'I can't . . .' she looked up and found that he was looking at her from under his eyebrows, chin on chest. 'Stop it, now. I can't.'

'April Summers is having a termination.'

'How in Heaven's name do you know that?' she said.

'Her mother told me.'

'Well, all right. We can talk about that then, if you like. But that's all.'

Maxwell was confused. He had rather thought that it was April who was causing the silence. 'What else has happened?'

'Just the day. You know. Not been back long, that sort of thing.'

'There's been another.' A guess was as good as a wink to Maxwell.

'Max! Who tells you these things?'

'In this case, dear heart, you did. I had no idea there had been another. I just thought I would try it out. But now I know, why not tell me about it?'

She sighed and sipped her drink, looking over the rim of her glass at him. 'This is just getting nowhere,' she said. 'All we get is another victim, then another . . . he's changing his MO as well, which is worrying.'

'Is he?' Maxwell asked. 'We don't know what he did to or with Josie Blakemore or Mollie Adamson before he killed them. We don't even know for sure if the man who abducted April Summers is the same one.'

'I won't squabble with the "we",' Jacquie said, 'or we'll be here all night. It's true we don't know, but we will soon. The latest victim isn't dead, but she is seriously hurt as well as being in shock. But although she can't speak to us yet, he was interrupted, so we have DNA and a rough description from the couple who scared him off. When we have the DNA from April, we will have a little more to go on.'

'Who was this girl?'

'Her name is Kirsty Hilliard,' Jacquie said. 'She was out with friends last night and he seems to have cut her out from the pack. One minute she was there, the next minute she was gone. Her friends didn't do anything about it because, to quote one of them, she had been a grumpy cow all night and they were glad to be shot of her.'

'Nice. What a lovely evening she must have been having.'

'Whenever I talk to girls, I am more happy than ever to have a boy,' she agreed. 'She had broken up with her boyfriend – her friends called him her partner – and she was out drowning her sorrows.'

'Oh,' Maxwell's relief was palpable. 'She's older, then.'

'You'd think so,' Jacquie said, swirling her drink. 'But no. She's fifteen, just. Apparently, it isn't very cool to say boyfriend these days.'

'It isn't very cool to say cool either, by all accounts, but I get the gist. So, another girl who is sexually active, then.'

'I gather so.'

'So, how does he do it? Does he chat them up? Surely it can't be as crass as simple exposure? "Ever seen one of these"?'

'I think girls want a little more than a randomly proffered penis, dear,' she said, with a smile. 'Things have changed since you were a lad.'

'Ah, the good old days,' he said, grinning back at her. That had been what the bike sheds had been made for; as well as parking bikes, of course. Once her sense of humour started to peer through the blackness, he knew she would soon be able to see the wood for the trees.

'So . . . he finds the vulnerable ones, the girls who their friends won't miss, ones they might even be glad to see the back of. Not ugly, though, are they, these girls he chooses?'

'Not at all. Quite the opposite, I'd say.'

'So, why do they just go off with him?'

'We're not sure they do. We think there is a degree of old-fashioned wooing in his methodology – it's a standard serial-killer phase, after all. The girls who were murdered were wearing clothes their families didn't recognise, clothes we have to assume he bought or at least chose. The clothes Josie was wearing were cheap and tacky, market-stall glitz. Mollie Adamson's were pricier, a better fit for one thing and also better labels. April tells of a bed strewn with rose petals in a hotel. That might not mean much, because how could a kid of her age know a good hotel from a hole in the ground. A couple of supermarket roses and some cheap plonk and it would seem like heaven to her.'

'Cynic.' He made a note to self not to buy supermarket flowers next time a bunch was in order.

'Perhaps. Anyway, this girl, Kirsty, didn't seem to even warrant that. According to her friends, she was only gone around half an hour – not that they noticed the very moment she disappeared. But around about that. When they were interrupted, they had already had sex, at least twice, according to the doctors, and he had his hands around his neck.'

'Not wooing, even by good old days standards,' Maxwell said.

'No. But also, quite good going, bearing in mind they were about ten minutes walk away from where her friends first missed her. She shows no signs of force – except around her neck, of course – no marks where he dragged her along, pushed her down, that kind of thing. There was no rape; she was as keen as he was.'

'So . . . apart from her age and the strangling, he did nothing wrong.'

She sat up sharply. 'I beg your pardon!'

'That's right though, isn't it? As far as we know he is a perfectly pleasant bloke to look at, who asks girls to go with him into the bushes, to a hotel, to a shop or market and they go along. What happens then seems to differ, but he doesn't have to use force. He uses force by choice. But what makes him do it? Two girls died, one had a taste of what he might do, but he didn't take it further and one girl almost died within half an hour of meeting him. There must be a trigger. Something that makes him snap.'

'I see what you mean . . . I think. You mean, he could be out there doing this on a daily basis, but only gets caught out sometimes, because something goes wrong.' Jacquie sometimes thought that Maxwell had a time twin working at Quantico.

'Precisely. He could be a perfectly respectable bloke, who goes out looking for girls. He could be a speed-dater, an online dater, he could have a wife and 2.4 kids for all we know. But one thing we do know, and I'm sure you have all worked it out for yourselves down at the Nick, is that he chooses the vulnerable, the lost and the needy and then makes them think he can fulfil their dreams. He obviously has a good eye for character and a lot of charm.'

She looked at him through slitted eyes. 'Not unlike your good self,' she said.

He smiled at her. It was good of her to look through the eyes of love. 'Perhaps in my day, Mrs Rose-Tinted Spectacles, but there was only a very narrow window of opportunity.'

'Which was?' She was always interested in filling in the gaps in his life, much of which had happened before she was born.

'Which was that heady year when I had learned a bit about life in general and kids in particular, and hadn't started losing my looks.' He lifted his chin and gave her a flash of his best side.

She dutifully mimed a paparazzi moment and he turned back to her, serious again.

'I don't want to teach my granny to suck eggs,' he went on, 'but that is the kind of person you need to be looking for. Someone who has reached his peak of perfection and has let it get out of hand.'

'We're all over the place at the moment. We've had a builder, a teacher and a solicitor in the frame so far, albeit briefly. The teacher and the solicitor have cast-iron alibis, the builder is far too old, though creepy and with a definite link to a victim. I personally would like to give him and his light o' love a kicking, but that's just me.' DI Jacquie Carpenter-Maxwell had no compunction in resorting to Old Time Copper Mode when the occasion demanded it. It made her husband proud.

'Solicitor?'

'Caroline Morton's husband, aka her soon-to-be-ex husband. His alibi is the best we've come across for ages; one for the memoir, I think. He was at Leighford Nick, called in as next on-call, when his wife clocked a policeman in pursuance of his duty, when she had come in to shop said husband for the murder of her sister.'

'Don't you just love it when that happens?' Maxwell asked, rhetorically.

'Indeed. I've never met Jack Morton myself but by all accounts he seems a very nice bloke, shackled to a jealous harpy. But he isn't a murderer. And, bless his heart, no Adonis either. Not someone to charm the birds from the trees, at any rate.'

'Our man may be more than a pretty face.'

'True. But April specifically said he was handsome.' Even as she said it, Jacquie knew that this was a huge generalisation. If everyone found the same people attractive, the human race would grind to a halt. 'And not just handsome, but quite stacked.'

'Stacked?' Maxwell raised a quizzical eyebrow.

'Fit, then. But on the other hand, fit also means handsome . . . I should check that. She definitely told me he was fit. I assumed, and I shouldn't have.' She reached for her phone and tapped in a memo, muttering.

Maxwell waited until the phone was stowed away again, then said, 'Last night's victim. Where did it happen?'

'Just off the Esplanade. In that park thing, you know where I mean.'

Maxwell did. It had been the favourite trysting place for Leighford Highenas, Old and Current, since time immoral and this rang a warning bell. 'It seems a bit rash, to take her there, doesn't it? Also, from what you've told me, he doesn't usually hunt in Leighford. He lives here, after all.'

'Hunt?'

'Well, it is a hunt for him, isn't it? Hunting, capturing. Power. I watch the telly. I know how these serial killers work.' He tapped his chest. 'Just call me Patrick Jane.'

Jacquie looked at him fondly. His eyes were either side of his nose and that was where his similarity to Simon Baker ended. 'No, darling,' she said gently. 'You're *mental*, please try and remember. He's the Mental*ist*.' With that cleared up to her satisfaction, she did give it serious thought, though. This was a hunt, a stalking, a capture. The elements were there, but the finesse had gone. Was he, as Maxwell thought, in a window of physical perfection that he could see nearing its end? While she was still thinking, the phone rang. Maxwell picked it up.

'Hello?'

Jacquie looked at him quizzically, but he held up a hand, listening.

'Are you sure it's me she wants?'

There was a murmur at the other end of the line.

'I'll go over there now . . . it's a bit late for rousting Mrs Troubridge out to babysit; I'll get a cab.'

He started to unfold himself from his chair, feeling around for his discarded shoes.

'Sylv, could you? That would be marvellous. Twenty minutes? I'll walk up to the corner. See you then.'

Jacquie kicked his left shoe across to him from and said, 'Sylv?'

'Thingee has asked to speak to me.'

'Sarah or Charlotte?' Jacquie knew the code. 'Is she all right?'

'Charlotte. She's in Leighford General. She went in for a termination but . . . well, there seems to have been a problem. They're keeping her in overnight. She wants to talk to me.'

'Why?' Jacquie knew that her husband's shoulder was a very sought-after item, but she also knew that he was hardly a by-word where obstetricians gathered. 'Why does she want to talk to you?'

'I'm not sure,' he said. 'Sylv was a bit cagey. I'll give you a ring from the hospital.'

'Do you have your mobile?'

He patted his pockets, looking around vaguely.

'Do you even know where your mobile *is*?'

He set his mouth in a rueful line and shook his head.

'Happily, I do. It's plugged in in the kitchen. Here,' she unwound herself from the chair, 'Let me get it for you.'

He slipped on his shoes and ran a cursory hand through his hair. It was still quite warm out, but he got his jacket from the peg on the landing; the jacket was like a badge and he assumed it was in his role as Universal Dad that Thingee wanted to see him. Jacquie came out of the kitchen with his phone and put it in his inside pocket, patting it for good measure.

'Off you go, then, Superman,' she said, kissing him on the end of his nose. 'I'll see you later.'

'Nightie-night, Wonder Woman,' he said. 'I'll let you know if I'll be late.'

She hung over the banisters and waved as he went out through the front door. Mighty Mouse. Superman. Green Lantern. Mad Max. Whatever you called him, he was there to save the day. It was only as the door closed behind him that she realised that he had told her nothing about his unusual day – hopefully, it could wait.

Sylvia Matthews arrived as Maxwell got to the main road and he squeezed himself in to her tiny car.

'Thanks for coming, Max,' she said. 'I tried to persuade Charlotte to wait until tomorrow, but the ward staff can't do a thing with her. They've had to put her in a side room. She's inconsolable.'

'What's happened, for heaven's sake?'

'They're not sure. She was due for the procedure today but there was some kind of crisis in the operating theatre and they had to bump half the list. In normal circumstances they would send everyone home, of course, and carry on as listed tomorrow, bring them back another time. But of course, as you can imagine, time is of the essence here, so they kept them in, pending an early start tomorrow. Then, after visiting hours, they found her . . . well, you'll see for yourself.'

'Who visited?'

'No one knows. The staff don't make any kind of list, you know. Those days are passed, if they were ever here. All they know is that when everyone had gone, a girl from the next bed rang her bell and they found Charlotte close to collapse.'

'Changed her mind?'

'That's what they thought at first. Idiot!' Sylvia suddenly yelled at a cyclist and by the time Maxwell's heart had left his mouth, she was speaking again. 'They asked her that. She just shook her head. Then, she asked for you. That's it.'

'We've hardly spoken since I left for America,' Maxwell said. 'I just wished her well, that's all.'

'Well, that may be it,' Sylvia said, swinging into the car park at Leighford General. 'Perhaps she's tired of the rest of us and our platitudes.'

'My platitudes are the same as anyone else's,' Maxwell pointed out. 'Look . . .' he waved a hand vaguely to the left. 'There's one!'

'Platitude?'

'Parking space!'

Sylvia turned into the space, cutting up an old lady in a car too big for her. 'No way she'd have got in there,' she muttered to herself. 'Well spotted, Max. For a non-driver, you are a great parker.'

'I *am* a driver,' he said. 'I just don't actually do it. I have a license and scarily enough could quite legally drive Jacquie's car any time. I'm on the insurance. No one ever asks when you drove last, just when you passed your test.'

Sylvia looked twitchy. 'You're not planning to *do* it, though, Max, are you?' she asked.

'God, no. I'm just saying.'

The school nurse blew her cheeks out with relief. 'That's all right, then. Okay, it's round here, to the left.' She ferreted for the change for the parking machine, muttering as she always did about NHS scams and dived into a rabbit warren of buildings, leading him round corners and across forgotten quads until they reached an automatic door which opened jerkily to let them in. After washing their hands at the next set of doors, they made their way down a dimly lit corridor into the ward and were about to turn into a curtained side-room when a bantam dressed as a nurse barred their way.

'What, may I ask,' she said, in her best and most piercing hiss, 'do you think you're doing?'

Sylvia stepped forward. 'This is Mr Maxwell. Charlotte Wilson is asking for him.'

The nurse looked him up and down and found nothing good there. Dirty old bugger, messing around with a girl less than half his age. It was a wonder his wife put up with it. 'She may have been,' she said. 'But she isn't now.'

Maxwell bit back a retort. It wasn't blowing a gale, nor yet snowing or hailing, but even so, he had been dragged out of his comfy home and from the company of his comfy wife on what seemed to be a wild goose chase. 'Madam,' he said and remembered just in time he wasn't wearing a hat so didn't make a fool of himself with an aborted doff. 'I was asked to come along here this evening and have done so at considerable inconvenience. If Miss Wilson is no longer asking for me, that's irrelevant, surely. If I pop in and see her for a minute, she won't be asking for me again when it is even more of a nuisance to everyone.'

The bantam ruffled her metaphorical feathers and looked smug. 'She may still be asking for you, for all I know. But she isn't doing it here. She's discharged herself. And we couldn't stop her; she hasn't had a procedure of any kind, so as far as it goes she is a member of the public. Pregnancy isn't an illness.'

'She's discharged herself?' Sylvia said. 'But she was hysterical. Pregnancy may not be an illness, but surely suicidal ideation is.'

The bantam pulled in her chin and looked at Sylvia down her nose. 'I see someone has been checking online symptoms,' she said. 'Miss Wilson showed no signs of suicidal ideation, as you put it. She is just yet one more girl who has found it hard to part with a baby. Happens all the time. We can't advise. Woman's right to choose and all that. She'll have to come back, though; she's left her things.' She turned on her heel and then stopped, speaking over her shoulder. 'So I would ask you to leave my ward, or I will call security.' And with that, she stepped smartly into her office and shut the door behind her.

'Ah,' Maxwell said, putting an arm round Sylvia Matthews' shoulder, feeling as he did so that she was trembling with rage. 'The caring profession – it's a vocation, you know. Like teaching.'

'Max, I . . .'

'Let it go, Sylv. Nurses haven't been the same since that nice Miss Nightingale retired. Let's get back to the car and we'll think where to go from here.'

They stepped into the corridor again and were hailed by a familiar voice.

'Mr Maxwell, Nurse Matthews. What're you doin' here?' Mrs B managed to look as though she had a fag-end in her mouth even in this strictly no-tobacco environment.

'Mrs B.' Maxwell said, unsurprised. 'I always forget that you work here.' The woman held the cleaning monopoly on the South Coast.

'Just onna bank, these days,' she said. 'Saving for Christmas, that kind of thing. Lots off sick, 'specially in this ward. That Sister, she's a tartar.'

'Is that the word?' Sylvia asked. 'I think she's more of a . . .'

'Sylv!' Maxwell warned. 'She probably has a heart of gold.'

'Not really,' Mrs B told him. 'She's a first class bitch and no mistake. Never mind, though, I'm mostly public areas on my shift. Don't really have to have much to do with her. But what you doin' here? Been visitin'? Mrs M's all right, I hope. Nobody poorly at home? Can't be Mrs Troubridge. I doubt she's ever seen the inside of a nanti-naval ward.'

'Errand of mercy, Mrs B,' Maxwell replied. 'Not really, no. She's fine. No, all well. No it isn't. I agree totally.'

Mrs B grinned. Mr M was salt of the earth, but you had to trot to keep up with him. Sometimes it was hard to tell what the mad old bleeder was on about. 'I best be off,' she said. 'I finish in an hour.'

'See you tomorrow, Mrs B,' Maxwell said. 'Up at the school.'

'Right you are,' she said, and, leaning on her trolley to give it momentum, wandered off up the corridor, singing under her breath.

'I wonder when she sleeps?' Sylvia asked, as they retraced their steps through the rabbit warren.

'Mrs B? I don't believe she does,' Maxwell said. 'Sleep is for wimps. She just hangs upside down in the wardrobe.'

'Is there a Mr B?' she asked. 'I've often wondered.'

'Mrs B's family is very complicated,' Maxwell said, 'and to be honest, I've never been sure about Mr B or even if he has ever existed. I think it might be rather like film stars when one is more famous than the other. So husbands just end up being Mr Whatever, using the wife's name.'

'Like Brangelina,' Sylvia said.

'If you say so,' Maxwell agreed, patting her. She was clearly tired. 'Here's the car. Let's work out Plan B.'

'Come back to ours,' Sylvia said. 'Guy is out at some team-building rubbish tonight. I have no idea when he'll be back.'

'I'll just ring Jacquie,' Maxwell said, producing his mobile with a flourish.

'My word,' Sylvia said. 'Is that what I think it is?'

'Indeed it is,' Maxwell said, punching keys with aplomb. 'If Jacquie ever finds out that I can use this thing, I'll know it will be you who told her.'

A tiny, tinny voice sounded from his palm and he put the phone to his ear.

'Sorry, heart, what was that?'

'I said,' repeated his wife, 'that you always forget that you have home on speed dial. It connects after the zero – no need for the other numbers.'

'Ah. Well, that proves I can't use it, I suppose. We have drawn a blank here. Old Thingee has discharged herself, so we need to find her. Sylv is a bit worried that she might . . . well, I don't have Thingee down as the suicidal type, but I expect that's what everyone says. I'll let you know how we get on.'

'Do you need any help? Shall I ring the Nick?'

'No, I think Sylv has her address?' He made it into a question and Sylvia nodded, turning the ignition key and reversing out of the space as she did so. 'We'll try there first and if no go, we'll have a think. See you soon. Love you.'

165

'Love you too. I'll wait up.'

'You're an angel. Mwah.' He pressed a key and put the phone back in his pocket.

'Max,' Sylvia said. 'I can still hear your lovely wife.'

Maxwell smiled happily. 'I often hear her voice in my head,' he said. 'It's nice it's not just me.'

'No, I think it's coming from your pocket.'

'Oh.' Maxwell foraged inside his jacket and fished out the phone again. He held it gingerly to his ear. 'I forget that every time, heart,' he said to it. 'Sorry. Mwah again.' He looked at the phone and very deliberately pressed another button. He smiled at Sylvia. 'Always doing that. Wrong button.'

'I thought that might be the case,' Sylvia laughed. 'Do you want to try Charlotte's house first? It's further out than ours.'

'No, let's get back to yours. We can ring her from there. She might even ring you.'

'True. I can't think what the silly girl is doing. She seemed to have sorted everything out when we spoke yesterday.'

'She's in a fragile frame of mind,' Maxwell said. 'Changing the subject for a minute, how's Guy's new school panning out?'

'It's hard work, compared to his last place. It's the kind of school that likes its pound of flesh. Lots of evening activities, that kind of thing. It used to be a Community School when that was trendy and for once it seemed to have worked. There are still a lot of things that the local people join in with; sports, drama, that kind of thing. Of course, Guy loves it. You know him and his rugger. He hasn't had a team to coach for ages. Even the girls play.'

'A whistling woman and a crowing hen are neither fit for God nor men,' Maxwell said, somewhat enigmatically.

'Pardon?'

'Women's rugger. Not natural.' Sylvia sketched a slap around his head. 'Sorry, I know that sounds sexist, but it just isn't right.'

'Perhaps not, but it shows they're keen and that's the main thing.'

'I daresay Guy is a bit of a draw,' Maxwell observed. 'He is a bit of a hunk . . . by all accounts,' he added hurriedly.

Sylvia laughed. 'He's not bad, for his age,' she conceded. No one except Sylvia and Guy knew quite what their age gap was, but they were such a perfect couple, after a while, no one noticed. On the few occasions that they and the Maxwell's had been out together, they looked like two couples; just not the actual ones.

'I'm glad it's going well, though,' Maxwell said. 'Moving schools must be a headache.'

'They're all different,' she conceded. 'But whenever he moans, I just remind him his Head could be Legs and he backs down.'

Maxwell snorted and settled back in the seat, bracing himself for the hairpin bend as they left Leighford Town Centre. Once that was over, it was just a couple of turns to Sylvia's house, a drink and a think. He felt his eyes closing and woke up with a jerk outside her semi.

'Come on, Max,' she said, poking him in the side. 'We're here. Guy still isn't back, so I'll park on the road. We don't want him boxing me in when he comes home.'

'I wasn't asleep,' he protested. 'I was just resting my eyes.'

'Of course,' she said. 'Come on, let's go in and try Charlotte's number.'

'It's worth a go,' he said. 'And where will we start if she doesn't answer?'

'My guess would be Andrew Baines' place,' she said, grimly.

'Which is where?' He had finally struggled out of her Smart Car and was brushing himself down on the pavement.

She tapped the side of her nose. 'I haven't spent the last Millennium working with you without something rubbing off, Peter Maxwell,' she said. 'I jotted it down today, in the lunch hour. I just had a feeling I might need to know it.'

He fell into step with her up the drive and put his arm around her shoulders. 'Sylvia Matthews,' he said, 'you are a marvel.'

'Why, thank you,' she said, putting the key in the door. 'You're right, of course.' She gestured to the sitting room, to the left of the hall. 'Make yourself at home. I'll just put the kettle on, then we can phone.'

Chapter Fourteen

The ringing phone woke her instantly, and DI Jacquie Carpenter-Maxwell was in day job mode before the receiver reached her ear.

'Hello. DI Carpenter-Maxwell speaking.'

'Jacquie.' Henry Hall never bothered identifying himself. There was no mistaking those clipped tones. 'Kirsty Hilliard is awake. The hospital are being cagey, there doesn't seem to be a very coherent memory there yet, but we need someone there, in case she remembers anything. I don't want anyone messing up things by asking the wrong kind of question.'

'Guv . . . Max is out and it's a bit late for Mrs Troubridge. Can someone else go?'

'I thought of that,' Hall said. 'Jason is on his way over. He can babysit.'

'Jason? Babysit?' The two words didn't seem to belong in the same sentence.

'I know he comes across as being a bit of a geezer, Jacquie, but Jason actually has a couple of kids of his own. He isn't actually living with them at the moment, but he knows which end is up and anyway, as I remember it, Nolan sleeps like a poleaxed steer once he's down. That's right, isn't it?'

'Yes . . . but, guv . . .' Jacquie ran through all the excuses but decided it was pointless. Henry Hall didn't often come the heavy. As bosses went, he was always very reasonable and he had after all let her go to LA, leaving himself with a hornets' nest of sickness, stress and mild incompetence. 'That's fine. I'll get down to the General now.'

'Thanks, Jacquie. Take a book or something. It may be a long night.'

'Sounds enticing. See you in the morning.'

'I'll look forward to it. Goodnight.' And with his usual briskness, Henry Hall was gone. Jacquie was still fighting off the pins and needles in her leg as she got reluctantly up off the sofa when the doorbell rang. Mary Poppins had arrived.

Maxwell was unsurprised to find that Sylvia Matthews had a phone and address book, kept meticulously up to date. That she had versions on her mobile phone, her tablet, her laptop and her PC he had no doubt, but thumbing through the pages felt a lot more natural to him and he quickly found Thingee's number, although oddly, under the Ws rather than the Ts. There was just a mobile number listed and he rang it, wondering as he always did why an eleven digit number for a mobile should seem so cumbersome and be so impossible to remember, when an eleven digit number for a landline should stick in the mind for ever. Ah, for the days of 'Press Button B, Caller.' He listened as it rang and then went to voicemail.

'The person you are calling is not available at the moment. Please leave a message after the tone. If you wish to rerecord your message . . .'

He rang off and sat waiting for Sylvia to come in with the coffee. Perhaps she was just out of signal. Perhaps she had taken a leaf out of his own book and had left the dratted thing at home in a drawer, although even as he thought it, he dismissed it as impossible. No one under forty ever went more than a linear yard from their phone if they could help it. No, she was either avoiding answering or she couldn't for some reason. He tapped his foot and tried to think things through rationally. Leaving suicide on the list of possible outcomes, but low on the list, there were a number of options. If he were in Thingee's situation, unlikely though that clearly was, he would go . . . where? Apparently not home to mother. She had confided in Sylvia and yet she wasn't here. So her own home would be the next place in line; the fact that she wasn't answering her phone was probably just a red herring.

'Penny for your thoughts.' Sylvia put down the tray of coffee and broke into his reverie.

'Sorry, Sylv. Just thinking about what to do next. She isn't answering her phone.'

'She may be asleep. She's had a bit of a trying day.' If there was one thing at which Sylvia Matthews excelled, it was seeing the bright side of things.

'Yes, but it isn't *late* late, is it?' Maxwell looked at his watch. 'Ten. That's nothing. Ten is the new eight, or so I'm told.'

'Even so . . . I may have over-reacted, Max.' Sylvia had unleashed the dogs of war and didn't even remember crying havoc.

'No, no, you were right to call. You're worried about her and no wonder. Where does she live? We'll go round.' He reached across and took a mug from the tray and took a swig. 'God, Sylv! How do you make coffee so hot?'

'Boiling water probably has something to do with it,' she said. 'Do you think we should check on her?'

'Let's make a plan and stick to it. If she isn't at home, we'll check on Andrew Baines' place, just to be sure and if she isn't in either place, we'll call it a night. Jacquie can have a clandestine check tomorrow to make sure she isn't in hospital anywhere, she can have a drive-past to see if there are signs of life at her house. If she doesn't surface, I daresay there are things she can do relating to mobile phones – I can't imagine what, but that always seems to work on TV.'

Sylvia smiled across at him. He was the oddest mixture of calming omnipotence and total naivety but somehow, it worked. 'Drink up, then,' she said. 'Sooner we're gone, the sooner we're back.'

'I've never really understood that,' Maxwell said, sipping gingerly at his drink. 'Look, Sylv, this is never going to cool down. Let's not drink it and say we did. Hmm?'

'You're right. I'll just leave Guy a note to say what's happening. The place looks like the Marie Celeste.' She scribbled on the pad she kept on the coffee table for all such eventualities. She might not be at the cutting edge of health care any longer, but old habits die hard.

Maxwell was already in the hall, opening the front door. 'Do you need me to navigate?' he asked over his shoulder.

'Are you going to do a takeoff of the woman on the satnav?' Sylvia asked, suspiciously.

'I may do, I may do,' he said. And he did, sort of – 'Let go of the steering wheel when it is safe to do so.'

'In that case, no. I'll take my chances.' She shooed him out and slammed the door behind her. 'It's not far. Let's go.'

They only took ten minutes and they were there, outside an anonymous block of flats with a keypad and buzzer at the door. 'Wilson' was marked as being in 302 and Sylvia pressed the relevant button. There was no reply.

'We could press for someone else,' Maxwell said, extending a finger to do just that.

'No, we couldn't,' Sylvia pulled his arm down and held on tight. 'That kind of tactic is best left to the police. We'll try Andrew Baines first.'

Jacquie opened the front door and let a slightly embarrassed Jason Briggs in.

'I hope you don't mind this,' he said. 'DCI Hall seemed to think it would be all right.'

'DCI Hall was in as much of a cleft stick as I am,' Jacquie retorted. 'If he wants me at the hospital, I need a babysitter.'

'I thought your husband . . .'

'Yes,' Jacquie again cut him off at the pass. 'He isn't under house arrest, though, and he happens to have gone out.'

'I didn't mean any offence, ma'am,' Briggs said, following her into the sitting room. 'I just heard that he was . . . well, very good at looking after the nipper.'

Jacquie relented. This situation was much worse for Briggs than for her. 'None taken,' she said. 'And please call me Jacquie when you are here as a babysitter. I'll just show you Nolan's room. He sleeps through the night about 364 days a year, and hopefully this will be one of them. If it turns out to be the other one, then just read him something and he'll soon drop off. Like a Gremlin, don't feed him after midnight.'

'Is your husband likely to be late back?' Briggs asked. He had no particular plans for the evening, but he wasn't sure how long he was expected to stay.

Jacquie looked at the clock and shrugged. 'He shouldn't be, but his plans are really dependent on other people. Look, Jason, why don't you stay over? I can't expect you to stay up all night just hanging around. The spare room is next to Nolan's. You could leave the door open – believe me, if he wakes up, the whole street knows about it. You won't miss it, I promise.'

Briggs perked up. He liked his bed and was good for nothing without eight hours shut-eye. 'Is that all right?'

'Of course,' she said, leading the way along the landing. 'This one's Nole's, this one's yours. Family bathroom along there; spare toothbrush in the cabinet, still wrapped. Help yourself. There's TV in the bedroom – no Sky in there, I'm afraid, but we do have films on demand so help yourself. Ummm – I think that's it. How are you at waking up in the morning?'

'Rubbish,' he grinned.

'I'll give you a shout, then,' she said. 'Call me if you run into any problems. Must go. 'Bye.'

And she was gone. Looking around, Jason Briggs made a note to himself; become a DI asap. And marry a teacher. The moaning buggers clearly earned more than they were willing to own up to.

Andrew Baines lived in an altogether more spacious house than Charlotte Wilson and it was easy to see why she would have wanted to bring up a child there rather than in her flat. It was a semi-detached, built between the wars and with a bow window, recessed porch and clearly a reasonably sized garden behind, judging by what they could see in the dark down the side alleyway between the house and next door. There was no garage, but half the front garden was given over to hard-standing and his car was there. Good news – at least he might be in.

Maxwell rapped on the door with his knuckles; the lion knocker was painted pretty much shut. They heard movement inside and then the door opened a crack.

'Max? Sylvia?' Baines opened the door. 'Is everything all right? Are you having car trouble or something?'

'No, Andrew,' Maxwell said. 'We're looking for Charlotte.'

'Gosh, this is embarrassing. I thought everyone knew we had split up,' Baines said, opening the door but not stepping aside.

'She discharged herself from the hospital today,' Maxwell said. 'She had gone in for a termination, but I'm sure you knew that. Look, can we come in? This isn't the kind of thing that really lends itself to doorstep chats.'

'Oh, sorry, yes, of course. Come in.' Baines stepped back and ushered them to the right into the sitting room, which was furnished in what Sylvia always thought of as bachelor eclectic. A sofa from his mother's, a sideboard from his gran and a computer desk from Ikea.

'Thank you,' Maxwell said, sitting down. 'We went to see Charlotte. She had become . . . well, somewhat distressed and she wanted to talk to me.'

'Why?' Baines didn't sit, but stayed standing in the doorway.

'I'm not totally sure,' Maxwell said. 'I think she just wanted to see a friendly face. Someone older. Not involved.'

'That must be hard to find,' Baines said, leaning against the door jamb. 'Charlotte seemed to be sharing her lot with anyone within earshot.'

'Andrew!' Sylvia said. 'The poor girl was upset. Scared of the future.'

'No need for that,' the PE teacher said. 'I would have looked after her.'

'Really? She seemed to think you were washing your hands of her and the baby.' Sylvia's words could have etched diamonds and Maxwell decided to give her her head.

'Well, I've got a new job, I suppose. I wasn't planning to move, though. I would have seen her all right.' He gave a harsh laugh. 'I don't expect the social services would have given me much option.'

'I think that what she was thinking of was support of a more personal nature,' Maxwell said. 'Not financial.'

'We hadn't been together five minutes,' Baines said, turning on the charm. 'Not in the scheme of things. She let me down, getting up the duff.'

Maxwell felt Sylvia tense and held her arm. 'I don't get the impression she did it deliberately,' he said, smoothly.

Baines shrugged. 'Whatever you say. Anyway, if she's decided to go and get rid of it, that's it, isn't it? Why are you here?'

'We told you,' Sylvia said through gritted teeth. 'Looking for Charlotte.'

'Well, she isn't here. Have you tried her flat?'

'She doesn't seem to be in. And she isn't answering her phone.'

'Let me try her.' He reached into his pocket and pulled out a mobile and punched a number. Still on speed dial, Maxwell noticed. They all looked around the room while they waited for her to answer. Then, Baines spoke urgently into the phone. 'Char? Is that you?'

Maxwell's head came up and Sylvia Matthews reached out for the phone, but Baines turned his back on them, finger in ear and head bowed.

'I've got Maxwell and Sylvia Matthews here . . . looking for you, it seems.' He swung back to face them and looked them one by one straight in the eye. 'Worried about you, babe. Yes . . . Do you want to . . .? I see. Yes. Laters.'

He broke the connection and went to the door and opened it, standing with it wide and inviting.

'She's fine. She's not answering the phone right now, but recognized my number. She doesn't want to speak to anyone at the moment and will probably not be in this week. That's it. I think we should all leave her alone, don't you? Thanks for dropping by.'

Maxwell's Return

Maxwell got up slowly and put a supporting hand in Sylvia's back as he shepherded her through the door. He couldn't vouch for her behaviour and wasn't too sure about his own.

'Thanks for ringing her, anyway,' he said. 'We feel a lot better knowing she's somewhere safe.'

'Any time,' Baines said. 'See you both tomorrow, I suppose.'

'Yes. Indeed.' Maxwell went out of the door and just as he reached the path, heard a voice call.

'Andrew?'

Maxwell turned and looked at Baines, who gave him a man-of-the-world grimace. 'Company,' he said, with a charming smile. 'Must go.' And he shut the door in the Head of Sixth Form's face. From the porch, Maxwell heard his footsteps thundering up the stairs. Eager. He hadn't let the grass grow under his feet, and that was a fact.

Back in the car, Sylvia gave vent to her feelings. And carried on giving vent until she dropped Maxwell outside 38 Columbine. At his age, Maxwell had not expected to learn any new words in the invective line and this was true of the journey – he just heard them in unusual combinations, some of which made his head spin. He went up the stairs and, pausing only to check on Nolan and trip briefly over the cat who was scratching at the spare room door, he went into the sitting room for a last minute drink and a think. Within minutes, he was asleep.

As Jacquie pulled up in the car park of Leighford General, she took a moment to clear her mind of what might be happening at home. That Nolan had woken up, freaked out at being looked after by a stranger and was inconsolable, had already had serious psychological damage done and would have separation issues for the rest of his life. If she knew her son, he would sleep right on till morning, but if not, then he would certainly have persuaded Jason Briggs that midnight feasts were de rigueur chez Maxwell and would be even now tucking into a short stack with bacon. She took a deep breath, picked up her bag and made for the main entrance.

Kirsty Hilliard looked tiny in her high dependency bed, dark circles under her eyes and a heart monitor on her finger. Someone had cleaned off her makeup which she had fondly imagined made her look twenty and her hair was slicked back from her face. It was hard to imagine that she had set off hardly twenty four hours before to paint the town red. Her eyes were closed but Jacquie, having spent many hours at bedsides waiting for information which often never came, could tell that she was asleep now, rather than unconscious. Her eyes were flickering to and fro and her mouth twitched from time to time, as her dreams tried to make sense of what had happened to her. Jacquie took out her book and settled down for a long wait.

She had only read a few pages when the bedclothes rustled and a quiet voice asked her, 'Who are you?'

She looked up and saw that the child had turned her head and was looking at her. Her eyes were extraordinary, a deep violet that didn't look real. They searched Jacquie's face now, trying to remember. Was the DI someone that she ought to know? Panic began to show and Jacquie put down her book and leaned forward reassuringly.

'It's all right, Kirsty,' she said. 'I'm Jacquie. I'm from the police but don't worry, you haven't done anything wrong. I just need to know a bit more about what happened to you, if you feel like talking. If you don't, don't worry about it. I've got my book and I'll just wait here until you fancy a chat. Do you need a nurse for anything? A wee? A drink?'

The girl licked her lips. 'A drink,' she said. 'Could I have a drink? My throat is really sore.' She tried a cough and winced.

'I'll just ring the bell. Hold on a minute.' Jacquie pressed the buzzer and a nurse came scurrying along the ward.

'Hello, Kirsty,' she smiled. Maxwell and Sylvia would not have recognised her as the same breed as the bantam in ante-natal. 'Nice to see you awake.' She looked at Jacquie. 'What do you want?'

'A drink,' the girl whispered. 'My throat hurts. Have I got the flu or something? It didn't hurt before . . .' Her pupils dilated and she tried to get up.

'Don't worry,' the nurse said, soothingly. 'The Detective Inspector will tell you all you need to know.' The woman was clearly happy to pass that particular buck. 'I'll get you a drink. Do you like orange or blackcurrant?'

'Orange. Please.' The girl waited until the nurse had gone and then turned back to Jacquie. 'What happened to me?'

'I'm hoping you can tell me a bit about what happened, Kirsty,' Jacquie said. 'I need to hear it from you first, you see. Then we can find out more.'

'I can't really remember much . . .' The girl closed her eyes and let her head loll on the pillow. The nurse crept back and put an orange juice complete with bendy straw in Jacquie's hand before tiptoeing away.

'Let's start from the beginning of your evening out, shall we?' Jacquie suggested. 'Where did you all get ready? There was quite a little gang of you, wasn't there?'

'We all got ready at Ali's. She lives nearest to the Esplanade.'

'There you are, you see. So you walked there when you were all ready?'

'Yes. Some of the girls were meeting lads when we got down to the Front. They went off then, so there were about six or seven of us at the finish.'

'Can you let me have their names?'

'Are we in trouble? We were in pubs . . . they shouldn't have served us. I don't want to get anyone in trouble.' The violet eyes filled with tears.

'No-one's in trouble, Kirsty. I'll tell you what; let me have their names later. Just tell me the story of your evening.'

'We went into a couple of pubs and had a drink in each one. I had a tequila slammer. Some bloke bought it for me – I didn't like it, but he said if I drank it quick, it would loosen me up a bit.' She coughed and closed her eyes, swallowing with an effort. Jacquie handed her the drink, which she sipped gratefully.

'This . . . this bloke. What was he like?'

'Old.' The eyes checked out Jacquie's face. 'Older than you. Bald at the front, with one of those . . .' the girl sketched a comb-over.

'Handsome? You know, fit?'

Kirsty smiled for the first time. 'Not him! He'd never been fit, not even when he was young. No, he just liked having a few young girls round him for a bit. We cost him a packet, then moved on.'

'Did he follow you?'

'No. Just as we were finishing up our drinks, some old woman came up to him and chatted him up. He was on a sure thing, I think. He certainly thought so.'

'So, you moved on and then what?'

'We walked along the Front a bit. It was still warm and there was a nice breeze off the sea.'

'Were there any boys with you?'

'No. They'd all gone by this time. We were going on to a club if we could get in. I know the others didn't want me with them. I'm too little to pass for old enough. They were walking on ahead and I was a bit upset.'

'Were they being nasty to you? Bullying?' Jacquie was beginning to see what Maxwell had meant, about their man cutting one out from the herd, taking the runt of the litter.

'I suppose so. I'm used to it.'

'Why do you go out with them, then?'

The girl shrugged, then winced. 'I don't fit in with the swotty girls. They don't talk to me much.'

'You seem a bright girl, Kirsty. Why don't the swotty girls talk to you?'

She blushed and turned her head away. 'I was in trouble at school last term,' she muttered. Jacquie had to crane across to hear her. 'The teachers found me with one of the boys in the gym.'

Jacquie said nothing, but patted the girl's hand.

She spun back to face the DI and shouted as far as her throat would let her. 'I didn't mean to let him do it. He said he fancied me. He said . . . he said you couldn't get pregnant if you did it standing up. I told him that was rubbish, but . . .'

'It's all right, Kirsty,' Jacquie said. No story had a simple beginning and there was rarely a happy ending. 'Don't worry about that.

I just need to know whether you were walking with the others, a bit behind, that kind of thing. Try and imagine yourself back there and tell me what is going on. Close your eyes if it helps.'

The girl lay back on the pillows and did as she was told. Her eyes moved from side to side – a good sign, because it meant she was picturing the scene. Then she spoke, in a husky whisper. 'I was behind the others. I was fed up and my shoes were hurting me.' Jacquie could just imagine her, clopping along on killer heels and hating every step. 'They were getting further and further ahead and I could tell they were laughing at me, because every now and then, one of them would look back at me and snigger. I wanted to go home, but my proper clothes were back at Ali's. My mum would have killed me if she could have seen how I was got up.'

The kid would realise in a minute that her mum now knew all about it, but let that realisation come when it would. For now, the narrative was running nicely. Jacquie offered the girl another drink and after she had drained the glass, she carried on.

'I suppose I was sulking a bit. Anyway, I was walking behind them when I noticed this bloke watching us from a doorway. He was just looking, you know, but he was well fit. Young. No, not young. Younger than the bloke in the pub, by miles. Older than the lads we know.' She stopped, clearly trying to find some kind of benchmark. 'Not as old as . . . you know, people like David Beckham. He's well old. But fit like him, you know. Probably about the same as my uncle Dan.'

'How old is he?' Jacquie said, with a smile.

'Thirty? Thirty five. Something like that.'

Jacquie made a note. So far this chimed well with April Summers' description. 'Was he dark? Fair?'

Again, Kirsty sketched in the hair. 'Gel. His hair was kind of messed up, but it looked good. It's probably fairish when it isn't gelled. He had nice clothes on. Smart, you know.'

Jacquie thanked heaven for a fashionista. 'Label?'

'Gap? That kind of thing.'

'So, then what happened? Take your time.'

'He stepped forward and smiled. He really was good-looking. He said something like, was I on my own? Had I had a row with my mates? They looked like proper slags, that kind of thing.'

Cut her out from the herd, Jacquie thought. Oh, but you are a cynical bastard.

'We were just on the edge of that bit of park behind the Esplanade and we went and sat on a bench.' The girl sniffed. She was back there well and truly. 'He smelt nice. Expensive, you know. Hugo Boss, but I don't know which one.'

Jacquie couldn't resist a laugh. 'Kirsty, you're one up on me. I didn't even know there *were* different ones!'

'My mum works in Boots. Anyway, he smelt nice and he was nice to me. He said I didn't need to trail around after the others. That I was the prettiest and he chose me. I . . . I was stupid, I know that now. But he was so *nice* to me.' The tears squeezed past her closed lids and she let them run down her face. 'He . . . he said, should we go for a walk and I said why not. But my shoes hurt me, so I took them off and he carried them for me. He held my hand.' She turned her head towards Jacquie and smiled. 'No one holds my hand. I liked it.'

Jacquie stroked her arm gently. 'Do you want to stop, darling?' she said. She knew it was wrong, but she was more mother than DI right at this minute. She didn't know how Maxwell stood this, living with the breaking hearts all around him and soaking it up and tamping it down so he didn't drown in it.

The girl shook her head. 'No. I want to tell it. Then I can stop thinking about it.'

Jacquie thought that was doubtful, but she took her metaphorical hat off to the girl for at least being prepared to try putting it behind her. 'Go on then. In your own time.'

'Will you hold my hand?'

'Of course.' Jacquie took it and rested it between both of her own, cradling it like a fledgling fallen from its nest.

'Right. We walked for a while and he asked me where I went to school. He asked me about my mum and dad, my sisters at home.

What I liked doing at the weekends. It was nice. People aren't usually interested in me, much.' She swallowed and touched her free hand to her throat. 'We went into the bushes in the park and he said shall we sit down. It hasn't rained for ages and the grass was dry, so I did. My skirt was tight and I couldn't get down for a minute and he laughed and picked me up and put me down on the ground. He was really strong. Then, he kissed me and I liked it. He hadn't been drinking or anything. His breath wasn't all fag smoke and beer. Then he pushed me down and . . . do I have to tell you this? It's embarrassing.'

'Just say what you're comfortable with,' Jacquie said, squeezing the girl's hand.

'Well, he . . . did it, you know. I didn't want to, but he'd been nice and he wasn't rough. I liked it in the end.' She half rolled over to face Jacquie. 'Is that wrong?'

'Of course not,' Jacquie said, letting go of her hand to stroke a lock of hair out of the girl's eyes. 'Of course it isn't.'

'Well, when he . . . you know, when he'd finished, he went all weird. He put his hands round my throat and squeezed really hard. I screamed, but he squeezed. Then . . . the next thing, I was here.'

Jacquie patted her hand. 'You've done really well, Kirsty,' she said. '*Really* well.'

'Will you catch him now?' the girl whispered. 'Put him in prison?'

'Yes,' Jacquie said and realised as she spoke that she actually did feel much more confident that they would indeed be taking this predator off the streets at last, and soon. 'Yes, we will.' She let go the child's hand ready to leave, but the girl clutched hers.

'Please don't go. Stay till I go to sleep. Please.'

Jacquie sat back down and nodded. 'I'll stay,' she said. 'Don't worry. I'll stay till morning.'

Somewhere in the house, an alarm was ringing and Peter Maxwell woke with a groan. Someone appeared to have put his head on backwards and half his body had been removed. After the initial panic at these discoveries subsided and he realised he was asleep half on and half off the sofa in his own sitting room, wracked with pins and needles, he opened his eyes slowly and stifled a scream.

'Mr Maxwell?' asked the stranger sitting across in his own favourite chair. 'I'm Jason, I work with your wife.'

Maxwell struggled upright and was not proud of how long that took him. 'What's happened?'

'Nothing as far as I know,' the stranger said carefully. He had heard how this old git managed to muscle in to all the cases his wife worked on and he didn't want to give him any info that could be traced back. 'The hospital rang last night and the guv'nor sent me here so I could babysit so the DI could go down there.'

'And Jacquie was all right with that?' Maxwell was surprised.

'Not at first,' he said, 'but she showed me where everything was and it was all fine anyway. Your lad is a good sleeper, isn't he?'

'Yes,' Maxwell said, finally gaining an upright posture. 'I'd better go and start getting him ready.'

'Oh, he's up,' Briggs said. 'I came in to check whether he is really allowed two bowls of Cocoa Pops and nothing else for breakfast.'

'Not really,' Maxwell said, silently applauding his son's chutzpah. 'But we'll make an exception for today. So, Jacquie is . . .'

'I rang the station, Mr Maxwell,' the sergeant said. 'She stayed at the hospital and then went straight in. She says to tell you see you tonight.'

'Right.' Maxwell was feeling a little redundant. 'I should ring to get Nole a lift to school.'

'That's no problem, Mr Maxwell,' the man was quick to save him the trouble. 'I have a kiddy seat in my car. I'll take him. Let you get yourself sorted ready for school.' Was there something more than a little condescending in that remark, Maxwell wondered. 'What time can he be there? Only, I don't want to be late myself. Apparently the DI found out some useful stuff at the hospital and I should be at briefing.'

Maxwell, the redundant, said, 'Eight o'clock there's someone there.'

'Brilliant.' The sergeant looked at his watch. 'Nole!' he called over his shoulder. 'Are you done in there? We need to get a wiggle on.'

Nolan appeared in the doorway, chocolate moustache well in place from his binge. Good luck to his teachers this morning, as he hit the ground running full of sugar and little else. 'Morning Dads. Did you sleep all night in here?'

'Uh huh. Are you all set?'

'Yes. Jason . . .' he caught Maxwell's expression out of the corner of his eye, 'Sergeant Briggs got me ready. Mummy had to go to work.' He bounced off to get his coat and there were sounds of jumping from the landing until he managed to knock it off its peg.

'He's a great lad,' Briggs observed. 'Bright.'

'That's right,' Maxwell said. 'Very like his mother, lucky boy.'

A tousled head topped with a cap on crooked stuck itself around the door and the child sketched a kiss at his father. Richmal Crompton, thou shouldst be living at this hour, Maxwell thought, throwing a kiss right back. With the usual noise of thundering feet on the stairs, the two were gone and the noise of a worryingly powerful engine echoed up from the street. Maxwell lay back on the sofa and waited for his joints to remember how to work, then, without even the benefit of shining morning face, went unwillingly to school.

Chapter Fifteen

Sylvia Matthews' face swam into focus. 'Are you feeling all right, Max? You look like shit. In fact,' she pulled his jacket to one side, 'isn't that yesterday's shirt?'

'I have several like this in fact,' he said, 'but, yes, it is yesterday's shirt. It's a long story but it isn't big nor is it clever so let's just leave it at the fact that I do feel like shit as well. I fell asleep on the sofa and feel as though I have been run over by a herd of stampeding buffalo.'

'As long as that's all,' she said, sitting down opposite him. 'Did you have any breakfast?'

'Yes, mummy, I did. I am also wearing a vest.' He looked more curmudgeonly than the occasion warranted and she waited for the second shoe to drop. 'I'm feeling old. Leave me alone.'

'Max, you sound like a four year old. Have you heard anything from Charlotte?'

'No. I checked with Thingee as I came in this morning. She hadn't heard. Nor has that rather scary woman Legs has installed in HR, the one with the single eyebrow. She put a pension forecast form in my pigeonhole at break. Is she trying to tell me something?'

'Only that you look like shit, I expect,' Sylvia said, comfortingly, 'and she's trying to be helpful. Did you talk to Jacquie about Charlotte?'

'No, she was at work, apparently. Honestly Sylv, it really *is* a long story. She was at the hospital, presumably with the latest attack victim. Our little problem is really not that big, not in the scheme of things.'

'Sorry.' Sylvia Matthews knew when enough was enough. 'Is she all right, the girl?'

'I don't know any details, but she's awake, which is more than the first two will ever be again. April got off lightest of all, if being pregnant with your abuser's child is light.'

'She's having a termination, though, isn't she?'

'So her mother says, but they are a very mixed up family, the Summers. So who knows what decision today will bring.' He glanced up at the clock. 'In fact, judging by the last two days I have been in this room at this time, I'm about due a visit from her mother.'

They both looked at the door, almost willing the woman to appear.

'I may have escaped my karma today. I could do with a nice normal afternoon trying to drum Nazi economic policy into Year Thirteen. Hector Gold did a first rate job, but he kept shelving this topic and who can wonder at it. Still, it will keep me awake just long enough, so I won't knock it. Guns or butter?' He held up each hand in turn as though weighing the options.

'What?'

'It was the choice that Herman Goering gave the German people when that nice Mr Hitler was in the Brown House. He expected them to choose guns, of course, but looking at his waistline, I suspect he had a bit of both.'

'I'll leave you to catch a few minutes, then,' Sylvia said, getting up. 'I just popped by to see if you'd heard anything.'

'No. Have you seen that slimeball Baines?'

'He did stick his head around my door. Just to say he hadn't heard any more. He is a piece of work, isn't he? I wonder who he had upstairs.'

'Some poor unsuspecting girl who doesn't know any better,' Maxwell said. 'I hope he gets a nice desk job soon so all those lovely abs and pecs go like jelly. Then he won't find receptionists so easy to fool.'

She ruffled his wiry hair, making no difference to the final appearance at all. 'I'm glad you're not bitter, anyway,' she said with a smile. She was still closing the door when he had put his head back against the chair and was halfway asleep again.

Jacquie finished her presentation to the team and stood in front of the white board.

'Any questions?' she asked.

'I have one,' a voice said from the back. It was one of the old stagers, a sergeant who had been around for what seemed like forever, never wanting promotion or indeed to do a hard day's work. He often had pertinent things to say, though, so the rest of the team turned in their chairs to look at him. 'I know it's a while since I went courting . . .' Guffaws met this. He had been married at twenty to a woman who had ruled him with a rod of iron ever since. '. . . but when I *did* go courting, one of the first things you asked each other was your name.' He put on a mincing voice, '"Oh, Sandra. My favourite name!"'

Jacquie smiled and waited for the laughs to die down. 'That's a good point . . . what's your name, by the way?' More guffaws. 'No, seriously, Den, that is a good point and one we hoped would take us forward in the April Summers situation. But he had gone to great lengths to make sure she never saw his post, never heard anyone else speak to him, didn't even answer his phone with his name. He called her by endearments all the time, said names were for strangers, or some such sloppy tosh.'

'So this one . . .?' Den persisted.

'She was swept up into his aura. He's very good at making a girl feel special, loved, even within the first few minutes.'

'Hypnosis?' a young WPC at the front asked and immediately regretted it. She'd been watching too much Derren Brown.

'No,' Jacquie said with a smile. She remembered how it felt to be the new kid on the block. 'Nothing like that. Just plain, old-fashioned charm. He holds their hand. Looks deep into their eyes. He took April Summers to a hotel and had the bed covered with rose petals.'

There were a few grimaces on the face of the back-row element but some of the women looked quite wistful.

'It wouldn't work on an older woman, one with a bit of experience,' Henry Hall chipped in, 'which is why he preys on the younger, more impressionable girl.'

'Is that why, guv?' Jason Briggs already had Brownie points to further order for babysitting the DI's kid, but a few more never hurt. 'I thought we were looking at the paedo lists.'

'No,' Henry Hall said, firmly. 'This is *not* a paedophile. We've talked to profilers and they all agree that this is not someone drawn to children. He is drawn to anyone he can manipulate. If he met a woman older than him who nevertheless was taken in by his rather cheesy charm, he would be onto her like a rat up a pipe. He just hedges his bets by going for the youngsters.'

Jacquie took back the conversation and stepped to one side and ran down the list of things known about their quarry.

'If you will just look at this list,' she said, 'and take it away with you, I would be grateful. I know not all of you are assigned just to this case, but see if anything else that comes your way rings any bells. Our man is aged between 25 and forty. We've stretched the limit a bit because we know kids are notoriously bad at guessing adult ages. He is fair rather than dark, but not very light blonde. His hair is long enough to gel and look 'bed-head' – any of you lads who don't know what that is, ask.' More laughter. Henry Hall looked on proudly – the girl was doing good. 'He is good-looking. Names mentioned have been Daniel Craig and David Beckham, who I know don't resemble each other, but I have taken it to mean that he has a pleasant face with even features and rather a twinkle in his eye. His height is not defined very well – both the girls we have spoken to are tiny, so if he is over about five eight, he will seem tall. Kirsty Hilliard's friends didn't see him to notice and April Summers' friends have all forgotten. The summer holiday is a long time when you're fourteen. He lives in Leighford, in quite a decent house, but April can't really describe it or where it is.'

'Is this April kid okay? You know, in the head?' Den was on his hind legs again. 'Surely, a kid of that age would know where she was.'

'She had been a virtual prisoner for some weeks,' Jacquie pointed out, 'and the man she thought loved her had just tried to throttle her. I suppose map references were not her first priority at that point.'

The sergeant nodded. The DI had a good point there.

'From talking with psychologists and looking at demographics, we think he may be either a professional or a high-functioning white-collar worker of some kind. We're talking perhaps solicitor, teacher, doctor, something of that order. And that is *not*,' she clarified, 'because there have been a solicitor and a teacher briefly in the frame. Both men have been cleared and they are no longer of interest. The builder who we were pointed at by a victim's parent is too old and frankly too plain to fit the bill. He also has a cast iron alibi for at least one of the murders.'

'Yes,' came an anonymous voice from the back. 'He was doing one of the victims' mums at the time.'

'Indeed.' Jacquie sat on that one quickly. Mrs Blakemore had nothing to be proud about, but she nor her dubious boyfriend had anything to do with the deaths either. 'So,' she picked up her bag and slung it over her shoulder, 'I haven't been to sleep since I woke up yesterday morning, so if I could just leave you to mull this over, I'm going home for five minutes' shuteye and a shower. In no particular order.' She walked past Henry Hall on her way out. 'Is that okay, guv?'

He patted her on the shoulder as the Incident Team broke up to go about its collective business. 'We all need sleep, Jacquie,' he said. 'I'll give you a ring if anything develops. Thanks for last night. How did Jason do at the babysitting?'

'Well, he's still standing. He said everything went well, except that for some reason, Max slept on the sofa. I'll get to the bottom of that tonight, I suppose. Never a dull moment. I'll see you later.'

'Tomorrow will do,' Hall said. 'As I say, I'll ring if I need you in the meantime.'

'That would be good. As long as you're sure . . .'

'Do it. Before I change my mind.'

Jacquie needed no second bidding and made for the stairs and, ultimately, bed.

Maxwell felt a little better after his workout with Year Thirteen. They weren't the brightest apples in the barrel, any of them, but he had tried his best to enthuse them about the banking metier of Hjalmar Schacht and now his brain at least had a couple of synapses which worked. Even so, the end of the day had never been so welcome and this early in the term the prognostications for his still being on his legs and functioning come December were not good. He stood irresolute at the sink in the corner for a moment, then decided to leave the coffee until he got home. It was Nolan's day for Beaver scouts and so Mrs Plocker was i.c. supper – perhaps tonight was the night he might actually get to eat something English for a change, something without added cheese from a can or maple syrup. He dried his mug from lunchtime, hung it on its hook and turned to go. And almost swallowed his tongue. Was today going to be the day he died of shock? The odds were looking good.

'Lindsey,' he said, trying to keep the tremor out of his voice. 'I don't think I heard you knock.'

'I didn't,' she said. 'Mr Maxwell, you've got to help me. April's gone.'

Euphemisms spun in Maxwell's head. Surely, a termination this early carried almost no risk of death, but there was always allergic reaction. Suicide! No, surely not . . . 'Gone?' was all he could manage in the end.

'I went to call her this morning, to go to the GP, you know, and she wasn't there.'

'Lindsey,' Maxwell said, reasonably. 'That was, what? Eight hours ago. Where have you been since then?'

'Out looking,' she said. 'We checked my mum's place, and all her friends from school. We checked . . . well, everywhere.'

'Have you been to the police?'

'No.' Lindsey Summers had the grace to look shamefaced.

'Why ever not?' Maxwell was appalled but not surprised. 'She was abducted for weeks in the summer and now she's disappeared again and you haven't been to the police? Lindsey, what are you thinking?'

The woman looked mulish. Maxwell remembered that look from her days at school, especially the day when she told him she was leaving to go and have her baby in a squat with a lowlife. That baby was missing now and she was still as stubborn as any donkey. 'They'll take my kids.'

'They?'

'Social Services.'

'Oh, *They*. I don't think you've averted that by not reporting it to the police, Lindsey, if I can be blunt.' Maxwell was not a cruel man, but his patience was being sorely tried. No man who has woken up to a sideways view of a complete stranger sitting in his house should have to cope with stupidity on this level. The woman's lip began to tremble and he sighed. 'Come on, Lindsey. Let's go and see what we can do. Look, I'll tell you what I'll do. I'll ring Mrs Maxwell at work, see if she can help us out. Is that all right?' He found himself bending down slightly, patronising away as though the woman were five. 'Yes?' She nodded and turned away.

Maxwell picked up the phone and dialled the number of Leighford Nick from memory.

'Hello. It's Peter Maxw . . . oh, do you? . . . Yes, I suppose it is quite distinctive . . . Oh, has she? Thanks. I'll try her there.'

He turned to the weeping woman. 'Mrs Maxwell has gone home from work. Give me a minute and I'll ring there.' This time, he rang without even looking at the phone. 'Hello, heart. Yes, they said. Have you had a kip, now? . . . Look, petal, I have Lindsey Summers here with me and she . . . well, she seems to have mislaid April. Could you . . . yes, we'll wait here.'

Again, he turned to his visitor.

'She's on her way. Would you like me to get someone up here until she arrives? Mrs Matthews, for instance.' He was silently begging her to say yes, but she shook her head. 'Would you like a coffee, then? Tea?'

'I'd love a nice cup of tea,' the woman answered and Maxwell wondered, not for the first time, how any crisis would manage without a nice cup of tea. Had anyone offered a nasty cup of tea in trying circumstances, he wondered. He put the kettle on and decided to wait until Jacquie arrived but in the end, he couldn't help himself.

'Where do *you* think April is?' he said.

'We've looked everywhere,' she replied, which was really no reply at all.

'I didn't ask that,' he said mildly, handing her her tea.

'I think she's gone back to that bastard, if I'm honest,' she said, cradling the mug.

'How could she do that? She doesn't know where he lives, does she?'

'She said not,' the girl's mother said. 'But I don't know whether we can believe anything she ever said about it. I think she knows quite well where he lives.'

Maxwell thought it was time to stand up for Plod-dom everywhere and his wife in particular. 'The police do know what they're doing, Lindsey. They know how to question people.'

'Yeah, but she's a lying little madam,' she said, bitterly. 'She's been lying nearly since she was born, that one. All that crying. Lies.' She hid her face in her mug, so he couldn't see her expression.

'I understand, Lindsey, really I do,' Maxwell said. He looked around his office, papered as it was with nostalgia and memories. He wondered how he would feel if anyone came in here and told him a few home truths about his heroes, his heroines. He knew they had feet of clay and he decided to ignore them – Shane might only be five foot two in his stockinged feet, but he could still outgun the best. If someone told him that Nolan was not his, if someone told him that Metternich was moonlighting as someone else's cat, called Tiddles and eschewing vole for canned tuna, if someone told him that Jacquie was . . . time to stop the ifs. Lindsey Summers' world was shaking apart and she was lashing out. But he needed to get her to see the facts, not to dismiss her daughter as a liar. 'I don't think we should jump to conclusions until my wife gets here. Had April talked to anyone else about the baby?'

'Just me and Phil. And my mum, but she just shouted, called her names. Called *me* names, come to that. That's why she came home. Mum isn't very . . . understanding. So that's why I knew she wasn't there, but we looked, all the same.'

'Has she told her friends, do you think?'

'I don't know. I doubt it, but I don't know her friends very well, what with her going to school near mum's. She sees her friends when she's there, really. Not at ours.'

'On her mobile all the time, I imagine?'

She managed a smile. 'Aren't they all? Texting, talking, Facebook, all that. I wouldn't have let her have one if it was just me, but all her mates have the latest thing. You know how it is.'

Maxwell had a drawer in his desk for the specific purpose of storing captured mobiles and he hadn't waited for that nice Mr Gove to tell him it was all right to confiscate them. He knew all right. 'Has she taken her mobile?'

'Yeah . . .' Somehow, the word came out sounding rather uncertain.

'Are you sure? Did you look?'

'Well, no. Her bag had gone, so we just assumed . . .'

'Is Phil at home?'

'With the little ones, yes.'

'Ring him. Ask him to look.' He nodded at the phone. 'Dial Nine for an outside line.'

Without taking her eyes off him, she reached for the phone and then glanced at it only for as long as it took to dial her home number. Then she fixed her eyes on his face again. 'Phil? It's me. Look, don't ask me why, can you just run up to our April's room and check for her phone . . . I know she doesn't ever go out without it, just check, will you?' She held the phone to her chest until an indignant quack made her put it back to her ear. 'Yes, I'm here. Is it? Oh, God, Phil. Where was it?' She waited while he explained and he clearly wanted to know more, but she signed off with a brusque, 'Gotta go,' and hung up.

'Still there?' Maxwell asked gently.

'Mmmm.' She nodded her head.

'Where was it?'

'Under her pillow. Where she always puts it at night.'

'When Mrs Maxwell gets here . . .' but he cut himself short at the sound of a well-loved tread along his mezzanine corridor. 'We'll let her take over now, Lindsey. She'll know what to do.'

Sylvia Matthews was putting the final touches to the emergency packs in her store cupboard when there came a tentative tap on the door.

'Yes?' She turned round and met the clear blue gaze of Sarah, known better to Maxwell as Thingee One. She had to bite back the name and instead managed to get it right. 'Sarah. How odd to see you in the afternoon. How can I help you?'

'I just wondered if you had any news of Charlotte. I tried ringing and she isn't picking up.'

'We missed her at the hospital yesterday, Sarah,' Sylvia said, still folding and counting under her breath. 'Mr Maxwell and I were a little concerned when we couldn't find her, but we went to Mr Baines' house and he managed to get through and she said she's okay. A bit confused, poor girl. The list went all to pot yesterday and she didn't have her procedure.' The euphemism ran slickly off her tongue. 'She discharged herself – she was rather upset and I can understand why.'

'But that's rubbish, Mrs Matthews, if you don't mind me saying so.'

'Sarah! What do you mean?' Sylvia was as shocked as she would be if one of Maxwell's posters had suddenly come to life. 'I can assure you . . .'

'I'm not calling you a liar, Mrs Matthews. Don't think that. But that bastard Baines, he's one and no mistake. He didn't ring Charlotte and if he did, she didn't answer him.'

'Well . . . couples, you know how it is,' Sylvia hedged. 'None of us knows what goes on behind closed doors.'

'Yes, I accept that,' Sarah said, sharply. 'But when it comes to Charlotte and that bastard, I do know. She blocked his number.'

Sylvia used a mobile, but wasn't really sure about everything it could do. If someone told her that theirs could cook the Sunday lunch, she wouldn't have dismissed it out of hand. 'I'm sorry, I don't really know what that means.'

'It means,' the girl said, speaking clearly as though to her granny, 'that if he rang her, it wouldn't get past him punching in the number. Her phone just wouldn't accept it. The call wouldn't go through. There would be nothing for her to answer, because it wouldn't ring at her end.'

Sylvia stopped folding and counting and looked at the girl aghast. 'So he made up that whole conversation? How extraordinary.'

'He's such a big headed bastard. He wouldn't want you to know that she wouldn't speak to him either. He didn't speak to her last night. Or for some time, when she had anything to do with it.'

'I didn't know it was as bad as that,' the school nurse said.

'God, yes. She hasn't made too much about it, but she told me. She thought he might not be too pleased about the baby, but he flipped. Told her that he was seeing other women, that they were all better in bed than her, she lay there like a dead thing, all that. The stuff blokes say, you know, when they want there to be no going back.'

Mr Matthews had been no prize, God knew, but Sylvia realised that perhaps with her history of him and Guy, she had had it easy.

'In fact, he told her, he was, almost as he spoke, giving one to that piece in IT, you know, the new one. The NQT who never made it.'

'We never met.' Sylvia was not surprised, however. The woman was clearly out looking for anything in trousers; it was all in the body language.

'Well, that lasted less than five minutes, but Charlotte had got the message. That's when she blocked his number and decided on the termination.'

'I didn't know Andrew Baines was quite as bad as that.'

'Anything with a pulse,' Thingee One said. 'I should know. He had me pressed up against the coat racks last Christmas, before he got round to Charlotte.'

Sylvia's eyes were wide. 'What did you do?'

'Kneed him in the nuts, Mrs Matthews, not to put too fine a point on it. Hats off to him for managing what he managed later with Charlotte. But he's hated me ever since. He doesn't like to be crossed. I may be over-reacting, but I think we should carry on looking for Charlotte.'

Sylvia drew herself up and decided to pull rank, although there was no actual hierarchy here except age and experience. 'I'll go and see Mr Maxwell, see what he thinks.'

'Mrs Maxwell is up there. And that woman, the one with the kid.'

In a school of well over a thousand pupils, that should have meant nothing, but Sylvia put two and two together. 'Right.' She rubbed her forehead, overcome with unfamiliar indecision. 'I'll go and see Andrew Baines, then. Is he still in the school?'

'Yes. But you'll have to be quick. He goes to do that gym club thing today. He's going to work there full time soon – good riddance to bad rubbish.'

'I heard he had a new job. Where is it?'

'Somewhere posh. Not sure where. Just not here and that's good enough for me.'

'I'll pop over,' Sylvia said. 'If you see Mr Maxwell – or Mrs Maxwell – can you tell them I'd like a word, please? And, Sarah . . .'

'Yes?'

'Thanks for all this. You're a true friend to Charlotte.'

'We Thingees have to stick together, Mrs Matthews,' the girl said. 'I'm sure she's all right, but I won't rest until we're sure.'

'Same here,' Sylvia smiled. She followed the girl out and turned right towards the gym. 'Can you text me your number?'

'Will do,' the girl said. How sweet, she thought, when these old dears use mobiles.

Chapter Sixteen

Lindsey Summers was feeling better than she had for ages. Mr and Mrs Maxwell were sitting one on either side of her and they were helping her to find April. Her life had been a series of alarums and excursions almost since her birth – having a crazy, shouty mother is no way to grow up calm. And yet, here she was, sipping tea while these nice people put her world to rights. When she came out of this fog, half Maxwell, have diazepam, she knew that everything would be fine, April would be a good little girl in pigtails and her coming baby would be a pink-cheeked angel who never cried. She switched off almost all of her brain and just drifted.

Jacquie reached round behind the woman and poked Maxwell in the back. He leaned forward so he could see her face and raised an eyebrow.

'I think we've lost her,' Jacquie mouthed. 'Is she on anything?'

Maxwell spread his hands. For all that he had seen more of this woman in the last three days than he had his own wife, he knew next to nothing about her. Her daughter was missing – what more did they need to know? Jacquie got up carefully and walked to the door, motioning Maxwell to follow her. They stepped out into the corridor, mercifully quiet now except for some distant hoovering and some incoherent shouts with more than a whiff of Mrs B about them. They left the door open and kept a weather eye out for Lindsey Summers falling off her seat and leaned in to each other so they could speak in mutters.

Maxwell went first. 'Where do you think she is?' he said.

Jacquie took a deep breath and bit her lip for a second, then said, 'Are you thinking Shannon Matthews?'

'I wasn't,' Maxwell said, surprised. 'You mean that you really think Lindsey has April stashed under a bed somewhere, waiting for the big reveal?'

'No. I just wondered whether you did.'

'No, I don't. I think that poor old Lindsey really has lost her daughter, but whether her daughter considers herself lost or just staying elsewhere is moot.'

'I would agree, except that with her history, we can't just wait and see. I spoke to the latest victim last night and it seems to me that this guy is upping his game. He's getting impatient. He can't be bothered with more than half an hour's chat now before he has his hands round their throats. Forget the slow seduction. It's all about the throttling now.'

'But why would he look for April again? He must know she will have been to the police.'

Jacquie smiled and patted his arm. 'The trouble with you, Max, is that you assume everyone is like you, thinking of every eventuality, relying on commonsense. He probably doesn't think anything of the kind. He has reached a point where he doesn't think these girls have any value unless he is in the frame. They don't exist except when in his company.'

'There must be a syndrome.'

'Pardon?'

'Well, you know how once upon a time, there were two sorts of people. People who conformed to the norms and people who didn't. The people who didn't were two sorts of people. They were either nicely eccentric . . .' he paused to see if she would make a sassy remark, but she settled for a sweet smile and a pat on his cheek, 'and those who were pretty unpleasant to be around. And that was about it. Then, the experts thought that perhaps some names for these different people would be handy and so the Syndrome was born. There's a kid in Year 9 – Nine Ell Pee if memory serves – who can't sit still and chats incorrigibly to his oppos during lessons. Once we would have called him a bloody nuisance, slapped him round the head and sent him down the Social. Now he is the

Syndrome Kid and he has to be allowed to express his individuality; the other twenty nine in the class? Who cares?'

'I think sociopath covers our man quite well.'

Maxwell was unconvinced. 'Let's see what his brief comes up with before we guess his label,' he said.

'Let's catch him first.' She glanced over her shoulder. 'Look, is Sylvia still likely to be here? I don't like the look of Lindsey at all. She seems to have withdrawn completely. That can't be good for her in her condition.'

Maxwell looked in through the open door, to where April's mother was sitting staring into her empty cup. 'That sounds like a plan. Then we can go and start looking for April properly.'

'*We?*' Jacquie looked quizzically at her husband. She could get away with a lot with Henry Hall, that was a given, but having Maxwell trotting through the streets of Leighford in a stab vest looking under bushes for a missing schoolgirl was not on the list of acceptable behaviour.

'You, heart, of course. I mean you. But I can help, surely? It was to me that she came, after all. I have her trust, all that kind of thing.'

'We'll have to speak to Henry. But meanwhile, can you ring Sylv?'

Maxwell crept into his room and picked up the phone, dialling the Sick Room's number by rote. He stood looking at Lindsey Summers while the phone rang in an empty room, then put down the receiver. 'Not there,' he mouthed at his wife, who gestured to him to come nearer.

'In that case, Max, I'm going to have to call the team. And an ambulance. This poor woman needs some proper care.'

'I wonder where Sylv is, though? She doesn't usually leave until everyone else has gone. I expect she'll be even worse now Guy is working at his new school – she was telling me last night, his hours are ridiculous.'

'Tried Thingee? Oh . . . is there a Thingee on this afternoon?'

'Yes, Thingee One is covering. She's become Thingee All The Time. I'll try her.' He tiptoed back to the phone and dialled zero. This time, the phone answered at once.

Maxwell's Return

'Yes, Mr Maxwell?'

He was always a touch startled when they knew who was calling but he rallied. 'Thingee, old thing, I was wondering if you knew where Mrs Matthews might be. We could do with her up here, if she's within hail. Oh, and there will be an ambulance arriving shortly – can you point the nice people in green in the direction of my office, please?'

'Ambulance? Is everyone all right?'

Maxwell paused as he always did when a cliché was offered him on a plate, but decided to leave it be. Why should there be an ambulance arriving, after all, if everyone was all right? 'Mrs Summers isn't feeling too good,' he said. 'Nothing serious. But . . . Mrs Matthews?'

'She was going to the gym,' the girl said. 'She wanted to see if she could catch Mr Baines.' Maxwell couldn't see the expression on her face, but her voice was quite a giveaway.

'I see.' He could get the details from Sylv shortly. 'Do you know, Thingee, I have absolutely no idea if there is a phone in the gym.'

'There's one in the office,' she said. 'They hardly ever answer it, though. It drives us mad.'

'Can you do me a favour, dear one?' he smarmed. 'Can you nip along there and see if she's still in the building? If she is, we really would appreciate it if she could come up to my office.'

'No problem, Mr Maxwell. I'll ring from there when I find out what's going on.' The girl pulled off her headset and went into the corridor. When all this was sorted, she really had to try and swap shifts with Charlotte. Afternoons were *so* much more exciting than mornings!

Thingee ambled along the corridor to the gym and pushed open the door carefully. There was a probably inaccurate but nevertheless amusing story about Mr Diamond once walking in to the gym unannounced and getting a basketball right in the face and although it was droll to have it happen to someone else, Sarah had places to be that evening which would not be enhanced by a couple of black eyes and a fat lip.

'Hello! Cooee!' The girl walked in a few steps through that old indefinable smell of ropes, sweat and liniment, then remembered the no-heels rule and hopped first on one leg, then the other to remove her shoes. 'Mr Baines! Mrs Matthews!' All she got was an echo mocking her from the wall bars, benches and other paraphernalia that she had been more than glad to see the back of when she left school. 'Is anyone here? It's Sarah. Mr Maxwell needs Mrs Matthews urgently upstairs.' She played her final sentence back and added, 'In his office.' She listened again and, opening the door, turned back for a final shout. 'Cooee?' There was clearly no one there. She put her shoes back on and went back along the corridor towards reception. Only another half hour and she could go home. The days were long now she was covering for Charlotte, but she would have a nice fat payslip next month, so she kept her eyes on the prize. She was just passing the mouth of Hell, aka the SLT corridor, when a voice stopped her.

'Sarah! I thought you were only here in the morning.'

She turned. Oh bugger. When Bernard Ryan called you by name it was never going to end well. 'Mr Ryan,' she said. 'I'm covering for Charlotte while she's not well.'

'I see. Can you type?'

Sarah was surprised that not everyone could type. She sometimes thought she had been born at a keyboard. 'Yes.'

'Could you come and do a couple of letters for me. I'm . . . a bit behind.'

'Yes, of course,' she said, adding in the privacy of her head, I bet you are. Being arrested and suspended will do that for a person. 'Can I just . . .' she gestured towards reception.

'It won't take a minute. It *is* rather urgent.'

'Okay.' Afternoons were a lot more interesting and this one became doubly so as the doors to the foyer crashed back and three paramedics trotted in. Raising her voice, she called, 'Up the stairs. Mezzanine. They're waiting for you.'

'My word, Sarah,' the new improved Bernard Ryan said. 'That's a nice bit of multitasking there. Anything I should know about?'

'A visitor, apparently,' Sarah said, taking care not to mention Peter Maxwell by name, 'taken poorly. Just a precaution.'

And she followed him down the corridor, all thoughts of Sylvia Matthews forgotten.

Maxwell and Jacquie followed the men in green down the stairs and watched from the foyer as they loaded an uncomprehending and uncaring Lindsey Matthews into the ambulance. She was walking, which disappointed them; they had just taken delivery of a new chair which could do stairs and they were dying to try it out, but never mind; there was always another crisis just around the corner. Maxwell felt he should wave or make some other social gesture, but in the end settled for putting his arm around Jacquie's shoulders.

'I wonder what happened to young Thingee?' Maxwell asked as they turned away.

They looked through the glass partition into reception and saw that the desk was empty.

'She can't still be scouring the gym, surely?' Maxwell said.

'How big is it?' Jacquie asked.

Maxwell looked at her. 'You do know who I am, do you?' he asked. 'I have quite literally no idea. In the good old days I invigilated exams in there, proceeding in a Westerly direction at two and a half miles an hour. But since the Exams Office Posse have taken all that over, I never set foot. Old men forget, but I wouldn't have thought it is that hard to find a fully grown adult in there. Never mind, crisis averted. I suppose you'll be off to the Nick now, starting the search for April.'

'That's right,' Jacquie said. 'And you can go home and get some shuteye. You look like rubbish.'

Maxwell bowed. 'Thank you,' he said. 'It's nice when a marriage keeps the magic, don't you think?'

She glanced around and, seeing no kids, kissed him briefly on the lips. 'I always feel a bit naughty doing that here,' she said.

'We could always pop out to the bike sheds if you would feel more comfortable,' he said. He held up his hand. 'But, time is short! I couldn't do myself justice. Anyway, there's probably a queue. Off you go, find April and come back and tell me all about it. I'll go home – if I drop off, Surrey knows the way – and you're right, I could do with a snooze.' With another slightly puzzled glance at the empty reception desk, Maxwell fished in his pockets for his cycle clips and gallantly opened the door for his wife. Two days down; only another million or so to go.

Thingee, released from Bernard Ryan's boring clutches and shaking herself free of letters to the multi-use playing field Stasi, half walked, half ran back to reception and immediately punched in Maxwell's extension number. It rang and rang and eventually she put down the receiver. He couldn't have wanted to know where Mrs Matthews was that much if he had gone home. She glanced at the clock. And now she could go home. Hurrah! She reached under the desk for her bag, snatched up her coat from the back of the chair and was out in the car park before you could say knife. Leighford High belonged to Mrs B and the cleaners now.

Maxwell reached home without needing to resort to White Surrey's homing instinct, but only just. He had hardly dismounted when Mrs Troubridge's door opened and the woman herself was approaching.

'Mrs Troubridge,' Maxwell said, hoping this might be something quick. 'How lovely.'

'I'm cut to the quick, Mr Maxwell,' she said. 'To the quick.'

'I can only apologise for the Count,' Maxwell said, automatically. 'We've tried to tell him about the vole innards. It's because he loves you . . . this isn't about vole innards, is it?' He had read her expression, which was beyond bulldog chewing a wasp and was verging on the Les Dawson with his teeth out.

'I was standing in my front window last night,' she hissed, 'as one does, and I saw a Man arrive. He rang the bell and very shortly afterwards, DI Carpenter-Maxwell left.'

Alarm bells were ringing. When Mrs Troubridge called Jacquie anything so formal, things were bad. 'Indeed. She was called in to . . .'

'*You*,' she said, poking him in the stomach with a bony finger, 'were out. With that Nurse from the school.'

'That's right, we . . .'

'I don't want to know about your private life,' the old woman sniffed. 'What you do behind closed doors is all the same to me. But to leave Nolan, that Dear, Innocent Child,' and the capital letters were enunciated with a snap of her chelonian jaws, 'in the care of a Stranger, well, that is beyond the pale, Mr Maxwell. I feel I should call someone in authority.'

'Mrs Troubridge,' Maxwell prepared to pour oil on troubridged waters. 'Firstly, Mrs Matthews and I were on a mission of mercy to a colleague in Leighford General. Secondly, the man you saw arriving was not a stranger, he was a very trusted colleague of my wife. In other words,' – he toyed briefly with his impeccable Sly Stallone, then thought better of it – 'he *was* the law. And thirdly . . . what *were* you doing at your window? It was quite late. That's why Jacquie didn't want to worry you.'

'Didn't want to worry me?' Mrs Troubridge drew herself up and still barely reached Surrey's handlebars. 'Didn't want to worry me? I have been worried all night and all day, wondering what might have happened to that Dear, Innocent Child.'

Maxwell found himself mouthing the words. Mrs Troubridge loved every hair on his son's head, of that he was sure. He only hoped that the lad would never disappoint the old trout by showing his feet of clay. 'Nolan was very well looked after. In fact, he didn't even wake up. He got two bowls of Cocoa Pops out of the deal, so he went to school happy.'

'I'm just saying.' Mrs Troubridge barred his way and the only method of getting into the house was to lift her bodily and move her aside. Unless . . .

'Mrs Troubridge,' Maxwell ingratiated. 'Nolan is with Plocker this afternoon. How would it be if I ring Mrs Plocker and ask her to drop him off at your house? He'll have eaten, but you can play Scrabble. He'll like that.' And the odd thing was, Maxwell thought as he formulated the plan, the kid would actually like it. He had found a way under the old bat's shell and had her firmly in the palm of his hand, mixing metaphors as if there was no tomorrow.

'I really wouldn't want to push myself forward where I'm not wanted,' she said, but they both knew this was just going through the motions.

'If you just budge over a second so I can get by,' he smiled, 'I'll make the call now.'

She stepped back onto her own path and he pushed Surrey up to the garage door and let himself in. 'You'll ring her now?'

'This minute. Bring him back when you've had enough.'

'Oh, Mr Maxwell,' she trilled, happy again. 'Don't say that or I might *never* bring him back. Oh,' and she skipped back to her door, 'I might just have time to make him some of his favourite brownies . . .' and with that, she was gone.

Maxwell stowed his bike, picked up the post, went up the stairs and was about to crash on the sofa when he remembered the night before. Instead, he went on up to his bedroom and sank gratefully onto his bed, still smiling. Brownies, indeed. Why that child wasn't the size of a house, he would never know. His mother's metabolism, that must be the answer. He quickly picked up the bedside phone and made his call. Mrs Plocker was an accommodating woman who had met Mrs Troubridge on numerous occasions. How the Maxwells could leave their lovely son with her, she had never really understood, but hers not to reason why. Maxwell was still smiling as his head hit the pillow and sleep came up to meet him with outstretched arms.

Downstairs in the sitting room, the phone's little red light flashed unheeded. 'You have two new messages' the sign marqueed across its base station. 'You have two new messages.'

The Incident Team had been working all day on various tasks and had got precisely nowhere, which was why they were looking so enthusiastic as they gathered yet again for a briefing. Jacquie was again in the chair and filled them in quickly on what she had managed to glean from Lindsey Summers and Maxwell. That she could now do this without mentioning her husband at all bore testimony to the number of times she had done it. The old stagers could tell that he was in the background; one mention of Leighford High School and ears were pricked and hackles raised before the sentence was done. However, a missing girl was a missing girl and the door to door and street interviews began as soon as they could all gather their coats and hats. As the room emptied, Henry Hall stood behind Jacquie and leaned forward to whisper in her ear.

'Where's Max, Jacquie?'

For once, she had no need to dissemble. 'At home. Catching up on his sleep after a night on the sofa.'

'You're sure?'

'Positive.' She too had rung Mrs Plocker, to be told that Max had already rung and arranged for Nole to go to that mad old bat next door, oh, I do beg your pardon, Mrs Troubridge. So he was clearly planning a good long sleep. It was nice to be able to tell Henry where he was and know it was right.

'That's all right then. Are you going out with the others or staying here to co-ordinate? I'll do whichever you don't do – I don't mind which.'

'I thought I'd go out, guv. I've met the girl and so that might be a help when they find her.'

'I thought that's what you'd choose to do. You have considered the possibility of publicity, I suppose?'

'What, the parents hiding her, you mean?'

He nodded. 'Hopefully nothing worse.'

'The mother seemed genuine. I know this isn't gospel, but Max said she was rubbish at acting at school, so I doubt she's improved now. She seemed to be in total collapse and the paramedics agreed.'

'You're checking the house first, I take it.' He didn't like telling his granny how to suck eggs, but this could be a media minefield.

'There's a team there now, guv. And the granny's. Not that you'd choose to stay with her if you were desperate. She is a truly horrible woman and it's not many I say that of, as you know.'

'We certainly do meet them,' he agreed. 'I'll make sure you get any updates. Who are you with?'

'Jason.' He wouldn't have been her first choice, but he was better than many.

'Fine. I'll be here.' And in his usual abrupt fashion, Henry Hall was gone.

Maxwell was dimly aware of a car drawing up outside and a voice that sounded very much like his son's briefly raised in song. A twitter that could only be Mrs Troubridge and the cheerful goodbyes of the Plockers, mere et fils, joined the mix and then peace again descended on Columbine and Maxwell dropped gratefully back to sleep.

The next noise came just a few seconds later by his reckoning, but in fact it was three games of Scrabble, two brownies and a glass of milk later. It took him a moment to work out what it was, then it resolved into the phone.

'Mmm?'

'Max?' A man's voice grated anxiously in his ear. 'Are you all right?'

'Sleepy,' Maxwell managed, licking his lips and struggling upright. 'Bad night last night. Catching up.'

'Oh. Max, it's Guy. Is Sylv with you?'

Against his better judgement, Maxwell couldn't help checking the room. 'No,' he said, after a cursory glance. 'Should she be?'

'No, no, it's not that. I know she was with you yesterday. You know, when that girl was in hospital. We didn't have much time to chat last night and I was gone this morning before she woke up.'

'I see.' Maxwell was concerned. This didn't sound like Guy and Sylvia of old.

'It's nothing like that,' the man said, hearing the tone. 'It's my new job. It's a killer. We're talking about moving nearer, but . . . well, these things take time.'

'Yes,' said Maxwell, getting into his stride. 'Have you no idea where she might be? It's not like Sylv to be dippy and disappear.'

'No, exactly. She's got that pad thing, you know, in the sitting room. She's absolutely rigorous about filling it in. Me, not so much, but I've never known her fail. Sometimes I've come in and she's put things like "I'm in the garden" or "I'm in the loo". She just hates to be off the radar.'

'I know. Medical training, I suppose,' Maxwell said.

'And a tiny touch of control freakery, but in a good way.' Maxwell sensed that Guy was beginning to wish he hadn't shaken this particular tree. 'Look, Max, sorry to have bothered you . . . she'll turn up in a minute, I expect.'

But Maxwell was sitting up now and taking notice. When had he last been aware of Sylvia Matthews being in the right place at the right time at school that day? She seemed to have gone awol around three thirty. He glanced at the clock. Gone seven now. That was a long time, in the world of Matthews.

'Guy, we need to talk. I've just got to pop next door and palm Nole off on Mrs Troubridge for the evening and then I'll be ready. Can you pick me up?'

'To go where? We can't just drive around looking for her, can we?'

'Well, it won't be quite as random as that, I hope. I have an itinerary in mind. But please, Guy, *please* leave a note on the pad!'

'Will do,' the man said, thoroughly rattled by now. He had rung Peter Maxwell up for reassurance and was now in the grip of full scale panic. 'I'm on my way.'

'See you shortly,' Maxwell said and crashed the phone back on the rest. He grabbed his coat from the rack as he hurtled past and was soon ringing Mrs Troubridge's doorbell. It went without saying that she would be delighted and scurried off to put a hot water bottle in the bed in Nolan's room, as her spare room was now called, down to the little plaque on the door. Nolan loved it now; it would only be in the years to come that the Bob the Builder decoration would come to be an embarrassment, when Sir Nolan Maxwell was Architect Royal to King William V. As Maxwell reached the pavement he stopped. Caught in the crosshairs of Metternich's disapproving glare he suddenly had lost the use of his feet. He tried to brazen it out.

'Count,' he said, curtly, and nodded, trying to sidestep the animal.

The enormous black and white beast didn't even blink. He got up from his classic cat-sat-on-the-mat position and stretched extravagantly. He then walked up to the man laughingly referred to as his master and sunk a thoughtful pawful of claws into his calf. Then he quietly walked away.

'I love you too,' Maxwell muttered and, hoping the blood wouldn't show on his dark trousers, limped in the direction that he knew Guy Morley would be approaching from – anything rather than stand there being eyeballed by a cat planning to sue for desertion. Guy's car came round a corner in what even Maxwell could tell was the wrong gear. He got in as the car slewed to a halt and fastened his seatbelt. It was going to be a bumpy night.

Chapter Seventeen

Thingee One, Sarah to her friends, was on her third drink before she remembered her promise to Sylvia Matthews. She had said she would text her number to her and it had gone right out of her head. And now, it was too late because she didn't know her number, not right off the top of her head, anyway. She could remember about half the numbers, but, she thought with a giggle, that wasn't much help with a phone number. It had to be right or not at all. She had taken her phone out of her bag, ready to text and sat there with it in her hand, irresolute.

'I'm glad you're enjoying yourself,' her date said, bitterly. He had picked this one at the Speed Dating evening at the Red Lion and was beginning to regret it. She was pretty enough, legs up to here, but she wasn't much in the way of company. She'd just sat there necking drinks at his expense and now she had her bloody phone out. Great. He started thinking of excuses to leave – even his missus was a better bet than this silly little chickie. There was raucous laughter from the bar – the yachtie crowd were out on the tiles. Starting early by their normal standards but they hadn't had much wind to keep them on the water and they were stuck for anything to do on dry land except drink.

'Sorry.' She looked up at him and his heart melted. Those big blue eyes – they did it for him every time. 'It's just that I promised I'd let someone have my number, for emergencies, if you know what I mean, and I forgot. Now I don't know how to get hold of her.'

'Emergency?' he asked. He had thought she was a receptionist or something. How many emergencies did they get when they weren't at work? Or when they *were* at work, come to that.

'It's a friend,' she began, and ended up telling him the whole story, leaving nothing out. 'And so,' she said, 'I ended up missing Mr Maxwell *and* Mrs Matthews, so now I don't have any way of finding out what's going on or whether Charlotte is all right.' Her eyes were swimming with unshed tears now and he was lost.

'Don't worry, Sally . . .'

'Sarah.'

'Sarah,' he said, scarcely missing a beat. 'I know Mr Maxwell's phone number. Both home and mobile.'

She narrowed her lovely eyes at him. 'Why?' she asked.

'Because,' he said, 'I am a reporter on the *Leighford Advertiser* and there isn't a reporter in the town who would dream of not having Mad Max's phone number in his little black book.'

'But Mr Maxwell never answers his phone. He's famous for it.'

'It's worth a try though, don't you think?' He smiled down at her. Oh, you lovely little thing, he thought. I do believe I may get lucky after all.

'Why not?' she smiled at him, and carefully wiped away a tear. You may have breath that can stop a clock, she thought to herself, but you have your uses. It's a shame I won't be paying in any currency you'd understand. 'Ben.'

'Bob.'

'Yes. Sorry. Bob.'

'Shall we ring or text? Mr Maxwell.'

'Oh, ring, I think, don't you? He might not know how to pick up texts.'

'We'll text if he doesn't answer. Okay?'

'That sounds good. Let's have your book, then.' She had her phone out in readiness.

'It's on my phone,' he smiled. 'I'll ring him. Hang on.' He whipped out his iPhone and scrolled through his contacts, choosing a name finally and holding the gadget to his ear. 'No reply,' he mouthed. Then he rang off. 'No point in leaving a voicemail. There's certainly no way he knows how to pick them up. Hold on, I'll text. What shall I say?'

'Just say it's Sarah and that I meant to leave my number with Mrs Matthews. Put my number in as a link, why don't you?'

'Yes, why don't I . . . tell you what, you can do it.' Bob Skinner had always pretended he was at the cutting edge of technology, but he knew his limits. He looked down at the girl, texting at lightning speed with her thumb and sighed. He felt very, *very* old.

Guy Morley and Peter Maxwell were sitting in Morley's car in a car park to the north of Leighford. They were hunched together over the satnav, trying to work out a plan. How a minute streetplan of Leighford could possibly be of help, Maxwell couldn't really see, but it seemed to please Guy and so he was happy to go along with it.

'So, Max,' the man said finally, sitting back. 'Where did you say this Charlotte girl lives.'

'I told you, Guy,' Maxwell said for the fifth time. 'I can take you there from Leighford General. I just can't point it out on this stupid thing. Have you tried her phone again? If she has been in the hospital, she'll have had it switched off.'

Guy reached into his pocket and flicked some screens around, finally putting the phone to his ear. He looked into the middle distance while he waited for a reply, but all he got was voicemail.

'That's funny,' Maxwell said. 'Sylvia's ringtone is the same as mine.'

'Really? That *is* funny.'

'Why? I thought they were all just preset on the phone.'

'God, Max, you *are* a dinosaur. I downloaded the theme tune from *Emergency Ward 10* from YouTube. That's her ringtone.'

'Oops. I've just missed a call, then.' Maxwell dug his phone out of his pocket. 'Yes. One missed call, one text.'

'It's probably Jacquie. Or Sylv.'

'No. I don't know this number. Hang on, let me open this text.'

As all people did when near Maxwell and a mobile phone, Morley held out his hand, but Maxwell shook his head.

'Jacquie says I have to do it or I'll never learn,' he said, pushing buttons at what looked like random. 'Here we are. Oh, it's from

Thingee One. She promised Sylv her number, apparently, but missed her this afternoon, so she's sent it to me. I expect that's in case there's any news on Charlotte.'

'Ring her back,' Guy said, nudging him and making him drop the phone. 'Oh, sorry.'

Maxwell scrabbled to pick up the phone and when he had retrieved it looked at the screen in disbelief. 'It's gone.'

'What has?'

'The message.'

'Please let me look, Max. No, look, here it is. You'd just minimised the screen. Ring her back. Perhaps she knows where Sylv is.'

'I'm not sure if she would have texted if she knew that. Although . . . I suppose if she knows she's with Charlotte.' The Head of Sixth Form was following a meandering train of thought. He would usually try this kind of thing out on Metternich, but Guy Morley would do just as well. He wasn't quite so black and white or indeed, so feline, but he would do. 'If she knows she's with Charlotte, why didn't she just ring her? And how does she know my number?'

'And why is that text not from Thingee's phone? Look,' Guy pointed, 'two different numbers.'

'I wouldn't have spotted that,' Maxwell said. 'Thanks for noticing that. So, with all these questions, I'll ask one more.'

'Which is?'

'How do I phone her back? I've never done this before.'

'Max, Max, Max . . . it is true what they say. Give me your phone a minute.' Morley punched a key and handed the mobile back to Maxwell. It was ringing. It was answered.

'Hello?' She had to cover one ear to hear him over the row from the bar.

'Thingee? I thought I'd ring you back.'

Sarah could hardly contain her surprise. 'Mr Maxwell. I wasn't sure whether you . . .'

'Thank you, Thingee my dear. I can use a mobile phone, you know. Anyway, I'm here with Mrs Matthews' other half, Mr Morley. We're a little concerned about her because she hasn't come home.'

'Not come home? Perhaps she's shopping.' Sarah always liked to look on the bright side, hence her weekly attendances at the Red Lion Speed Dating Nite.

'No, she always leaves a note. Tell me, did you see her to speak to this afternoon?'

'I popped in. To her office, you know.'

'When was this?'

'Just before I spoke to you. I . . . well, I went to ask her if she had heard from Charlotte and ended up telling her what I thought of that pig Baines.' She looked up and saw Bob Skinner jotting down a note. He smiled at her and put the book away. Just because he had other plans for this evening didn't stop him being a journalist and this had the smell of something that could be quite juicy.

'Whanhstiyhsbit?'

'Pardon? Mr Maxwell, keep your head still. The signal isn't very good.' She wanted to scream at the yachtie yobboes to shut up.

'Sorry, Thingee. I said, what did she do then?'

'Well, like I told you, she went to see Mr Baines in the gym.'

'Did you find her there?'

'No. I was coming back to tell you that they weren't there when Mr Ryan grabbed me to type some letters. When I got back to reception, you and Mrs Maxwell had gone.'

'And Mr Baines and Mrs Matthews?'

'What about them?'

'Had they signed out? You know, fire regs, all that kind of thing.'

Thingee was pained. '*You* never sign out, Mr Maxwell,' she pointed out. 'Or in.'

'No. But that's me. I'm talking about *Mrs Matthews*, the woman who never met a rule she didn't like.'

'Now you come to mention it,' the girl said, 'they hadn't signed out, no. That *is* odd, they're both usually so good about that kind of thing.'

'Yes. It is odd,' Maxwell said, thoughtfully. 'Well, thanks, Thingee old chap. Give my regards to Bob Skinner, by the way.'

'Mr Maxwell!' Sarah looked around, expecting the old bugger to be at the other end of the bar.

He chuckled. 'It's not magic, Sarah,' he said. 'I know all the *Advertiser* staff have my number. Only the school and my family and very close friends have it apart from them. Of the journalists, only three are men. One is a hundred and specialises in obituaries, which he is careful to check each week in case one of them is his. One is as far as I know is currently undergoing gender reassignment and don't ask me how I know that. The other is Bob Skinner. Tell him if any of this reaches the paper, we'll know who to sue. 'Bye, Thingee. Thanks for your help.' He turned to Guy Morley who was reaching for the ignition. 'That was Thingee,' he said, redundantly. 'I think we need to get round to Andrew Baines' house asap.'

'Where is it?' Morley asked.

'Sadly, I can only find it from your house. But after that it will be plain sailing. So, off we go.'

'What was all that?' Bob Skinner asked.

'Mr Maxwell says hello,' was all Sarah could manage.

Skinner looked at her and was similarly lost for words. As if in chorus, they both caught the eye of the barman.

'Same again.'

April Summers was not hidden in the house, nor that of her repellent grandmother. Her friends had all been visited, courtesy of the numbers on her mobile phone. She wasn't there either. This was a negative result, it was true, but it meant that the door to door teams could coalesce on areas where she might be instead. Jacquie looked again through the file. She had been held, if that was the word, in an 'old' house, not on an estate, in a 'proper' road. April had not remembered a garage or much of a garden and it definitely wasn't part of a conversion, like a flat or maisonette. Some of the older beat coppers had been set to blocking out areas where such houses could be found, within a reasonable distance from where April had reappeared as if by magic on that August day. She had estimated a ten minute journey with her lift, who had never been traced. Traffic had been analysed for the day in question and soon they were down to only a few thousand houses. Jacquie was kicking herself that they had not made this effort when April had reappeared, but with the girl well and unharmed, it was wasted manpower. And now, Kirsty Hilliard was in the hospital, lucky to be alive. Jacquie, stuck in traffic, punched the steering wheel in frustration. Jason Briggs bent to his map and pretended not to notice.

'We'll find her, ma'am,' he said, keeping it formal. 'We're really fine tuning the search now. She can't be far away.'

'Perhaps. Or perhaps she's on the dunes, perhaps she's tossed off a cliff, perhaps she's . . .'

'. . . perfectly safe and enjoying giving everyone the runaround. Girls are like that, guv. They don't always think about how parents worry.'

'You sound like an expert,' Jacquie said, smiling at him.

'Not really. I don't see my girls as much as I'd like and they're a bit small yet for that. But I have three sisters – I tell you, Jacquie . . . I mean, ma'am, you have no idea how lucky you are to just have a boy.'

'He is more or less according to the order form, I'll grant you,' Jacquie said. 'Just like his father.'

'I thought he was just like you,' the sergeant hazarded.

'Thanks,' she said. This conversation had wandered into personal territory and it was time it was brought back on track. 'So, where are we heading?'

'We've got this block here, look.' He traced a rough rectangle out towards the east. 'There are door to door teams canvassing; we're there for backup or for liaison.' Jason meant well, but Jacquie could do without a blinding glimpse of the obvious about now.

'Any news yet?' she asked, taking a left at a T junction.

'I'll check in,' he said. 'Hang on.' He dialled a number on his phone and listened carefully, marking areas on the map. He rang off. 'There have been a few what might have been sightings, but they have all been checked and didn't come to anything. The girls have all been spoken to and crossed off the list. Some of the teams haven't got very far – that's these . . .' he pointed to an area where the houses were subdivided into flats in the main, 'but some are almost done. Do you want to try a bit of door knocking yourself? I'm up for it – it's ages since I had any hands on.'

Jacquie looked at him and saw the enthusiasm shining in his face. The hunt was up, the game was afoot. Why not – it would be good to be at the sharp end for a change. 'Why not? Call in and tell them where we'll be working. If we go towards a team from the edge of a block, we won't double up.'

'Okay guv . . . ma'am. Will do.' And he took out his phone again, hot to trot.

'There are an awful lot of policemen about,' Guy Morley observed as they drove through town towards the hospital, watching his speed carefully.

'I think my lovely wife may be the cause of that,' Maxwell said, and filled Guy in on the April Summers saga, as far as he knew it.

'That's dreadful, Max,' the man exploded. 'How could he keep a girl captive like that without anyone knowing? And grooming the others – how did he do that?'

'The first two aren't telling, being dead,' Maxwell said, perhaps a little more shortly than he had meant to sound. 'April isn't very coherent at the best of times, according to her mother, lying, changing her story and whatnot. But this is one clever psycho, Guy. He seems to have some kind of . . . well, I don't know, Svengali like charm that they all fall for. We don't even know if he always targets youngsters. The smart money, apparently, is that he is just out to control. All they know is that he's a good looking bloke, indeterminate age, bright . . . that's it. It could be you, for all the description they have.'

'Thanks for the vote of confidence,' Morley said and drove on in silence for a while.

'I didn't mean to imply . . .' Maxwell said, into the awkward quiet of the car.

Morley looked surprised. 'God, no. Max, sorry, I hadn't taken offence. I'm just worried about Sylv. Oh, God! Should we have called the hospital? The police? In case there's been an accident.'

'Well . . . let's go into casualty when we finally get through this traffic and ask. You'll get more information in person than on the phone, at any rate.'

'True,' the man conceded. 'And, we're actually here, so that's good.' He turned in to the car park and then the search began for a space. 'Oh, for God's sake, why are things so difficult all the while?'

Maxwell put a calm hand on his arm. 'Look, Guy, pull up here and I'll just run in, yes? Yes. I won't be a minute.' Anyway, he thought as he trotted up the slight incline to the entrance, there was bound to be an Old Leighford Highena somewhere in the building who would help. And there was – there on the reception desk, sat Angela Cannon, of blessed memory. Four As at A level and working reception at Leighford General, for heaven's sake.

'Angela!'

'Don't panic, Mr Maxwell.' The girl held up a restraining hand. 'I'm only here until I go back to start my MSc at Imperial in October.' Then, she remembered herself. 'How can I help you?'

'Angela – congratulations, by the way. Imperial, well done. Has Mrs Matthews been in today? I mean, as a casualty.'

'Mr Maxwell! Is everything all right?'

Now he came to think of it, Angela could panic for England. Not the perfect appointment, perhaps. 'Everything's fine, Angela. We've just mislaid Mrs Matthews, that's all.'

'If she comes in . . . er, that is . . .'

'No, no message, Angela. Thanks so much.' And he was gone, jacket flapping in the breeze of his passing.

'Not there,' he said to Guy, settling back into the passenger seat. 'So, it's on to Andrew Baines' place now, I think. See what he has to say for himself as the last person to see Sylv as far as we know.'

'God, Max. Do you have to put it like that?'

'Sorry. You know what I mean. You'll have to go out of that exit . . . no, that one, over there. Yes, that's right. And don't you think you ought to put some lights on.'

Guy Morley felt as though he was in a computer game, with his car being driven by a remote control.

'Don't interrupt me or we'll go wrong. Now, you need to go along here to the lights.' Maxwell sat, drumming his fingers irritatingly on his leg. 'Guy, is that all right?'

'You said not to interrupt.'

'You can say "yes", helpful things of that nature.'

'Sorry. Yes.'

'Now then . . . there should be a row of shops along here in a minute. When we get to them, we need to go round the next roundabout and go off at one o'clock.'

'For a non-driver, you're very good at directions,' Guy observed.

'I've had this conversation with Sylv,' Maxwell said. 'She says I'm not allowed to mimic the satnav.'

'That sounds like a good rule,' Guy said, smiling at the deliberate use of the present tense regarding the school nurse. 'Here we are. One o'clock, is that right?'

'Yes. Then, along here it gets a bit more hazy. It's one of these roads, but I'm buggered if I can remember which . . . go slower. Let me see . . . No, it isn't these. These are battles in the Boer War; I'd remember if it was one of these. I wonder whose idea it was to name a blameless suburban road Spion Kop Close?'

'Can you remember anything about the address?'

'No . . . hang on, it's something to do with trees. Or birds. Nature, anyway.'

'There are loads of police about. Perhaps we could ask one of them what roads are round here.'

'If you had a proper map, Guy . . .'

Morley decided not to answer. His heart was beating so hard that he was afraid that if he opened his mouth, Maxwell would be able to hear it thump.

'There!' Maxwell's shout filled the car and Guy braked hard.

'God, Max. I nearly shat myself. Don't *do* that!'

'Sorry.' He shook the man by the arm. 'That's it, though. There.'

'A bird or a tree?'

'Or a range of mountains. Nature, that's what I said.'

'Dolomite Road.'

'That's the one. But I don't know the number. Let's park here and walk up. Then we have the element of surprise.'

Guy grabbed Maxwell's sleeve. 'You've done this sort of thing before,' he said, his voice husky with fear. 'What are you expecting, Max? Has he hurt Sylvia?'

'No, of course he hasn't,' Maxwell said. 'But he is a smarmy bastard and it would give him a lot of pleasure not to tell us what he knows, just to see us squirm. He didn't like us turning up here last night – he's the sort to bear a grudge. We need to catch him unawares. Then he will probably just tell us what you've forgotten, that Sylv has started Pilates, is having her nails done.' He shook him off and patted his shoulder. 'Do you see? Guy,' he looked into his face, 'do you see? We have to stay calm. For Sylv.'

The man nodded and they got out of the car. Down the road ahead of them, pairs of police were ringing doorbells, rapping knockers. They were coming their way in a slow but inexorable tide. Maxwell hoped they had not already visited Baines. That wouldn't please him at all and all their courtesy would probably be no good. He pulled Morley around the corner and they walked off down Dolomite Road, Maxwell looking for clues. It was an obvious one in the end – Baines' car parked on the hard standing just under the bow window.

'That's the one,' Maxwell said, pulling on Morley's sleeve. 'There. Now, I'll do the talking and please, Guy, no rough stuff.'

'I take that as an insult, Max,' the man said. 'I don't have a hot temper.'

'Perhaps not. But this is not one to mess with,' Maxwell said. 'He's not tall but he's wiry and don't forget, he has a good few years on you, no offence. Add to that the fact that he's a PE teacher and I wouldn't take any bets on you winning. So, leave it to me, please.'

Morley nodded and dropped a few paces behind as they approached the front door.

Jacquie parked the car and reached into the back for her bag. 'Hang on a minute, Jason, would you?' she said. 'I just want to ring home, see how things are going.'

Politely, he got out and waited on the pavement. It was at times like these he wished he still smoked; it would have given him something to do with his hands.

She chose 'Home' in contacts and waited while it rang. After a moment, it was picked up.

'The Maxwell residence,' said a voice that sounded as though it was squeezing its way through a mouthful of marbles.

'Mrs Troubridge?' Jacquie's heart contracted. 'Is everyone all right?'

'Nolan is all right,' Mrs Troubridge answered, 'as am I. I can't speak for Mr Maxwell, because he isn't here.'

Jacquie heaved a sigh. She knew he *had* been there, because he had sorted out Nolan with Plocker's mother and Mrs Troubridge, but where the devil was he now? 'Has he left a message, Mrs Troubridge?' she asked. 'He will have left it on the whiteboard in the kitchen.'

'I'll go and check,' she wheezed. 'Nolan, talk to Mummy while I go and check.'

'Hello Mummy.' Jacquie could just picture Nolan, sitting on the arm of the chair, phone in both hands. 'We've come round to get my jamas.'

'Jamas, darling? Why?'

'Daddy came round and said could I stay and Mrs Troubidge said yes . . .' Nolan could still only manage one of the 'r's in Troubridge – it varied which one. 'And so now, I need my jamas.'

'Of course you do, poppet. Don't forget to feed the Count while you're there. Did Dads say anything about where he was going?'

'No. Just could I stay over.'

'Right. Darling, is Mrs Troubridge on her way back from the kitchen?'

'No. She had to come back for her glasses.'

'Okay. Sweetie, can you go and . . .'

'There are two messages on the phone. Would one of those be Dads, d'you think?'

'Clever boy. Can you play them for Mummy, please?' As soon as she said it, Jacquie regretted it. What if the message was not suitable for little ears? But it was too late. There was a click and a whirr and a mechanised voice said, 'You have two new messages. First new message. Message received today from caller withheld their number at thirteen twenty. Mrs Maxwell. As someone who has expressed an interest in soft furnishings . . .'

Jacquie raised her voice so Nolan could hear. 'Skip this one, sweetie.

Another click cut off the furniture salesman in full flow. 'Second new message. Message received today from,' and the voice turned into Jacquie's own for a brief moment, 'Sylvia Matthews,' then back to mechanised, 'at sixteen twenty. Max, Jacquie,' Sylvia's voice sounded strange, as though she were whispering in a huge space, with no ambient noise to give a clue, 'I missed you at school I think. Look, I'm very worried about Charlotte. I've spoken to Andrew and he's been very cagey, to say the least. I know he's lying about calling her last night. I don't know why he doesn't tell me what's going on . . . Oh, hold on, he's come back. Speak later. Message ends. To hear this message again, press one. To save it, press two. To delete it, press three.'

'Press two, darling,' Jacquie said.

'What was the matter with Sylvia, Mummy?' Nolan's voice was a bit wobbly and Jacquie ached to hug him.

'Nothing, poppet. It's a joke, I think. Look, off you pop with Mrs Troubridge and Mummy and Dads will be home soon.'

'Will you come and get me when you get home?' he asked.

'Of course we will,' she promised. 'Tell Mrs Troubridge we will knock when we get back. Don't forget, will you?'

'No, Mummy. Mummy . . .'

'Yes, poppet?'

'I love you.'

'I know that, sweet stuff. Now, take care of Mrs Troubridge and the Count and we'll be home soon, okay.'

'Mrs Troubidge is back now, Mummy.' She heard him hand over the phone and the marbled tones of her neighbour filled her ear.

'No message, I'm afraid, Jacquie,' she said.

'Not to worry, Mrs Troubridge,' Jacquie told her. 'Nolan will tell you our plans for tonight. I must go. Bye bye.'

She got out of the car and leaned on the bonnet to gather her thoughts.

'Jason?'

'Yes'm?'

'I think we may have a bit of a situation here. Listen up . . .'

Maxwell's hand was still raised to grab the knocker when the door swung open. Andrew Baines stood there and this time he didn't even feign courtesy.

'Max. Does this qualify as stalking? And you've brought a friend again. How nice.'

'Andrew,' Maxwell said in a conversational tone. 'This is Guy. He is Sylvia's very significant significant other and we were wondering if you knew where she was.'

'I saw her at school this afternoon. Other than that, I have no idea where she might be. Shopping?' Baines showed his teeth but it couldn't be called a smile. 'The ladies do love to shop, don't they?'

'I believe so,' Maxwell said. 'The thing is, we can't find anyone who saw Sylvia after she came looking for you. She didn't sign out.'

'Nor did I,' Baines preened himself in the doorway, catching his reflection in the hall mirror. 'Back way, past the tennis courts. Saves trouble. I try to keep away from whatshername, Sarah. She's always hated me since I turned her down at the Christmas party.'

'I don't go to the Christmas party,' Maxwell remarked.

'No.' Baines was unimpressed. 'So I've heard. Look, Max, it's lovely chatting, but I have a date. I must get a bit of a move on. Can't keep the little ladies waiting, can I?'

Guy Morley had been coming to a slow boil since Baines had opened the door. Already a gentleman when they met, Sylvia had honed him over the years to be almost as near to being an honorary woman as Maxwell was. And Maxwell had a trophy from the textiles department to prove it. Now, he burst into Baines' hall and pushed him in the chest with a flat palm.

'Look here, you little shit,' he said. 'If I find you've laid a finger on Sylvia, I'll knock you from here to kingdom come.'

'Hands off,' Baines shouted back at him, recovering from the shove and squaring up to the bigger man. 'No one pushes me around, you arsehole. I wouldn't lay a finger on Sylvia, to use your phrase. Not that she hasn't made it more than clear that she wouldn't mind what I laid on her, if you know what I mean?' Baines couldn't help running his fingers through his hair as he taunted what he saw as an old bloke, well past it and Morley was in like a rattler, punching the PE teacher full in the face with all his weight behind it. There was a sickening crunch as Baines' nose broke and the blood spurted in all directions.

'Nice one,' muttered Maxwell. He had always sensed a hidden power in Guy – it was just that the only example of it he had ever seen was that time when he had opened a very problematical jar of Branston.

'You've broken my nose, you bloody maniac,' Baines screamed, albeit rather indistinctly. 'I'll have the police on you, you . . .'

'Maniac.' Maxwell leaned forward. 'I always find a bit of repetition at this point lends weight to the insult.'

'Shut the fuck up, Maxwell,' Baines said, his hand across his face. 'I'm suing you as well, for bringing this whackjob here to beat me up. All my cosmetic procedures will be on you, believe me. You'll be bankrupt by the time I'm done. He broke my bloody nose.'

'Never mind,' Maxwell said soothingly. 'I understand it isn't even your second best feature. You'll probably have the girls at your feet with the plaster and everything. You know how the girlies love a wounded hero.'

Baines' eyes flickered. There might be something in what the mad old bugger said. But meanwhile, he just wanted them out of his face. 'Just get out,' he snarled. 'I'm calling 999 and not just for an ambulance. I'm calling the police as well. They'll throw the book at you. Both of you. And it won't help the little woman's career, will it, Maxwell? Having her old man done for GBH.'

Maxwell held up his hands. 'I haven't touched you. And I have restrained Guy, haven't I, Guy?'

'You certainly have, Max,' Morley agreed, stepping back. 'You did your best.'

'But on the other hand,' Maxwell said, 'I am old and past it, so what could I do, in the end?'

'Nothing,' Guy said. 'Nothing at all. You couldn't even stop me when I pushed this little shit over,' and he suited the action to the words, 'and searched his house, to see if he has anyone here he shouldn't have. Such as Sylvia.'

'That's true,' Maxwell said. 'But I will admit to having followed you, to make sure that you don't do any damage.' He pushed past Baines and managed to bash his face against the wall again. 'Ooh, that must be painful,' he said. 'If I were you, I'd sit down for a while.'

Baines crept down the hall towards the kitchen, his face a mask of blood and his eyes blurred with tears and Maxwell watched him go. The chances were that there was a back door but he didn't see Baines as a flight risk. He was too careful to play the injured innocent for that. As he disappeared into the gloom of the kitchen, Maxwell noticed something which made him go in for a closer look. It was a metal staple on the door jamb. And on the door, a hook. Maxwell looked at it for a moment, puzzling out its purpose. He and Jacquie had changed the hook on the bathroom door into one like this, high up, when Nolan had started to walk. It was to stop him locking himself in the room when he was by himself, but this had the look of keeping something in, not a safety precaution.

Bells and whistles started going off in Maxwell's brain and he called to Morley. 'Guy, come down here a minute. I think we need to make sure Mr Baines doesn't go for a walk. Don't you, Mr Baines?'

'What are you talking about, you mad bugger?' Baines' voice sounded muffled and strained. 'I need a doctor. I'm calling 999. The police.'

Guy stepped over the broken hall table and into the kitchen. Baines was at the kitchen door, struggling with a bolt. It was hard with one hand, and the other was busy pressing a handful of paper towels to his gushing nose.

'Surely, your phone is in here, isn't it, Mr Baines?' Guy said, swinging him round. Suddenly, the man who could still, after all these years, make Sylvia Matthews' world spin faster, gave a grunt and went down like a felled tree. Baines stood there at bay against the door, a bloody carving knife in his hand.

'I really shouldn't leave these things around, should I?' Baines said to Maxwell, taking a step forward around the table. 'I hate untidy people as a rule, but I just haven't had a minute to clear up. I keep it nice and sharp. My dad taught me how to keep things nice. Nice and clean. He was a bit of a perfectionist, my dad.'

'No! Really?' Maxwell had never seen a textbook case walking towards him with a bloody nose and a bloody knife. He was thinking fast. He knew Guy was alive, but he could hear his breath coming as tortured wheezing and knew too that he probably had a punctured lung. Sylvia would know the proper term, no doubt. So running wasn't an option. Before he got to the door, Guy would be dead from another knife wound and Sylvia would be condemned to join him. Because Maxwell was convinced she was in this house somewhere and the chances were she wasn't alone. But meanwhile, Baines was advancing, step by slow step, knife held out although his hand was trembling.

'I knew you'd be a sarcastic bastard, Maxwell,' Baines said. 'Sarcasm is the lowest form of wit, did you know that? Of course you did, because you know everything, isn't that right? Charlotte, when she told me she was up the spout, she wanted to talk to you. "What a shame Mr Maxwell isn't here".' He mimicked the girl, cruelly. 'You don't even know her name. You don't care about her. *I* cared. I bought her flowers. All that stuff. And in the end, she wanted to leave me. Not to have my baby. She couldn't get enough of me, then she didn't want my baby growing inside her. Bitch!' He choked on some blood dripping from the back of his ruined nose and gagged but didn't take his eyes off Maxwell.

'It was easy to get her out of the hospital. I visited in the afternoon and got her worked up. Then, I slipped in and got her to come back here with me. She was scared, but she came. She can't resist, you see. Can't resist the old Baines charm. That's what my dad used to say. He used to bring women home with him when my mum was out at work. They can't resist the old Baines charm, he'd say to me. He used to lie there in the bed and I used to have to see them out.'

'That must have been difficult for you,' Maxwell said softly.

'Not at all,' Baines shouted, and coughed again, spitting the blood on the floor. He looked down at the mess. 'One of the bitches can clean that up.'

'Any one in particular?' Maxwell asked, listening to Guy's breathing getting more ragged, more uneven.

Baines shrugged. 'Charlotte. Sylvia.' He looked at Maxwell, appraisingly and stepped forward, two, three steps but the fencer buried deep in Maxwell was ready for him and he kept the distance between them the same.

'April?' the Head of Sixth Form asked.

'Yes. April. She's puking up, though. Not as far along as Charlotte. She might not be up to it.'

'What about Mollie and Josie?'

Baines laughed and spat again. 'They're not going to be much good at cleaning up, are they, Maxwell? Because they're *dead*, see. And that other tart, the other night. Dead.'

'Well, not really,' Maxwell muttered.

Baines stopped his advance and lowered the knife a touch. 'What? She's dead. Sure to be. I'd finished when that bloody couple came barrelling out of the bushes. She's dead.'

'No, she's not,' Maxwell repeated. 'She spent last night talking to my wife. I would be surprised if the police took much longer to get here.'

'You won't be in any condition to be surprised or anything else, you old git,' Baines growled and lunged with the knife, which scored the inside of Maxwell's arm, just above the elbow. It had been so long since Maxwell had had so much as a hang nail that the pain jolted through him and he slipped, his arm clamped to his side and his knee cracking on the wall. Baines brought his boot high into Maxwell's ribs and the Head of Sixth Form rolled on the ground. 'Well, you weren't hard to bring down in the end, were you, Fantastic Mr Maxwell? The only question is, do I finish you off first or the fists of righteous harmony over there? Maxwell?' Baines leaned in nearer. 'Maxwell!' He slapped his face, 'I want you to hear all this. I want you to know who killed you.'

Maxwell groaned and rolled his head to one side, his eyes slits and his mouth a line of pain.

'It's not everyone who is killed by someone as perfect as me, Mr Maxwell. My dad, he used to tell me, when he was in his bed, resting after he had given some slag the old Baines charm. He used to tell me, son, I'm good, but you're better than me. He chose my mum, you see, for her looks. Not her brains, that's for sure. Anyway, he bred me to be perfect. Like a flower, you know. Weed out all the bad ones. Keep the best. That's what he did.'

'You mean . . . he killed his children?' Just breathing was taking its toll.

'No! He just bred to be the best. He had other kids, but he left them. It was only me he stayed with. Because I was the perfect one. He showed me how to keep fit. And then he showed me the old Baines charm. We used to go out together when I was older. He was getting on a bit by then, but he still had it. We used to pull some right old boilers. For practice. So when I was out on my own, I could just pick the best ones.'

'To breed some perfect children.' Maxwell's voice was weak and Baines slapped him round the face again to bring him round.

'That's it,' he said. 'I found some really good specimens at St Olave's, when I did the PE club there. But after the first two didn't pan out, I had to move on. I found April on the Esplanade. We got talking. She was a pretty little thing and she told me everything. God, that kid could talk. But she told me about her mum being some kind of maths genius or something. I thought I could do with some brains in the mix. Charlotte was up the spout, I didn't count that kid. She's all right to look at, but nothing special. She was kind of . . .'

'Practice?' Maxwell croaked.

'Yes. I suppose you could say that. Practice, yes. So, April got pregnant, but I didn't know. She hadn't done the test when she was living here. I found out when her dippy mother came to visit you.'

'How did you find that out? I don't see much of you on my floor,' Maxwell managed to gasp.

'Somebody in the staff room remembered her from when she was at Leighford High. God, some of you are old! You've been there for ever! Catch me staying in the same job for a lifetime. Anyway, somebody said she was some kind of maths whizz who had left to have a kid. Then when I heard you'd called your missus in to talk to April, I did a bit of digging and there you are! I found out all about what the little slag was planning to do. It's amazing what people tell me when I want them to.'

Maxwell's eyes rolled into his head and Baines brought his face in so they were inches apart and the Head of Sixth Form could feel the PE teacher's breath on his cheek.

'So, I went to April's place. I knew where she lived; like I said, she told me everything. She just never shut up. I threw some gravel up at her window. Like a cheesy romance it was – she lapped it up. She came downstairs to let me in, but I grabbed her and got her into the car. She was whining she'd left her phone behind and I admit that was a bit of a facer, but it was too late by then. Never mind, it won't make any difference at the end of the day.'

Whether it was the final cliché or the fact that Guy Morley's breaths were now frighteningly far apart, Maxwell never knew. All he knew was that the time had come and he took it. He brought his head up sharply and rammed hard into Baines' already broken nose. The man shrieked, throwing up both hands to clutch his face and the knife skittered under the table somewhere, out of reach.

Maxwell's plan only half worked, because Baines fell forward, pressing hard on his already injured knee. Maxwell writhed with pain and above his ruined face, Baines' eyes were triumphant. He pressed again with all his weight. The pain was worse now than when the knee had first crashed into the wall and Maxwell's chest hurt so much he couldn't even summon up a groan, let alone a yell.

Then, suddenly, the weight had gone and Baines was the one who was yelling. The Head of Sixth Form could hardly believe his eyes. Sylvia Matthews was standing over him, like the Angel of Mons, if the Angel of Mons had ever held a PE teacher by the hair and slammed his head into a door jamb until he was unconscious. She looked at Maxwell and assessed him briefly as potentially walking wounded and turned to Guy, lying curled in the foetal position now and gasping with frightening intensity as if each breath might be his last.

'Guy,' he heard her murmur, 'Guy, it's Sylvia. You're all right now, baby. I'm here. Look. I've put my hand over the hole in your side. It's only a pneumothorax, Guy. Come on, darling, you're all right now. Come on. Just breathe, poppet.'

Maxwell closed his eyes and managed a smile. He knew Sylvia would know the proper name for it. And if there was a woman in the whole wide world who could be relied upon to save the day, when Jacquie wasn't handy, it was Sylv.

Maxwell felt Baines begin to stir and knew he had to get help and somehow he scrambled to his feet and half ran, half fell into the hall, into the arms of Jason Briggs and then, in quick succession, those of his wife. He looked into her face and then his eyes flickered to the staircase, where two pairs of anxious eyes were looking down at him. He looked back at Jacquie and almost managed a smile.

'What are you doing here?' he muttered, passing out as she replied.

'Oh, dear, Max,' she said, holding him tight. 'Now I'm going to have to kill you.'

M J Trow